D0871520

THE HIGHLAND TWINS AT THE CHALET SCHOOL

'Oh, Flora! It's the Erisay Chart they want!'

PAGE 194

THE HIGHLAND TWINS AT THE CHALET SCHOOL

BY

ELINOR M. BRENT-DYER

W. & R. CHAMBERS, LTD.
LONDON AND EDINBURGH

Latest Reprint, 1952

Printed in Great Britain
by T. and A. CONSTABLE LTD., Hopetoun Street,
Printers to the University of Edinburgh

CONTENTS

TO MY DEAREST

AUNT ELIZABETH

WITH LOVE FROM

ELINOR

CHAPTER I

JOEY GETS A SHOCK

'POSTY!' Daisy Venables, who had been sitting curled up on the grass, jumped to her feet and made a bee-line for the drive, up which a familiar figure was to be seen slowly advancing. Evan Evans, 'Posty,' was none too young, and this was a very warm day for September.

Joey Maynard, once Joey Bettany of the Chalet School, looked after Daisy with a laugh. 'She's nearly sixteen, but she doesn't get any more grown-up for all that. Rob! What on earth has she done to her frock? It was clean this morning, and just *look* at it!'

The girl to whom she spoke lifted a curly black head from the daisy-chain she was making with the assistance of Joey's triplet daughters and glanced after long-legged Daisy, whose pale-green cotton frock looked as though she had wiped the chimney liberally round with it.

'Mercy! What a sight! *I* don't know what she's been up to, Jo, so it's no use asking me. Here she comes with the letters, anyhow, so you can find out from herself.' Daisy, with a handful of letters, came flying back to the group on the lawn.

Jo, not looking any older than she had been since she had made her escape from Austria and the Gestapo at the time of the Anschluss *—and a thrill-

* See *The Chalet School in Exile*.

ing adventure it had been!—promptly acted on the advice.

'Daisy Venables! What *have* you done to your frock? It looks as if you'd used it for a floor-cloth. You *are* a messy brat!'

Daisy glanced down at herself, unperturbed. 'I forgot. I meant to change it and rub it through. I was up the beech tree after Primula Mary's balloon, and that beech tree isn't what you'd call clean.'

'Did you expect it to be? Trot in and change, and be quick about it. You can't go round looking like that at three o'clock in the afternoon. Give me the letters first, though—you featherhead!' For Daisy was preparing to obey without handing over the mail.

She came back, and presented them. 'There you are. Don't look so cross at me, Auntie Jo. I'm sorry about the frock, and I really will wash it myself. You might give me a smile, there's a dear.'

'You baby!' But the corners of Jo's lips were going, and there was laughter in her eyes. Daisy saw it, and flung herself tempestuously on her aunt-by-marriage, as she always explained the connection.

'You're a pet, and the most precious aunt that ever lived! I'm truly sorry about the frock. Kiss me, and then I'll go and change while you read your letters. It wouldn't have happened if Prim hadn't let her balloon go up aloft.'

Joey gave it up, laughed, and kissed her, and then pushed the lanky schoolgirl off her lap. 'Run, you scaramouche! And do something about your hair while you're busy. If you can't keep it any tidier than that it'll have to be cut again.'

'Never! What would Gwensi and Beth say? We're *all* having pigtails. I simply couldn't be the only one not to. You'd never ask that!' She took a flying leap over a flower-bed, and vanished into the house, singing at the top of a high, sweet voice.

Jo looked after her with a grin. 'What a babe she is! Well, let's see what we've got today. "Miss Robin Humphries"—here you are, Rob—"Mrs John Maynard"—"Mrs Maynard"—"Mrs J. Maynard"—"Miss D. Venables"—"Miss Humphries"—from Lorenz, Rob; I recognise her writing—*and* "Mrs Jack Maynard"—from Jean Mackenzie. Dear me! It isn't a week since she last wrote, and I haven't answered it yet. What can she want, I wonder?'

'Open it and see,' advised Robin, who was opening her own missives. 'This other letter is from Elizabeth Arnett. She said she'd write and let me know her results when they came.'

Joey paused with her letter half-open. 'Has she passed?'

Robin glanced hastily through the sheet of scribbled writing. 'Yes; credit in English, French, and botany; pass in maths and Latin. Oh, well done, Elizabeth! And she's heard from Biddy, Nicole, and Myfanwy, and they've all passed too. Biddy and Nicole have distinction in French and Myfanwy has credit in Latin and botany. She doesn't know about the rest. I'll read it properly, though, and leave you to see what Mrs Mackenzie wants. Run away, Triplets, and get more daisies. We'll begin another chain when I've read this.'

The red-headed triplets trotted off cheerfully to gather more daisies and amuse themselves till their elders were free to attend to them again, and the other two settled down to their letters. There was silence for a brief space in the sunny garden, which Joey broke with an exclamation of, 'Oh, my hat!'

'What's up?' demanded Robin, glancing up from the lengthy screed she had received from her great chum, Lorenz Maïco.

'Just you listen to this!' And Jo, ruffling back to a sheet or so, read aloud, '"And now, Joey, I'm going to make a demand on you. I shouldn't do it if I didn't know that you had plenty of room now that Frieda has a house of her own, and Simone has betaken herself and her small Thérèse to Cumberland. But I know you don't want evacuee children if you can help it with the precious three, and you *know* that as soon as it's known that you have two or three rooms to spare you'll be landed. That's what comes of living in a safety area, my lass! It's a long story, and I'm going to tell it in full, for I want your sympathy. And believe me, you'll need all the sympathy you've got to spare, and all the understanding too, for what I'm asking you to take on is a problem.

'"Do you remember my telling you of a holiday I once spent with some distant connections of my mother's? It was on a tiny island in the Outer Hebrides, and with some cousins of hers—McDonald by name. At that time, there were Cousin Duncan and his wife, Cousin Morag, and their three children—Archie, who was my own age, Shiena, who was three years younger, and Hugh, who was about four. Since then, there have been another boy, Kenneth, who must be about fifteen now; and twin girls who are eleven—Flora and Fiona. When the twins were two, Cousin Morag died of pneumonia, and Shiena, who was twelve at the time, became mother to the entire family, so far as I can gather. I never went back, altho' it wasn't for want of asking. But first I went to school in Paris; and then there was that trip I took with Mother and Dad to America; and then I met Ken and married him. After that, as we know all too well, the war broke out. Alan arrived to complicate matters; and then it was a case of trot through Great Britain to keep with Ken as far as I could.—By the way, there are rumours that his squadron may be going East, in which case I shall go home to Edinburgh for the time being.

'"Well, to continue my story. One evening, about six weeks ago, Ken brought in a couple of his pals for supper; and no sooner did I see the younger one than I exclaimed: 'Archie McDonald!' And Archie it was. Of course we had a great chat, and I heard all the news. It seems that Cousin Duncan died about eighteen months ago, and Shiena, Kenneth, and the twins had gone on living in the Great House, as they call it, on Erisay, their island. I should explain that Cousin Duncan was very much of a recluse; never would send any of his children to school, and refused to allow any casual strangers to land on Erisay. The children were all educated by the minister until Archie was eighteen. Then Archie, who is now twenty-four, insisted on going to Camberley as he was mad on flying; and Hugh gave his father no peace till he got leave to try for Dartmouth—which he got into by a scrape of two days. He would have been over-age if they'd left it any later. Shiena and the others carried on at the Great House, and it almost looked as if it would continue for ever.

'"I rather think it must have been the war that finished off Cousin Duncan. At any rate, he died, and Archie got special leave to go home to settle up things. He wanted them to leave Erisay and go to Scotland somewhere, but they refused. They are all as shy as young fawns, and the thought of having to meet strangers was too much for any of them. You can't wonder at it, can you, considering how they've been brought up? So he had to go back to his squadron, leaving it at that, and there, when he came to our house that night, they still were.

'"Two days ago, he arrived in a state of what I can only describe as *dither*. The Admiralty have got their eye on Erisay for some fell purpose of their own. They have commandeered the whole island for the duration of the war, and Shiena and the children have to turn out at once. She, I suppose, will have to join one of the women's forces; Kenneth is to go to school; and *so must the twins*. Now do you see what I'm driving at?

'"They are singularly badly off for relations—Cousin Duncan was the only child of only children; and Cousin Morag's only brother lives in Canada, so he's no use to anyone at present. They can't go to our place—there won't be room if I have to go with young Alan. When I married, Mother and Dad moved into a flat, as Mother felt she'd had enough of a house; and they have just the one room to spare for us.

'"I think Archie had been hoping they would be able to come to the rescue, for his face fell a yard when I told him that, and he was more upset than ever. I felt I simply must do my best to help him out, poor fellow; and then I remembered the School!

'"But, Joey, can you imagine what being plunged straight into school life would be like to two children of eleven who have never seen a soul, beyond the thirty or so people who lived on Erisay, in all their lives? It would be cruel to try it. Don't you agree? They *must* go, of course; but not at once. Let them get accustomed to meeting strangers first.

'"So this is what I've thought of. You've got the rooms to spare. And I want you to take Shiena as well as the twins for a week or two till she's called up. You're accustomed to girls of all kinds—look at your books! Robin is gentle and not alarming, either. And then there are your delightful triplets to help break the ice. Will you have them for a few weeks and let them get used to your household? They could have till half-term, anyhow. And then, when Shiena will have gone—as I expect she will by that time—let them be daily boarders as Robin *was*, and Daisy and Primula *are*, for the rest of the term. After that, if you want the rooms, or it seems better, they can become full boarders. What do you say?

'"Don't rush off to answer this at once. Take time and think it over. Discuss it with Madge and Robin, and get their advice. You were very good to me and Alan while we were with you, and I do feel that if Shiena and the twins can come to you it will help them all through what must be a horribly difficult time. I don't ask you to have Kenneth—and boys are different, anyhow. Archie and Hugh seem to have managed all right, and I expect he will. But when I think of poor Shiena and those scared bairnies of eleven, I do feel that they need a little breaking-in.

'"Be a dear, Joey, and agree. I'm sure you will when you've thought it over. I'd take them myself if I'd somewhere of my own; but I haven't—and if Ken goes East, then goodness knows when I shall have. Look on it as war work, if you like—but *do* it!" And the rest,' concluded Jo, folding up the sheets, 'doesn't matter. But did you ever hear of anything to beat that? What on earth should I do with three wild, shy Highlanders here? Jean Mackenzie must be mad. She knows what this house is like. We're a regular port of call for all the clan. Her timid trio *would* get a benefit if they came here to be broken in to meeting strangers. When it isn't Madge and Co., it's the School. Or if it isn't them, it's safe to be someone from Armiford.'

Robin nodded, her eyes fixed dreamily on the triplets who were picking daisies industriously at the further side of the lawn. 'Yes; there certainly is something in what you say, Joey. And yet——'

'And yet—what?' demanded Jo as she broke off.

'Well, Mrs Mackenzie is right, you know, when she says that you understand girls. Look what you did to Gwensi Howell when we first came here. And you helped Elizabeth through that bad time she had with Betty Wynne-Davies when she first broke away from her.'

'That's quite another thing; and it was just as well for Elizabeth that she did have the sense to break away. I can't understand how it is that Betty Wynne-Davies has never been expelled yet. She asks for it on an average of twice a term, I should say.'

'I don't think it's as bad as that—though she goes to the very edge of it, I know. Well, perhaps she'll settle down this term,' said Robin hopefully.

'At seventeen? Not a chance of it, my child. She's one of the few really unsatisfactory girls the School has had. The leopard will change his spots and the Ethiopian his skin before Betty Wynne-Davies will become a decent member of society,' retorted Jo emphatically.

'I hope not.' Robin had been gazing up into the delicately-cut face that was to her the dearest face in the world. Now she turned back to watch the babies once more. 'Look at them, Joey,' she said, waving her hand towards them.

Joey's splendid black eyes softened as they fell on the three little girls who were her pride and joy. But she only said, 'What about them?'

'Suppose something should happen so that Len and Con and Margot were brought up like these twins—what did you say their names were?'

'Flora and Fiona. And *that's* mad to start off with. What d'you bet that any school where they go makes Flora and Fauna of it before they've been there a week?'

Robin doubled up in wild giggles. 'Oh, Jo! I

hope not! How like you to think of it, though! But, Joey,' she turned round, laying an arm on Jo's knee, and looking up into the black eyes above her with all her heart in her own dark ones, 'suppose—just *suppose* something should happen like that? I know it's not likely; but it might. Wouldn't you be glad to know that there was someone who would help them out when they first came back? Wouldn't you, Joey?'

Jo was silent. Then she nodded. 'Yes; I should.' She stooped, framing the lovely face upturned to her with long, slender hands, and looked deep into the pleading eyes. 'You're right there, Rob. And I suppose I'll do it in the end. But I must say I never expected Jean, of all people, to give me the shock I've had today. And though I've had experience of most kinds of girls, they've always been girls who've grown up normally, and however we shall get on, I *don't* know.'

'We'll manage all right,' said Robin confidently. 'It isn't as though you'd be alone, you know. I shall be at home a good deal of the time, now that I'm only working for Higher Cert. The Abbess said I need go only three days in the week. I'll be with you the other four. And Daisy and Primula will help, I know. Look how shy Prim is, even now. And Daisy's accustomed to *her*. If you explain, I know she'll help. Think it over, Joey. I know you'll want to say "Yes" when you do.'

'Oh drat!' said Joey crossly. 'I suppose I shall. But don't talk about it, Rob. And say nothing to anyone till I give you leave. I must talk it over with Madge before I do a thing. I'll go up there this evening, and you can put the babes to bed for me for once. I shall have to have Peg, and Bride, and Sybil at any rate for the term, as you know. If I take these McDonalds as well, the house 'll be packed out.'

'It 'll be that, anyhow, if you don't,' said Robin placidly. 'And they might take you for war work, now the triplets are nearly two. You don't want that—at any rate not until we see how Margot weathers the winter.'

A look of fear came into Joey's eyes. Last winter Margot, the youngest of the triplets, had nearly died of bronchitis, and she was by no means as sturdy as her elder sisters, even now. Most emphatically her mother did not want to have to leave her to the care of anyone else at present.

'I 'm not unpatriotic,' she said slowly, 'but I don't want to do anything that takes me from the babes just yet. I 'll see what Madge says; but I expect I 'll agree, Rob. We may as well begin to make plans, for I see no way out of it.'

CHAPTER II

A TRYING JOURNEY

SIX o'clock in the evening, and Newcastle Central Station at its worst and rowdiest! Platforms were packed with sailors and soldiers; little groups welcoming returned fathers, sons, and husbands alternated with others that were saying farewells.

People from the various smaller towns on Tyneside or up Tynedale, who had come into the city for a day's shopping, were scurrying to secure seats in the already crowded compartments; engines were hooting or blowing off steam. Altogether, it was a scene calculated to strike terror into the hearts of any folk as unused to such bustle and confusion as the little cluster of three which stood timidly on one platform, gripping gladstone-bags, suitcases, and rolls of rugs, while they kept an eye on the three trunks piled up against one of the pillars that supported the roof.

More than one person turned to look at them, for, even in these days of cosmopolitan dress to be met with everywhere, it is not customary to see three girls clad in full Highland kit, with kilts of Macdonald tartan, black cloth coats, plaids of the same tartan clasped on the left shoulder with great pebble brooches, sporran, hose-tops, and Glengarry bonnets complete with eagle's feather. Moreover, it was a hot evening, when most other girls were sporting light cotton frocks if they were not in uniform, and such hats as were to be seen were big shady ones.

'Iss this our train?' asked one of the younger girls as a monster came snorting along the platform, to pull up clanking, when doors were flung open and crowds began to descend, many of them heavily laden with baggage of one kind and another. '*Iss* it our train, Shiena?'

Shiena McDonald shook her head. 'I do not know. I must ask someone.' Summoning up all her courage, she took a step forward, and addressed a big, burly man in sergeant's uniform. 'Oh, pleass, woult you tell me if thiss iss the train for Leeds?'

He paused on his way to look down at her—Shiena McDonald was small and very slight—and something in her worried face roused the fatherliness in his heart. 'Aye; 'tes t' traa-in arl reet, laass,' he said. A kindly curiosity lit up his face. 'Goain' by't, eh? Wal, rackon tha'll be arl reet if tha staand 'ere till 'tes time. 'Ere! Bide a moment!'

His broad Yorkshire accent was puzzling to the three outlanders, but they managed to grasp the fact that he would help them, and they were to stay where they were for the present. He vanished before shy Shiena could pluck up courage again to thank him; but only for a few moments. Presently he returned with a fellow-sergeant to whom he introduced them.

'This is Sergeant Purlbeck. Aa's goain' t' 'Arrogate, and 'aa'll see tha gets in arl reet, an' thi luggage, an' all,' he added. 'Tha'll be saafe noo. S'long!' And once more he vanished, leaving them with his friend.

Sergeant Purlbeck gave them a keen look, and summed them up at once as 'gentry.' In peacetime he was chauffeur to a very great gentleman, and he prided himself on being able to gauge a person at the first look. Now he made up his mind to see that these three frightened creatures were safely bestowed as far as he could manage it. But he rather wondered that they had been allowed to travel by themselves, so plainly were they unused to it. It was a pity that it looked like being a bright, moonlight night—just the night for 'Jerry.' Still, if Leeds were their destination they might get there safely. He asked them this, and Shiena shook her head.

'Oh, no,' she said, her soft, Highland accents sounding strangely in his ears. 'We haf to go much further—to Armiford. But we go to Leeds first; and then to Stockport. Then we get the train to Armiford.'

'Oh, aye,' he said. 'Wal, Aa'll see tha into t' train, and Aa rackon summun'll 'elp t'other end.'

His accent was not nearly so broad as his friend's, and Shiena was able to understand him at once, and thank him shyly. Then they all stood waiting, till the last of the outgoing passengers had cleared away, and the Sergeant was able to put them into a compartment, with all their hand-luggage beside them. Their trunks he saw into the van, and made interest for them with the guard—a fellow-Yorkshireman, who promised to see them safely out at Leeds. He came back to tell Shiena what he had done; and then with a kindly 'Good-neet!' departed to seek his own place with the men of his company.

Left alone, the three settled themselves as well as they could. It was a new thing for them to make train journeys. Until a week ago, they had never even seen a train, and it is not too much to say that the twins were terrified of the snorting monsters which dashed along the lines, making such blood-curdling noises and hissings. Fiona, the elder of the pair, vowed that it was worse than the Kelpie; and far, far worse than the tiny coasting steamer which had taken them from their beloved Erisay to Oban, whence they had travelled to Glasgow first; then on to Edinburgh where Jean Mackenzie's parents had taken them in for a couple of days. They had left Edinburgh that morning, and reached Newcastle in the afternoon; and now, here they were, on the road again, for the last part of their long journey, and Erisay seemed almost as if it belonged to another world. Even Archie, who had been their stand-by in Glasgow, might have been in Mars now. To the untravelled McDonalds it was all very dreadful. And when they did reach the end of the journey, it was to be with total strangers. It is true that Jean Mackenzie and her mother, Mrs Robertson, had assured them all that young Mrs Maynard was delightful, and very ready to welcome them, while her triplet daughters were a real joy to look forward to—as Flora had said, 'I've never seen triplets except in music'—but even this could not alter the fact that they were going to total strangers, and they had rarely seen any until this last week or so.

At the moment, the compartment was empty save for themselves. The twins snuggled up to Shiena, who was their one stand-by now, and Fiona asked earnestly in the Gaelic that was as much their mother-tongue as the English they spoke with such a pretty West Highland accent, 'Will we be long in going, Shiena? Will it be very long, think you?'

Shiena shook her head. 'Indeed, Fiona, I don't know. But there is one thing I do know,' she added with vigour, 'and that is that you two *must* remember to speak English all the time now.'

'And forget the Gaelic? Shiena! You don't mean that?' gasped Flora.

'Of course not. But we are going to be with people who won't have the two languages, and—honestly, Twins, your English iss not as good as it might be. I noticed when Archie wass talking how fery differently he spoke from us. We must try to speak better, now that we must live away from the Highlands for a wee while.'

'*I* thought Archie spoke Englishy,' returned Fiona with a twist of her pretty mouth. 'It wassn't like us at all.'

'But if we are living with the English, we must speak like them or they may laugh at us,' argued Shiena shrewdly. She knew her twins. They hated nothing more than to be laughed at.

'I ton't see why we must give up Erisay to any-one,' put in Flora. 'It wass *ours*—it iss Archie's. Why shoult we have to go away from it? It iss preaking our hearts we will all pe——'

'Flora—Flora! You must speak better!' cried Shiena in dismay. 'You can do it, for I haf heard you. Why must you be so bad?'

'I'm a Highlanter. I want to show these people I am Highlant,' returned Flora stubbornly. 'And you cannot say much yourself, Shiena. You speak nearly as Highlant ass we do.'

'I must be fer—*very*, I mean—careful, then,' returned Shiena gravely. 'Twins, it iss bad enough as it iss. Don't make things worse for us all by being naughty.'

More there was no time to say, for the door opened, and some girls in W.A.A.F. uniform got in with wide-eyed, curious glances at the three in their alien dress. The twins hushed at once in the presence of strangers, and Shiena, though inwardly she felt as shy and uncomfortable as they, was thankful for the invasion. She had no wish to spend most of the trying journey arguing; and her small sisters could be very argumentative on occasion. She got down a bag from the rack, fished out books for them, and buried herself in her own, to all appearances, while furtively eyeing the newcomers.

She was fascinated by their make-up. She herself wore none, of course. Lipstick, rouge, and face-powder had not penetrated to Erisay yet. These girls, with their 'permed' curls, their carefully made-up faces, scarlet-bowed lips, and plucked eyebrows were like beings from another world to the untravelled Highland girl. She envied them their smart appearance, little realising that they were envying her her naturally wavy brown hair, pink and white skin with its delicate bloom which came from no box, but from the soft airs and rains of Erisay, and admiring the long brown lashes that curled upwards, giving her grey-blue eyes such a starry appearance.

'I'd give her a pound apiece for 'em!' murmured one young lady to her friend. 'Wonder what she puts on 'em to make 'em grow like that?'

'Nothing, I guess. It's natural. Look at the kids; they have the same,' replied the other girl in the same low tones.

The first realised, as she glanced at the twins, that it was true. Fiona's dark eyes were fringed with black lashes, and Flora's blue ones had quillings of light brown; but they were of the same length and ray-like appearance as their sister's. Similarly, they had curly hair straying over their shoulders; Fiona's black, Flora's so light as to merit the word 'linty.' All three had the same oval, high-cheek-boned faces, with delicately aquiline features, and pink and white skins. Without being pretty, they were an attractive-looking trio, and there was no denying that their Highland dress suited them down to the ground.

Shiena presently became conscious that they were attracting more attention than she relished. She wished now that she had taken Mrs Robertson's advice, and invested in more ordinary dress for them all. But the twins had objected so strenuously, and she had so hated the thought of wrestling with the shopgirls, not to mention the complication of clothes coupons, that she had agreed to let them travel in their usual attire. And this was the result. They were stared at as if they were a show!

She knew that when they reached Armiford they must get clothes like those worn by other people in England, and she had been afraid to use their coupons until she was with someone who could go carefully into the matter for her, and advise her just what they ought to get. On Erisay the question had scarcely arisen. They all wore hand-woven clothes; and when it was necessary to see about underthings, Ian McDonald and his wife, Tibby, had crossed to Oban, and thence to Glasgow, where they had bought great rolls of the fine white nainsook and cards of the delicate lace which, Tibby was convinced, were alone suitable for summer underwear for young ladies. As luck would have it, the last expedition had been made just the month before clothes rationing had begun. Tibby and Ian had brought the usual great rolls of materials to Erisay, and they had all set to work to make the garments by the patterns which Mrs McDonald had brought there with her when she came as a bride. So while all of them had trunks filled with dainty underclothes, none of them were in the least like those worn by most girls nowadays. And the hand-spun, hand-woven tartan, which was made to withstand every kind of weather, is hard-wearing in the extreme. Nor did they know anything about the gossamer silk stockings girls wear now. They had silk stockings for best, it is true; but stockings that had been their mother's and grandmother's; fine, but so closely woven that no glimmer of skin could be seen through them.

'And indeed,' thought Shiena to herself, 'I would not like to be wearing such things for everyone to see.'

At eight o'clock, when they were well on their way, the W.A.A.F.s produced packages of sandwiches and biscuits, and thermos flasks of tea and coffee, and proceeded to make a hearty supper. The McDonalds had sandwiches and cake and bannocks in one of their baskets, but they were too shy to open them and eat in public; though by this time the twins felt faint with hunger, for their last meal had been in the train from Edinburgh, where they had been lucky enough to be alone in their compartment. As for Shiena, she was not so hungry; but she was very thirsty. She thought longingly of the coffee in the flasks kind Mrs Robertson had put up for them, and the big bottle of milk as well; but it was no use. They must just wait until they were alone. Then they could have a meal.

One of the girls, glancing up, happened to notice Fiona's eyes on her plums, and she promptly held out the bag with a hearty, 'Have one, kiddy? Yes, do! There are heaps more than I want. Take one, and your sisters as well. Do try one! They're awfully sweet and juicy.'

Fiona went crimson, and Shiena had to come to the rescue. 'It iss fery kint of you,' she said in her soft voice, rather more Highland than usual in her shyness. 'Put we haf some supper in our basket.'

At the quaintly foreign-sounding accent, the girls exchanged glances. Then their new friend laughed. 'I'll bet you haven't plums—not like these. My uncle brought them home today—he's a farmer, and they've got a peach of an orchard. Take one, anyhow, just to try them, and see what you think of Alnwick plums. Can't you get your basket down? It's getting on, and we shan't get into Leeds before the refreshment rooms are closed—I can tell you that. Lucky if we get in by midnight!'

'Oh!' gasped Shiena. 'Put our train for Stockport leafes Leeds at elefen o'clock. We shall miss it! And there issn't another. They said so at the station. Whatefer shall we do?'

'Don't worry,' laughed another. 'Your connection isn't any more likely to be punctual than this is—certainly not if Jerry's on the go.'

It was so much Greek to Shiena, but she gathered that she need not worry unduly about trains. Meantime their first friend was still offering them the plums, and another had jumped up, and was looking at the piles of luggage on the racks above them. 'This your tuck-basket?' she asked. 'Yes? Here you are, then. Sit down, and let's mug up and be 'appy and chatty.'

She handed down the basket, and the twins were persuaded to take a plum each. Shiena shyly offered bannocks and cake in exchange, and the W.A.A.F.s accepted on condition that the trio would share what they had. So after all, they got their meal in comfort, though Fiona and Flora never spoke, and their sister could utter only a few shy sentences in reply to the girls' kindly chatter. They learned that she expected to be called up soon.

'Joining us, then?' asked their first friend, whose name they had learned was Effie Maitland.

'I ton't know,' said Shiena. 'We are going to a frient—at least,' she corrected herself conscientiously, 'she iss not a frient yet, for we ton't know her. But she will pe. She will atvise me, I think.'

'Join us,' advised Miss Maitland. 'It's a ripping Service—the best of the bunch. Oh, I know the W.R.N.S. are older. And there are the A.T.S. as well, and Red Cross, and so on. But we are the latest. Join us, and help to make history!'

Shiena looked bewildered at this spate of letters, and another, Margery Bain by name, said abruptly, 'How old are you? Twenty-one? Then how've you got out of joining before this?'

'We knew nothing about it—away ofer on Erisay. I kept house for my father, and Kenneth and the twins. But now they haf taken the islant from us, and we haf to come to England, and so I must join, they say, for Kenneth iss at school, and the twins will go soon,' explained Shiena.

'Erisay? Where's that?' asked another. But she was fated to receive no answer, for the train, which had been thundering through the twilight, suddenly pulled up in a tiny wayside station, and as the rumbling of the wheels ceased, they heard, thin, eerie, and horrible, a wail that seemed to break through the grey mists, now rapidly darkening to the blackness of night, and with one cry the twins threw themselves on their sister, clinging tightly to her.

'Jerry!' said Effie Maitland disgustedly. 'He's early, confound him! All right, kiddies. That's only the siren—sounding to tell us that he's on the way. Nothing to be afraid of. He won't bother about us. I wonder where he's going this time?' she added reflectively.

'Who iss Jerry?' asked Fiona, her curiosity getting the better of her shyness.

'German planes,' explained Effie. 'They're away to bomb somewhere. But d'you mean you've never heard the siren before?'

'No; nefer,' replied Shiena. 'What a dreatful sound it iss!'

'It's pretty ghastly,' agreed their new friend. 'Still, as long as it gets no worse than that—I mean, as long as there are no bombs to worry about, I guess we can stand it.'

'The worst of it is there's no saying how long we may be held up,' put in another, one Joan Tully. 'The train won't go on till the "All Clear" sounds, and that may be for hours yet.'

'"It may be for years, and it may be forever," in

fact,' laughed Margery Bain. 'There they go! Hear the engines? You can generally tell a Jerry by the note. Well, there's one thing. If he does try to get us we've a couple of St John's people next door. I saw two girls from "canny Soo' Shields" get in that I know—Dolly Scott and Gladys Anderson.'

She had barely finished speaking, when their ears were assaulted by a terrific explosion, and they were all hurled on to the floor of the compartment in one wild heap. Screams rose from the twins, who were convinced that they were killed, and even Shiena uttered a cry. The more experienced W.A.A.F.s made little sound, but one or two of them swore at the shock, greatly to the scandal of Shiena when she had time to realise it. At the moment, she was more concerned with getting her sisters on to their feet again, when a sound even more frightening than the siren's wail came through the air, and Effie pulled them all down, even as there came another explosion.

'Keep down!' she ordered. 'Here, you two kids; get under the seats and do it quick. You'll be safer from falling glass there.'

Kind hands pushed the terrified twins under the seats, and the rest of them settled themselves as well as they could on the floor, prepared to fling themselves face downwards at the least sign of another bomb.

It came three minutes later, but further away, and though the train once more rocked with the concussion, the glass in the windows remained intact. It came with that horrible shrieking noise, and Effie, when the explosion was over, explained that these were 'screaming' bombs.

'I suppose they think the noise will frighten us. They don't know much about the British,' she said scornfully. '*Down!*' For again came the wild sound, and this time there was a tinkle as glass further along the carriage went with the force of the blast. Their own compartment had its windows cracked, but that was all.

The twins were sobbing with terror, and even Shiena, if there had been any lights, would have been seen to be white to the lips, though she pluckily kept from any outcry. There was nothing they could do but wait; and, luckily, they had not much more of the ordeal. That was the nearest bomb. Ten minutes later, the last of the planes had passed over, and in half an hour the train moved ahead, travelling swiftly to make up as far as possible for the delay.

Effie left their compartment, and went to find out what damage, if any, had been done. She returned to say that except for cuts and bruises none of the passengers had suffered; but it was rumoured that a house had been struck by one of the bombs, and the station wall had collapsed at one end. But this was all so far as they could find out.

'And quite enough, too,' added Margery Bain, who had produced a travelling washing kit, and was engaged in sponging Flora's face and hands to rid them of the worst of the dirt. 'But if you people really haven't met much of the war till now, you've had a baptism, I can tell you. There you are—Flora, isn't it? Take that towel and dry your face while I see what I can do for your sister. Then we'll have a cup of coffee all round, and that'll make us feel better—though how we'll manage in the dark without spilling is more than I can say.'

Spilling there was, though surprisingly little when one comes to remember that all the lights in the train had gone, and they had to feel as best they could, since no one could lay hands on a torch. Half-way through the little feast, an official came along, however, to see that all was well with them. He had his flash-lamp, and he waited till they had produced five torches among them, and then left them to get on with it. Finally, two hours later than they had expected, the train drew up in Leeds station, and there the McDonalds had to say good-bye to their new friends, for all the girls were going to a post midway between Leeds and Skipton-in-Craven, and they themselves had to hurry to catch their Stockport connection. As there were practically no porters, they had to make shift to drag their trunks along themselves, and it was with a bare half-minute to spare that they finally settled down in the new train, worn out with all they had undergone. However, after that, it was more or less plain sailing. It is true the train from Stockport to Cardiff, which had been their final change, was held up for an hour and a half while the German fiends tore back to their bases, after spreading death and ruin along Mersey-side; but no bombs were dropped this time; and presently they were able to draw the blinds and let the blessed light of day pour into the carriage, while Shiena, white and drawn and grimy, her shyness forgotten for the time being, handed out the last of the sandwiches and cakes, and gave her sisters the final flask of coffee, which was lukewarm by this time, but very grateful nevertheless.

Finally, nearly six hours after they were due, they tumbled out on to the platform at Armiford, and looked round for their hostess.

CHAPTER III

PLAS GWYN

JO MAYNARD had begun the day early. She expected her Highland guests to arrive at about half-past six in the morning, so it was barely a quarter-past five when she stole down the passage from her own room to Robin's after a peep into the night-nursery on the way, where her three daughters lay in the profound slumber of healthy babyhood. Jo paused by each of the cots to touch her lips softly to the shining waves of hair but, mindful of the need for haste, she was careful not to wake them. Then she slipped out, and went on to the pretty chamber where Robin, her long black curls escaped their bed-time ribbons, lay almost as fast asleep as the babies. Jo bent over her, and shook her gently.

'Wake up, Robin *liebchen!* I'm just going, and I want you to take charge till we get back— Oh, I say! Be careful! That was my eye!'

Robin, who had flung out one arm as she woke, sat up in bed, her hair tumbling wildly round her, and grinned up at her adopted sister. 'You shouldn't wake me so suddenly. I've heard Jem say it's very bad to startle people awake. What did you say, Jo? Going? Whatever time is it? You'll have *hours* to wait on the platform, you know. I'm certain the train will never be on time. Don't you remember Frieda's was two hours overdue when she came back from settling Simone at Penrith?'

'I can't bank on that. Ten to one if I'm late the train will be on time, and those three poor creatures will have to wander about the station till I turn up. They must be feeling quite awful enough, if all Jean Mackenzie said about them is true, without having *that* added.'

'Have you had some coffee? And something to eat?'

'Yes; Anna left me a flask full of coffee, and she'd also made me some sandwiches. I disposed of them while I was dressing. Now listen, Rob. It's quite likely that you are right, and I'll have ages to wait. Don't get alarmed if we don't arrive for two or three hours. If there's likely to be any really bad delay, I'll ring you up from the nearest call-box. Warn Daisy to keep herself fit to be seen; and give an eye to Primula, won't you? I'd like my family to make as good an impression as possible to start with. Goodness knows it can't last long! Still, let's begin as well as we can. Anna will see to the house, and Daisy can help you with the children. I've put out clean frocks for them on my bed; also overalls. And tell Len that if she's naughty about hers, Mamma said she was either to wear it or stay in bed. She hates pinnies, that child!'

Robin laughed. 'I didn't exactly love them

myself. But you'd never keep them in clean frocks if we didn't do something of the kind. Very well, Joey. I'll see to them. And Daisy will be a great stand-by. She always is. I hope you won't have too long to wait in Armiford, but you never know what to expect nowadays. The rooms are all ready for the McDonalds; and Anna will have the furnace going thoroughly, so that they can have hot baths at once if they want them after an all-night journey. Unless you ring up, I'll have breakfast waiting for them about half-past seven. Will that be all right?'

'I should think so. I hope,' added Jo anxiously, 'that they don't want porridge, for I don't believe there's a soul in the house who can make it decently. I must get the eldest McDonald to show me how while she's here. The children ought to be having it in the winter.'

'Well, I certainly shan't attempt it. Bacon and eggs and toast and marmalade they shall have; and a choice of tea or coffee. But that's the best I can do. And once the hens stop laying, the eggs will be a problem. We've managed very well so far; and Anna informed me with much triumph that she had two hundred put down in waterglass. But they won't go far with the houseful we'll have here—the triplets; Daisy and Primula; Peggy and Sybil and Bride; Anna; our two selves; and now these three—and Jack, when he comes on leave.'

'Those hens were certainly an idea,' mused Jo. 'And you deserve a vote of thanks for suggesting them; never to speak of the work you and Daisy have put in on them. Well, I must get off. Bye-bye for the present. And try to have the family looking somewhere near respectable when we get back, won't you?'

Robin nodded. 'Don't worry. I'll see to them. Is Anna up yet?'

'I heard her moving about when I left my room. The children ought to sleep for another hour or two. Dig Daisy out at seven though. She's a lazy young monkey.'

Robin laughed as Jo left the room. 'I'll dig her out all right. Don't fuss, Joey! And hurry up in case the train *is* on time for once.'

Jo went leaping down the stairs, and Robin, left to herself, glanced at her wrist-watch which was lying on the bedside table. 'Twenty to six. Jo will have to buck up if she means to be at Armiford station by half-past six. Not that I think it'll do any good. Well, I'll just have another chapter or so of *In the Steps of St Paul*, and then I'd better get out. But it's not worth while going to sleep again.' She pushed up her pillows, pulled a woolly round her shoulders, for her night-gown was sleeveless, and the morning air coming in through the wide-open window was sharp, with just a touch of frost, and settled down to a half-hour of enjoyment.

Meanwhile, Jo ran round to the garage at the back of the house, unlocked the door, and five minutes later was driving down the short drive in her own little car. 'Thank goodness I'm up on petrol for once!' she thought as she turned out into the road. 'Much better bringing them in Boanerges than having to take a taxi. I hope I can recognise them all right. Jean gave me very little idea about their looks. Still—one grown-up girl and two babes of eleven; they ought to be seen easily.' She changed gears for the steep hill, driving carefully, for the road was not wide, and many motor lorries were already speeding past her.

Half-way to Armiford, she passed the new, big aerodrome where already a large village of houses had grown up, and aeroplanes were taking off, arriving, or, in the sheds at the far end—about a mile away—being tinkered at. It was a self-contained community—a little town to itself. After the war, it was intended to form one of the big civil aviation centres. At present it was the home of bombers, Spitfires, fighter-planes of all kinds; and Jo knew that the thick masses of bush and scrub hid anti-aircraft guns, many of them of amazing calibre.

Once past this place, she had the road to herself for a little, and she pushed ahead, for before long she would turn on to the main road between Armiford and the next nearest county town, and she knew well that the chances were that she would find it packed with lorries, army vans of all descriptions, and marching men, never to mention its more normal travellers—cattle returning to pasture from the milking-sheds, and sheep being moved from one field to another. Part of the way lay past a series of hopyards, where already workers were busy on the vines. The School had taken four cribs in aid of the local county hospital, and several of the elder girls had returned early from their holidays to pick hops, as well as two or three of the Staff. She herself was too busy for more than an odd afternoon or so in the hopyard; but Robin and Daisy had already rendered yeoman's service, and would have gone again this morning if it had not been for the arrival of the McDonalds. It was pleasant, healthy work, and the long days in the open air had done both girls good; while at night they went early to bed, and slept, as Jo once remarked disgustedly, like a pair of guinea-pigs in winter. She used the quiet two hours or so after they had gone to get on with the book she was writing; for Jo, in addition to her many domestic activities, was a writer, and already had five gaily-jacketed books for girls to her credit. Another ought to arrive some time during the next month, and her plans were already laid for a seventh. But this one on which she was busy while the girls slept was a novel—her first—and she had a good deal of work to do in connection with it, for it was historical, dealing with the South Sea Bubble of 1720, and that meant much reading of history to be sure that she got all her facts correct. Taken by and large, she was not really sorry that Robin and Daisy were ready for bed by half-past eight or nine each night.

It was just twenty-past six when she entered the built-up area of Armiford, and was obliged to reduce her speed considerably as she went down the long road with its houses on either side which began below the railway bridge. She made the sharp turn where the Sors road runs into what is known as Fairmount Road, crossed the old stone bridge which has seen eight centuries, and turned into King Street, and thence through Broad Street, past the cathedral —largely spoilt by 'restoration' at the beginning of the present century—and then through the bottle-neck of High Street, and across the fine quadrangle of High Town where most of the best shops in

Armiford stand. Past the Old House—a Jacobean house once kept as a museum of Jacobean relics and now used for the Citizens' Bureau—and so down narrow St Stephen's Gate into the magnificent sweep of Broome Road with the big chapel and bus-station at one side, and then up the station approach, till she drew up at one side of the station square. Here she parked the car, and having made sure that it was safely locked up—a fine six weeks before for leaving it unlocked had made heedless Jo very particular about this—strolled across to the station just as the cathedral clock chimed half-past six. No train stood in the station, nor were there any signs that one was expected shortly. Jo passed through the booking-office into the station, looking for someone to whom she could show her platform ticket, and finally ran to earth a solitary porter who, in answer to her questions, informed her that the train from Stockport would be considerably overdue.

'Why?' demanded Jo.

'Air-raids up north,' he said laconically.

'Air-raids! Oh, Jehoshaphat!' Jo was upset at this. After living for so many years in the peace and quiet of a tiny island, what would the Highland girls make of such an ordeal? 'How late is it likely to be?' she asked anxiously.

'Three hours, I reckon,' he told her. 'Any'ow not before 'alf-pars' eight—if then. Likely 'alf-pars' nine. Better go 'ome again, lady.'

Jo considered this, and decided against it. 'I think I'll go to some friends—I've come from Howells village, and I haven't got an awful lot of petrol,' she said. 'The car'll be all right out in the station yard, won't it? I can walk there—they only live in Weonister Road.'

He nodded. 'She'll be safe enough if you've locked 'er. Where've you parked? Best lemme see 'case she'll be in the way of the army lorries.' He escorted Jo to the station yard, approved of the place in which she had parked the car, and then left her, for a local train was due at seven, and already it was ten minutes to the hour. Jo popped a shilling into his hand on his undertaking to keep an eye on Boanerges, and departed by a side track from the road above the station to seek the home of Mrs Lucy, a close friend of hers, there to demand breakfast when it was ready. She had no fears of disturbing the household. Janie Lucy was the mother of five healthy children, and Julie, John, Betsy, Vi, and Barney were early birds like her own trio.

When she reached the house ten minutes later, she found the family all racing about the garden, and was welcomed vociferously.

Julie Lucy, a dark, handsome child of ten, came running to open the gate for her, with a demand to know why she had come so early.

'I've come to meet some girls from Scotland,' explained Jo as she ruffled the thick black hair that curled all over Julie's head. 'Is Mummy up yet, Julie? Run and tell her I've arrived, honey.'

'You needn't tell me that,' called a sweet, fresh voice from an overhead window. 'What on earth are you doing in Armiford at this hour, Jo? Half a minute, and I'll come down. I'm just finishing off Barney. Julie, take Auntie Jo into the drawing-room; and Betsy, run and tell Michelle to squeeze the pot for her—you could do with a cup of tea, couldn't you, Joey? Breakfast won't be ready for nearly an hour yet.'

Betsy, a quaintly puckish-looking little person of seven, very like her mother in appearance, trotted off round the house to the kitchen, and Julie pulled her brevet-aunt up the short flight of steps, and into the pretty drawing-room, while John, aged nine, and Vi, a dainty little maid of four, followed them. Mrs Lucy arrived almost at once, her younger son tucked under her arm, and a slight girl of twenty behind her. Jo gave a cry of surprise on seeing her.

'Nan Blakeney! When did *you* turn up? This is a surprise.'

'*We*,' began Janie impressively, 'have an unexpected leave. *And—we*—no; be quiet, children! *I'm* telling this piece of news!—*we* are engaged! What do you think about that, Joey?'

'Engaged? Really, Nan? Oh, what fun! And when is the wedding to be? And who is he? Tell me all about it at once!' cried Joey.

Nan laughed, while she blushed furiously. 'You're as bad as Janie is, Joey! That's just the way she rushed at me last night when I got home and broke the news to her. You two are awfully alike in lots of ways. It's David Willoughby, and it only happened three days ago. As for when we are to be married, let me get used to being engaged first! And just answer a question or two yourself, please. Why are you here at this hour of the day?'

'It's this way,' began Joey, sinking into a huge chesterfield, as Michelle, Janie Lucy's little Guernésaise maid, appeared with a tray of early morning tea. 'I'm meeting three wild Highlanders who are coming to live with me—at least, the twins are——'

She got no further, for she was interrupted by peals of laughter from both Mrs Lucy and her young adopted sister. 'Twins again! I don't wonder you rose to triplets! You couldn't have done anything else!'

'Well, *you* can't say much,' argued Jo. 'You've got five of your own—oh, thank you, Nan—and Anne has a positive swarm. Even Elizabeth had twins. You've twin nephews and twin nieces. I think the less you say about twins the more you'll shine.'

Janie made a face at her. 'I may have five of my own, but at least they're singles. However, get on with the story while we have the tea.'

Thus adjured, Jo repeated the tale her friend Jean Mackenzie had written to her, and wound up with the explanation the porter had given her for the lateness of the train. 'So I thought I'd come and see if you could give me breakfast,' she concluded. 'Do you mind, J.?'

Janie laughed. 'Not in the least. D'you want bacon? I thought not. You aren't very English where breakfast is concerned, Jo. All right, Julie; run and tell Michelle to lay an extra place, please. Take Barney with you, Betsy, and all of you run off to the garden till you hear the bell. Run—shoo!' And she chased her family off to the garden.

When she came back, she found Nan asking questions about Shiena McDonald, for she was naturally interested in this girl who was, from Jo's account, only a year older than herself. 'You say she's kept house for her father all these years, and never seen a stranger till she left this island—what is it—Erisay?'

'So Jean says in her letter. That's all I have to go upon.'

'And she's joining up soon? Do you know which Service she'll have?'

'Not an idea. Her eldest brother is in the Air Force, and the second one is in the Navy, so I suppose it'll be either the W.A.A.F.s. or the W.R.N.S.; but which she's likely to choose, I couldn't tell you.'

'I hope it'll be the W.R.N.S.' Nan, a W.R.N. herself and the daughter of a Naval officer, though he had retired four years after her own birth, nodded her head with its coronal of black plaits over sea-blue eyes, which, with her pink-and-white skin, made such an attractive little person of her. 'Of course, she may prefer nursing, or the A.T.S. You can't say, can you?'

'You certainly can't after the queer bringing-up she seems to have had,' agreed Janie. 'And how is all your family, Jo? What's the latest?'

Jo chuckled, and settled down to recount the latest adventures of her own flock, which included not merely her triplets, but Robin, her adopted sister, and Daisy, her niece-by-marriage as well. Then breakfast came, and after breakfast she made tracks for the station once more. She was told that there was no hope of the train arriving for at least another hour, so she took the bus into town and did some shopping, returning to the station just as the train from Stockport steamed in.

It was some moments before Jo could get a sight of her quarry. Then she suddenly uttered a whoop which brought more than one curious pair of eyes on her, and dashed up to the spot where three bedraggled and begrimed girls were standing beside a pile of luggage, looking forlornly about them. They only could be her guests, for no one else was likely to be travelling in full Highland dress on a warm day in September, so she had no hesitation in demanding, 'Are you the McDonalds? I'm Mrs Maynard—Joey Maynard. What an awful time you seem to have had of it! You poor lambs! Come along to the car and we'll get home as quickly as possible. I'm sure you could all do with a good meal and a nice, hot bath. Give me those cases. Here comes my porter to take the trunks. I can manage that bundle of rugs as well if you'll shove them under my arm. Now come along, and let's get you to Plas Gwyn as fast as we can.'

The shy trio were swept away on the flood of her forcefulness. Almost before they knew where they were, they were across the bridge, through the booking-office, and over the station yard to the car at the far side, with Jo directing the grinning porter how to pack the trunks on the luggage carrier, while she tucked the twins into the back of the car, built them round with piles of bags, cases, and rugs, and ordered Shiena to the front seat beside her, with an airy warning of, 'Oh, mind how you stretch your legs, won't you? There's shopping down there.'

The McDonalds were quite stunned. Never, in all their lives, had they met anyone quite like Jo. On Erisay, life had flowed along smoothly and quietly, and there had been none of this rushing about and hurry. The clipped English accents of

Mrs Maynard sounded almost foreign to them, though her black eyes and hair were not so strange. Shiena wondered rather wistfully if *she* could ever become as competent as this girl who was plainly not much older than herself—if she was older at all. Joey by no means looked her nearly twenty-four years, despite her many responsibilities, and Shiena was inclined to think that she must have married in her teens. As for the twins, they had nothing to say, but sat like two little mutes in the back of the car, and longed for Erisay and the dear familiar things that all seemed so very far away now.

Still chattering, as much from nervousness as anything, Jo started the car, and presently they were driving through the now busy streets of Armiford. Then they flashed under a railway bridge with a train on it and into a country road with fields and hedges on both sides, and, in the distance, the long, gentle slopes of the Black Mountains. Jo pointed them out, explaining that some of them were more difficult than they looked, and then swung the car round a sharp corner, past the aerodrome, and so up the slope of a steep hill. At the top she changed gears, and they coasted down another slope, with the land rising on either side.

At one meadow she nodded, and told them that her sister, Lady Russell, lived in a house among the trees. 'At least, it's not exactly among the trees,' she added. 'Really, it stands above them. It's an old Georgian hunting lodge, and it has a glorious round room for the—well, I suppose you'd call it the living-room. There's a farm attached, and so my sister has her work cut out, what with all her family, and four of my brother's kiddies, as well as her own three to look after. You do know that we run to heaps of babes, don't you? Did Jean Mackenzie tell you about my triplets? And then I have Robin, and Daisy, and Primula who is Daisy's sister. However, you'll see them all presently. Now we turn down here—that road leads to Plas Howell where the School is—and we'll be home in two wags of a puppy-dog's tail.'

It was a very few minutes more before she turned into the short drive leading up to the open door of Plas Gwyn, where Robin and Daisy, attracted by the sound of the car, were already waiting for them, while on the lawn three small people with gleaming red hair and a little girl whose short, straight locks were primrose yellow, looked up, but remained where they were till they were called.

'Here you are!' exclaimed Robin, running down the wide, shallow steps to fling open the door of the car. 'Oh, how tired you must be! Jo rang up to tell us about the air-raids. I've got breakfast all ready for you and then baths will be waiting, and you must just go to bed for the rest of the morning and have a good nap. You'll feel better then.'

And that was their welcome to Plas Gwyn.

CHAPTER IV

FIRST DAYS

LONG after, when anyone asked them what their impressions of the first day at Plas Gwyn were, not one of the three McDonalds could say.

'It wass all so strange, and there wass so much to do,' Shiena explained to Jo once. 'You were all fery kind, but I felt so muddled.'

'I don't blame you,' returned Jo, looking up from the tiny white vest she was knitting. 'I know I thought you three were the shyest people I'd ever met—shyer even than Elspeth Macdonald when she first came to the Chalet School, and that's saying something, I can tell you!'

Once they were inside the house, where they got an impression of coolness, and peace, and the scent of flowers, Jo had taken Shiena up to the bathroom, while Robin and Daisy marched the twins to the little cloakroom off the hall so that they might wash the first thicknesses of grime from their hands and faces. There was plenty of hot water, and when the frightened pair had finished with the towels, Robin produced brush and comb, and insisted on brushing out the thick curls which did not reach much below their shoulders, while Daisy, wielding a stiff clothes-brush, did what she could for their clothes. When they were done, the two elder girls ushered them into a pretty room where big bowls of roses scented the air, and the sunshine came in through the open windows. A table had been set in one of the windows, and Fiona was able to note that it was laid ready for a meal. Almost at the same time, Mrs Maynard came in with their sister, who looked more like herself, and seated them round the table, taking the head of it herself.

'Ring for Anna, Daisy,' she said in the lovely, golden voice all three had noticed, scared though they were, when she first spoke to them. 'Can you and Rob manage a cup of coffee with me while these folk have a good, square meal? Then ask her to bring cups with her for us three.' Daisy ran out of the room, her short yellow plaits flying out from her head, calling for Anna in her high, sweet voice. Jo looked after her with a grin. 'Daisy is going on sixteen, though you mightn't think it,' she said. 'When you two go to school,' with a friendly nod to the twins, 'she'll look after you for a bit till you've felt your feet. Rob won't be there quite so much, as she's nearly eighteen, and her work doesn't need her as I do. You know I have triplet daughters, don't you? They'll be three on the third of November, and that means that someone has to be running after them all the time. I've got no one but Anna to help, so Miss Annersley, the Head, agreed that Rob need not go every day. So this next term she'll be there on Wednesdays, Thursdays, and Fridays only. Mondays and Tuesdays she'll be at home with me. This is a biggish house to run with only one maid and my large family, you see.'

The twins were silent; but Shiena, feeling that politeness demanded some answer from her, asked, 'Why iss it so hardt to get servants, Mrs Maynart?'

Jo's brows went up slightly at the Highland accent, but she took no other notice of it. 'Most of the girls have gone into one of the Women's Services,' she explained. 'I have a woman who comes for the day on Wednesdays, but Anna and I have to manage alone otherwise.'

At this point the door opened and Daisy came in again, followed by a sturdy person in blue print and spotless cap and apron. Her flaxen hair was worn in wreaths of plaits about her head, and her frock had short sleeves. She gave the strangers a pleasant smile as she set the big salver with tea and coffee pots before her mistress, and then turned to take the silver entrée dish from Daisy to set it before Robin. Toast in two big racks followed, and then Anna left the room, and they began—the visitors on their breakfast; Joey, Robin, and Daisy on cups of the delicious coffee which was so refreshing.

Jo talked, to quote herself, 'even on,' partly to help the newcomers to get over their shyness, partly because she herself felt nervous. Daisy, troubled by no such feelings, kept chipping in at intervals, and Robin, with her grave, sweet smile, saw to it that everyone had enough to eat. Finally, when Flora shook her head at the last bit of toast, and Shiena refused another cup of coffee, the mistress of the house arose. 'Five minutes to meet our babies,' she announced, 'and then baths and bed for you three. I'm sure you'll be glad of both.'

She ran to the window, and called, 'Prim—Primula! Fetch the triplets and come along and say "how d'you do" to Shiena and Flora and Fau—I mean Fiona!' She gabbled the last with a very red face, but they were all too tired to have noticed her slip. Besides, Primula came running up, the three tiny girls trotting behind her, and in the excitement of meeting their first triplets, the McDonalds paid no heed.

'Oh, *issn't* it funny to see three so much alike!' cried Flora, forgetting her shyness all at once. 'They *are* PRETTY! What are their names, pleass?'

Jo had dropped to the floor, a proceeding watched with some amazement by her eldest guest, and the trio had tumbled into her arms. 'This is my eldest daughter,' she said, with a smile at the grey-eyed baby. 'Lady Brown-eyes is really Con; and this little person is our baby Margot. Isn't it a mercy their eyes are all different? I'd never know them apart, otherwise.'

'But their hair iss different, too,' said Shiena after a careful look at them. 'The little one—Con—her hair iss darker than the others'; and wee Margot, she iss fairer. You woult know by their hair, too.'

Jo put her daughters back from her to look critically at the silky waves of hair tumbling over the small heads. 'I—believe—you're right,' she said slowly. 'Rob! what do you think—and you, Daisy?'

'I've seen it for the last few weeks,' said Robin calmly, 'but I didn't say anything. At first I thought it must be my imagination. Then I thought I'd better wait till you found it out for yourself. They are *not* going to be images of each other as we've all fondly imagined. Con will be dark—perhaps as dark as you, Joey. I've heard Bill say that red hair does sometimes turn black later on. And Margot is going to be quite fair. So far, Len seems to be going to be the only one who'll be really chestnutty. Not that Margot will ever be as fair as Daisy and Primula,' she added, with a glance at Daisy and a touch on the cheek of little Primula. 'She'll be reddy-gold. But I do think Con is going to have black hair like yours in time.'

Daisy burst into a peal of laughter. 'Oh, what *will* Jack say? He's been so proud of their all being so much alike! What a shock he'll get when he comes home again!'

'Well, that won't be for many a long day,' said Jo with an involuntary sigh. Her doctor husband had sailed for the East only two months before, and she knew it was likely to be a long time before he came back. Then she remembered her guests, and brisked up. 'I don't think I'll tell him. Do you hear, you people? You're to say nothing to him. Let him see them first. It'll be a pleasing little surprise when he *does* get back.' And she grinned impishly, looking ridiculously youthful to be the mother of even the three babies. 'Go and kiss Auntie Shiena, girlies, and tell her we're glad to have her, Flora, and F—Fiona here.'

The triplets were not shy. They left the shelter of their mother's arms to advance with tiny hands held out.

'Ve'y g'ad,' lisped Len. And the others repeated the words after her.

Shiena dropped on her knees. 'Dear lambs!' she murmured in Gaelic as she caught them in her arms. 'Oh, little flowers!'

The babies looked at her as the strange words rippled from her lips.

'Is that Gaelic?' asked Jo with interest. 'I never heard it before. It's not unlike our Tyrolean German, is it, Rob? Now, you two,' she added, turning to Flora and Fiona, 'this is Primula Venables, Daisy's sister. She's only nine, so two years younger than you, I think. And now, as you've met all my family—except my husband, of course—I think baths and bed are indicated. Take the babies back to the lawn, Daisy, and Rob will come with me to show Flora and Fiona their room. Come along, and we'll soon have you feeling more like yourselves again.'

Daisy and Primula led the small girls out to the lawn again, and Jo and Robin took their visitors upstairs to show them their rooms and the bathrooms, of which—as Jo pointed out with some pride —there were two.

'One must have been a dressing-room,' she said, as she gave Shiena a big bath-sheet, and pointed out soap and loofah and sponges, all new and waiting for her. 'With the gang we have here, it's just as well it was turned into a bathroom. Do you like bath salts, Shiena? Those are verbena, and here are lavender. Which will you have?'

Shiena stared at her. 'I ton't unterstant,' she said shyly.

'Oh, they just soften the water and make it smell nice,' said Jo, opening the jars. 'Which do you like best?'

Shiena sniffed timidly at them. 'I think thiss one,' she said, pointing to the lavender. 'But iss it necessary?'

'It's better for your skin,' said Jo solemnly as she tossed a double handful of the salts into the steaming water. She had just realised that such things were unknown in Erisay. Then she glanced round to see that her guest had everything needful, and withdrew to leave Shiena to slip out of her dressing-gown, and into the silky-feeling, scented water where she set to work to scrub all the dirt of that awful journey off herself.

Meanwhile Robin, having seen Flora safely into the bath, went to turn down the two little beds in the pretty green-and-white room allotted to the twins, and chat with Fiona to keep her from feeling alone.

'When you have had a good nap, we'll unpack your trunks and put everything away,' she said. 'Then you can feel at home. I hope you soon will feel as if you belonged to us,' she added. 'Of course, we know it can't be like your own home; but we do want you to feel happy.'

Tears welled up in Fiona's dark eyes. 'Inteet, you are fery, fery kind,' she faltered. 'We will try to be happy here.'

Robin slipped an arm round the thin shoulders, and bent and kissed her. 'You will be. Everyone is—or if they aren't, it's their own faults. And you'll love the School when you get used to it. I've been at it for eleven years. I went first when I was only a baby of six—younger than Primula. My mother had died, and my father had to go on a journey to Russia and couldn't take me. He gave me to Mrs Russell—I mean,' she added in some confusion, '*Lady* Russell. It's so dreadful, Fiona. Jem—Sir James, I mean—only got his baronetcy at the Birthday Honours, and we're having such a time remembering that they are Sir James and Lady Russell now, and not Dr and Mrs Russell. And Jo *will* rag them about it. Madge—that's Lady Russell—goes all purple when she's given her title. He got it for the work he's done for T.B.—tuberculosis,

I mean. He's made things a lot better for heaps of people. I tell Jo not to be so silly. Her Jack is just as likely to get into the Honours List some time, and then it'll be her turn to be teased. But she only grins and says, "I'll wait till then. And *I* shan't turn a beetroot red." I don't think she will, either,' added Robin reflectively. 'Jo's not that kind. And, of course, now that Jack has gone to the East, it's taking him off his proper work.—Oh, here's Flora! Nice and clean now, Flora? To-morrow, you shall both wash your hair, and then you really will feel clean. But just for today, you'd better rest as much as you can. This is your bed, dear. Get in, and I'll come and tuck you up when I've seen Fiona to the bathroom and run her water for her.' She gave Flora a smile and ushered Fiona across the landing to the bathroom, where she ran the water and saw that the small girl had all she needed before she went back to the bedroom where Flora was already lying in the little bed under the east window. Fiona's had been placed near a south window, but the twins were quite near each other.

Flora lay looking round the room which was very unlike the somewhat dark long slip of a chamber she and Fiona had shared on Erisay. The walls were white, with a border of green leaves running round them below the picture-rail and above the skirting-boards. A green carpet lay on the floor, and the white-painted bedsteads had green eider-downs on them to match. Two wicker chairs stood on either side of the fireplace, with green cushions in them, and the curtains were of white cretonne with a pattern of green leaves running all over it, and green linings which, with the dark green blinds, made a perfect black-out. The lights had green shades, and the hearth was tiled in green. A book-case with about a dozen books of various kinds stood against one wall; a pretty dressing-table, set in the best light, was across a corner. Twin ward-robes stood against the other wall. There were two or three cane-seated chairs, and a big, fleecy white rug before the hearth. It was as fresh and dainty and spring-like as it could be, and Flora, who was an artist at heart, and who had never been in such a gay, pretty room before, revelled in it, even though she was so sleepy, what with her adventures, the good meal, and her hot bath, that she could scarcely keep her eyes open. Robin saw how it was, and quietly drew the curtains across her window.

'You must sleep,' she said. 'Don't try to stay awake for Fiona.'

She need not have spoken. Already Flora was far away, and when Fiona came back from her bath, her sister was sound asleep. Robin only waited to tuck her up and draw her curtains too, and then she slipped out of the room knowing that both children were sleeping sweetly, and went to seek Joey and the others. She found them all on the lawn, and Jo, who, for once, was busy sewing, looked up with a fond smile at the slight girl coming across the grass to them.

'All safe in bed?' she asked, as Robin dropped at her feet.

'Rather! *And* sleeping like the Seven Sleepers all rolled into one. Poor babes! They could scarcely keep awake long enough to get there!'

'That's rather what Shiena was like. I expect they're worn out. She told me they were actually bombed on the journey from Newcastle to Leeds and held up between Stockport and here. I don't wonder the train was late. We must all be very quiet not to disturb them. I want them to sleep as long as they will. So mind you don't do any of your usual yelling about the place, Daisy. You sing so much, you often forget to be quiet, even when the babies are having their afternoon nap.'

Daisy chuckled. 'Well, at any rate I don't go giving our guests nicknames before they've been in the house an hour. Auntie Madge told you you'd call the kid that to her face if you went on about "Flora and Fauna," and she was quite right, as she usually is.'

Jo went pink. 'I don't think any of them noticed it. And *you* can't talk! You've been doing it yourself all this week. You just mind *you* don't come out with it. It would be a bit of a shock for her, I should think.'

'I did it myself,' confessed Robin with a laugh. 'It's awfully easy to make a slip of that kind. Well, what do you think of them all, Joey?'

'Too soon to tell. They're painfully shy, poor lambs; though Shiena tried to talk a little. But I could see what an effort it was for her. We shall have to go slow with them, and let them get accustomed to us before we let the rest of the clan loose on them. Did you get any sort of conversation out of either of the twins, Rob?'

'A few sentences—nothing much. And I think we shall like them when we get to know them.

But Jean Mackenzie was quite right to send them here first before they went to school. They'd be overwhelmed if they were sent straight to school. What about Shiena—or should Daisy and I call her Miss McDonald, Jo, do you think?'

Jo laughed. 'Actually, I haven't been given leave to call her Shiena myself. But she looks such a babe, I couldn't help it. *I* don't know how ever she'll get on in any of the Services. She's so totally unlike most of the girls in them. And her clothes! Lovely things, all most beautifully made; but they've evidently stuck to the same pattern for the last fifty years or so. I shall have to say something, for some of the others might laugh at her, and I should think she's very easily hurt by anything of that kind. But it'll be difficult, and my dearest friend can't say that tact is my long suit.'

'Get Auntie Madge to do it,' suggested Daisy.

'Yes; that's an idea. I think I will. Well, what are you two going to do with yourselves this afternoon? I expected we'd get here sooner than we did, and then I was going to suggest you went to the hopyards at twelve. But it's nearly one now, and it would be close on two before you got there. It might be as well if you just stayed here.'

'I've got stockings to mend,' said Robin with a grimace. 'If I get them, what about us all sitting here this afternoon, Jo? Daisy can read to us while we get on with the sewing. Then we'll be on hand if we're needed.'

Accordingly, when Shiena came down to the garden at four o'clock, she found Jo and Robin busy with their sewing, while Daisy was reading aloud from *An Inland Voyage*; and the triplets and Primula were playing in the sand-heap at the far side of the house. Of her own small sisters there was no sign. Jo, glancing up, saw her first, and held out a welcoming hand to her. 'Come along and sit down. Did you have a good sleep? You look heaps better—all rosy and fresh.'

'Yess, thank you. I slept fery well,' said Shiena, sitting down in the deck-chair Daisy pulled forward for her. 'Oh, I wass tired! I haf nefer peen so tired in my life pefore. And the twins—are they asleep now? I haf not seen them.'

'Fast asleep when last I looked in on them—which was about half an hour ago when I took my family in for a wash after their afternoon nap,' said Jo cheerfully. 'Do you want to go and have a peep at them? I'll take you up, shall I? And then you can feel sure they are all right?'

Shiena shook her head. 'If you say they are, Mrs Maynart, I am sure they are. And they were so tired, poor wee lassies. Flora cried with tiredness in the train, and Fiona wass not far from it. I woult rather they slept till they woke, if you ton't mint.'

'Of course I don't mind! Let them sleep the clock round if they like. Probably the best thing they can do. But there is one thing I mind, Shiena. I don't like to be Mrs Maynard to people who are making their homes with me. I call you Shiena—I admit without any permission—but couldn't you follow my example and call me Jo or Joey?'

Shiena went crimson. 'But—it seems so rude

and forward. It iss different for me; but you are marriet——'

'What on earth difference does that make?' gasped Jo.

'It makes it different.'

'Can't see it myself.'

'But it *iss* so,' persisted Shiena. 'A marriet lady hass more dignity than a maiden girl. I woult not like to take a liberty.'

'Well! What are you two giggling about?' demanded Jo indignantly of Robin and Daisy who had collapsed at Shiena's last speech. 'As for taking a liberty, Shiena, there isn't any, when I've *asked* you to do it. If you come to that, how about me using your given name from the word "Go!" almost? Of course, if you want to be "Miss McDonald"—' She stopped tantalisingly, and Shiena began to utter wild protests.

'Inteet, I nefer meant that! I hope you will always call me Shiena. It iss kint of you, and I like it. And I will say Jo if you wish it. It was shust I coult not forget you are marriet, and a matron!'

Whereat Robin and Daisy gave up all attempts at self-control, and shrieked with laughter, while Jo, more startled than ever—she had never thought of herself as a 'matron,' and Shiena's statement came as a shock to her—after flinging them a look of scorn, replied, 'But I honestly would much rather you made it "Jo." I—I don't *feel* like a—a matron. —*Will* you two stop that idiotic yelling? Do you want to wake up Flora and—Fiona?' She ended lamely, for she had come within an ace of making 'Fauna' of it, and she judged that Shiena might not appreciate such humour as yet—wherein she was right. There had been no jokes of the kind in Erisay—indeed, only Archie had been treated to an abbreviated form of his name, the rest being religiously kept to those by which they had been baptised.

Robin and Daisy, guessing shrewdly what was happening, redoubled their wild shrieks of mirth, and then the curtain at one of the windows overlooking the part of the garden where they were was swept aside, and two tousled heads, one fair, one dark, were poked out. The twins were awake at last, and wondering what all the laughter was about.

CHAPTER V

THE SCHOOL MEETS THE HIGHLANDERS

IT was a week later when the School made the acquaintance of the strangers. By that time the Highlanders had become more or less—chiefly less—accustomed to Joey and her household. Jo herself was still very much of a mystery to them. How anyone who was married, and the mother of three daughters, could still lapse into schoolgirl gigglings, and behave as if she were fourteen instead of almost twenty-four, was beyond them.

'But don't you think my daughters will prefer it to a mother who is all prim and sticky?' Jo demanded when Shiena shyly said something about it to her. 'I hope I never come to that. As far as possible, I want to be a chum to them. I certainly don't intend to be one of those *bossy* mothers who think that they can and should order their children about as if they were so many little slaves. Apart from anything else, it must have an awful effect on a child's manners if she never hears her mother say, "Please will you?" to her, but always, "Do this—do that!" *I* think you should be as courteous to a child as you are to anyone else. I don't see how you can expect courtesy from them if you aren't.'

Shiena turned this over in her mind—Jo had discovered that she generally considered a thing before she gave her opinion on it—then she nodded. 'Yess; I can see that you are right, Joey. A child learns more py example than py preaching. If your babies see that you are polite and considerate to eferyone, efen themselves, then they will grow up thinking it iss only right they shoult pe so, too.'

Jo nodded. 'Exactly. You've got my idea. From the very first I mean them to be accustomed to being spoken to nicely. Then, if I hear them being rude to anyone else, I can pull them up for it with a good deal more effect than if they can think—whatever they may or may not say—"Oh, it's all very well Mamma talking, but I've heard her speak just as rudely to us, so why should *we* bother?"'

'I see. And you play with them, and laugh and joke with Daisy and Robin and them so that they may think of you as a playmate. It iss fery nice for them, and I wish,' Shiena spoke a trifle wistfully, 'I wish all parents thought like you. My own mother was fery dear and good to us, but I cannot efer remember her playing with us. And my father nefer did, of course. He wass a student and he did not bother with us so long as we had food and clothes and a roof ofer our heads. He thought it wass enough.'

'Men are like that,' agreed the experienced Jo gravely. 'Well, I am going to take you all up to Plas Howell this afternoon—where the School is, you know. They came back yesterday, and they'll be longing to see us all. Daisy can't go, poor lamb—not with that swollen cheek, anyhow; and Rob went off an hour ago. But we'll pack the babies into the car, and run the lot of us up the hill. It's high time Flora and Fiona began to meet some of their future little playfellows!'

So it came about that that afternoon saw Jo's little car packed to the brim with Shiena and the twins, each nursing a baby, and herself as driver, making its way up the long winding drive that led from the high-road to Plas Howell. The twins were inwardly excited and also half afraid. Jo had insisted that while the warm weather lasted they must have cotton frocks to wear, so they made their first appearance looking, as she thought to herself, just like any one rational. Flora wore forget-me-not blue and Fiona soft green, while Shiena was dainty in wild-rose pink. They had never had such frocks in their lives, for their father, proud of his Highland descent, had insisted that they keep to the national dress on Erisay.

When they finally drew up before the wide, semi-circular steps at Plas Howell, there came a wild shout, and then, or so it seemed to the startled McDonalds, the whole place was boiling over with girls. Girls came tearing along the grassy terrace on either side; girls came racing round the bend in the gravelled path that ran below it; girls poured out from the wide-open door; two girls even hung out of an upper window, and called down joyfully, 'Joey Maynard! At last! Wait for us—we're coming down at once!' before they disappeared to arrive presently among the throng that were crowding round Joey and her family, all exclaiming and welcoming at once.

'Joey Maynard! Why haven't you been up before? We expected you to be here to welcome us, but never a sniff have we had at you till now!' scolded one ruddy-haired damsel, whose clear pallor and dark brows and lashes made her stand out among the more ordinary crowd.

'Couldn't fix it,' returned Jo. 'I've been entertaining visitors, and now I've brought them to see you. Congratulations on your results, by the way, Elizabeth. You've done well. You, too, Enid,' to a merry-faced, blue-eyed person of seventeen, who came up now and tucked her arm through Elizabeth's. '*And* all the rest of you! I was thrilled to see the list in the "Armiford Times." The School has certainly done itself proud this time!—Oh, Julie,' as that young lady's black curls suddenly bobbed up among the others, 'you're the very person I want to see. Where are Nancy and Vanna and Nella? Go and fetch them, honey, will you? I want you four.'

Julie ran off, and presently returned with the three Jo had named—a dark-haired, dark-eyed little person of her own age, and two people a little older, who combined golden locks with big brown eyes very charmingly. These three hailed Jo and the babies with squeals of joy, but Jo became very business-like, and turned to the Highland twins.

'Flora and Fiona, these are Julie Lucy, Nancy Chester, and Vanna and Nella Ozanne who are all about your age. You four, these are Flora and Fauna McDonald, who have come from the Outer Hebrides, and are going to live with me for a while. They'll be coming to school presently, when they've got accustomed to us. That will break them in for all you wild hooligans. And don't yell at me, you folk, or I'll go away at once.'

'We'll see to them, Auntie Jo,' said Julie, who was not shy. She turned and smiled at the twins. 'Come along with us, and we'll show you our form-room and the form garden and everything else.'

Flora and Fiona were too much overcome to do anything but go with her and the others, and they all vanished into the house while Jo, with laughing eyes, looked at Shiena. 'There now; the first of our problems is solved. By the way, though, those four are only ten—at least Vanna and Nella are almost eleven. Aren't *your* twins eleven?'

'Yess,' agreed Shiena shyly, 'but they will pe glat to pe with such girls, I know. And I shoult not haf thought them younger than my two.'

The girls looked interested at the soft, Highland accents, but they were too well drilled to do more, and Jo promptly began to introduce everyone within reach. 'Girls! This is Miss McDonald, Flora and Fauna's sister, who is staying with me for a few weeks——'

'What's that? *What* did you say were their names, Jo?' demanded a sturdy, jolly-looking girl of seventeen, with short thick brown curls that showed reddish glints in the sunlight, and who had a pleasant, good-tempered face which was attractive without being in the least pretty.

Jo had the grace to blush as she replied, 'Oh, forget it, Jocelyn—do! It was only one of the more stupid of my jokes. Their names are Flora and Fiona.'

'*That* wasn't what you said!' retorted Jocelyn. 'What was it—*Fauna*? Oh, I see. How exactly like you, Jo! And how rude!' And she went off into peals of laughter, while Shiena turned puzzled eyes first on her and then on the sheepish Jo.

That young lady, having been well and truly found out in a misdeed, decided to put the best face on it that she could, and explained in her airiest fashion, 'The fact of the matter is, Shiena, that I rechristened your twins Flora and Fauna when Jean Mackenzie wrote to me about you all. It was tempting, but I oughtn't to have done it. Rob kept telling me I'd do it in public, and so did Madge. How they'll crow when they hear I have, too! You don't really mind, do you?' And she looked anxiously at Shiena, wondering how her eldest guest would take the joke.

Shiena stared for a moment. Then a smile dawned on her face, and she began to laugh, her low, rippling laugh that struck the girls as one of the prettiest things they had ever heard. 'But it iss really clever. I shoult nefer haf thought of it myself; but I do see how clefer it iss.' And once again her merriment pealed forth, while Jo heaved a sigh of relief, and mopped her brow exaggeratedly.

'What a relief! I was so afraid you'd be offended—or hurt, which would have been worse. I'm sorry, Shiena, but I'm dreadfully afraid I've saddled Fiona for the whole of her career here with a nick-name. These young wretches will never forget it, I know, and it'll go the rounds, now.'

Shiena nodded. 'What if it does? That iss one of the things one has to enture at school. I know, for Archie said so, and so did Hugh.'

'Thanks, Shiena. And now let me get on with my job. I was introducing you.' And Jo turned to the laughing girls, and presented them quickly. 'This is Enid Sothern who comes from Devon; and here's her chum, Elizabeth Arnett. And these are Nicole de Saumarez, Mary Shand—whose home is in America, by the way, only she can't get back, so has to stay here—Myfanwy Tudor, and Jocelyn Redford, who proposes to become a gardener. Now you know the most important people in the School—the prefects, I mean. The rest of this gang are hoi polloi or riff-raff—' She got no further, for she was howled down by the indignant members of the Upper Fourth and Fifth Forms who happened to be present.

'Riff-raff yourself, Joey Maynard! What a nerve!'

'We'll punish her—let's kidnap the babies!' suggested a bright-eyed person of between fifteen and sixteen. 'Come on, you people! Bags me Con!' And she made a dive for Jo's second daughter, and, picking her up, hared off along the path, followed by a crowd who had made off with Len and little Margot, who went quite willingly with them, much to the amazement of Shiena; while Jo sent after them a wail of, 'My precious babies! Mind what you do with them among you all! And *don't* give them raw gooseberries to eat!' Then she agreed to going into the house with the rest, her arm tucked through Shiena's, and chattering nineteen to the dozen as she congratulated successful examinees, asked questions about holidays, and poured forth her own news all in almost the same breath.

Meanwhile, the twins, having been borne off by the four cousins—Julie Lucy had once said, 'Aren't we almost a *school* of relations!'—were being introduced by them to their first glimpse of school life. They were taken into a big, sunny room, furnished with folding desks, oak chairs to match, and long, low shelves, running round two sides of the room, and filled with books. On the walls hung copies of famous pictures—only three or four—and the broad window-sills bore flowering plants and vases of roses. Short net curtains fluttered in the breeze that came through the open casements, and some one had twined sprays of silvery honesty and flaming Chinese lanterns in the bars of the big, old-fashioned grate. Anything less like the somewhat gloomy apartment which had been the school-room at Erisay House the twins had never imagined. They were so surprised, they forgot to be shy, and Flora said eagerly, 'But you ton't mean that you do lessons here? This issn't where you learn, surely?'

'Of course it is,' said Vanna, the darker of the Ozanne twins, though she and her sister were far more alike than Flora and Fiona. 'Look at the desks! What do you think they're here for? Of course we do lessons here. And what's more, we have to work jolly hard, let me tell you.'

'Where've you been at school before?' asked sunny-faced Nancy Chester.

'We haf nefer been to school anywhere,' said Fiona. 'Shiena—that iss our sister—taught us at home—on Erisay. Ant Mr McInnes, who wass the minister, he taught us Latin and sums, for Shiena does not know them fery well.'

'You talk a bit like Gwensi Howell when we first came here from Guernsey,' remarked Nella Ozanne with interest. 'She doesn't do it often now—only when she's mad about something. But I liked to hear her. Say some more, won't you? It is so pretty to hear you.'

Fiona crimsoned to the roots of her black curls. No one at Plas Gwyn had made any comments on their speech—not to them, at any rate—so Nella's blunt remarks rather took her aback.

Vanna rushed to the rescue. 'Nella Ozanne, how *rude* of you! Never mind her—what is your name, by the way? I didn't catch what Auntie Jo said.'

'It iss Fiona; and my sister, she iss Flora,' said Fiona with an effort.

'Fiona? How pretty! And we haven't got a Fiona or a Flora, either,' said Julie with interest. 'But it didn't sound like Fiona when Auntie Jo said it. It was something different—what was it?—I can't remember.'

'Something like Fawns,' said Nancy thoughtfully. Then, with a sudden burst of intelligence, 'I know!

It was Fauna! Oh, what a joke! Don't you see, you people—Flora and Fauna—like in the j'ography book.'

'My name iss *Fiona*,' cried that young person rather indignantly; and the rest all hastened to smooth her down at once.

'Oh, of course! Auntie Jo was only joking. She's always at it. You'd never think she was a mummy, would you?' asked Nancy of her cousins.

'Auntie J. is a bit like it, too,' said Nella. 'That's why Bill—he's one of our brothers, Fiona—always calls her our "best aunt." He doesn't mean that Auntie Anne (who's Nancy's mummy) isn't a dear, too; but Auntie J. is always laughing and teasing, and Auntie Anne hasn't time.'

'She couldn't have—there's such a crowd of us,' agreed Nancy. 'And Nella's and Vanna's mummy (who is our Auntie Elizabeth) is too grown-up to do it, somehow. Auntie J. isn't—same as Auntie Jo.'

'Daddy says she never *has* grown up, and never will,' said Julie. 'I heard him one day when he'd been chasing her round the garden for something, and caught her. "You're a real kid, J. You've never grown up in spite of our large family and you never will, even when you're a white-haired old lady with great-grandchildren!" That's what he said.'

'It must be fery nice,' said Fiona, with a wistful remembrance of the grave, pale-faced scholar she had called 'father.'

'*I* think it's just as well Auntie Elizabeth doesn't do it,' said Nancy decidedly. 'Bill's more than enough for one family.'

'He can be *awful*!' agreed his sister. 'Well, have

we done here? Let's show them the garden next, shall we? Come on, all of you.'

They all turned and went out of the room, and presently Flora and Fiona were running with the other four down a narrow path which led between rhododendrons to a great space surrounded by chestnuts, limes, and one or two huge old oaks. Here were situated the school gardens, long, wide strips of ground, one to each form. The schoolgirls pointed out the big bed which the Sixth had dedicated to the growing of cabbages, sprouts, turnips and carrots, and beetroot. The Fifth Form had had theirs filled with potatoes, but these had been 'lifted' or dug up in June and July, and were now given over to the growing of scarlet runner, broad, and kidney beans, most of which were dried and stored for winter use. The Upper Fourth had a huge asparagus bed, and had surrounded it with strawberry runners; while at the foot of it were some very healthy-looking artichokes. The Lower Fourth grew, as they had done ever since they had begun, all kinds of salads; and lettuce, endive, chicory, spring onions, radishes and even sorrel and dandelions—the latter very carefully kept in order—had given the School many a deliciously cool meal during the summer, and even now there were lettuces and one or two other varieties of salads. The Third Form had gone in exclusively for onions, but these, like the potatoes, had been lifted in July, and the girls were now busy hoeing and raking in readiness for spring cabbages, leeks, and autumn turnips.

'And this is *ours*,' said Julie, leading the way to a series of fruit cages, where healthy raspberry canes, gooseberry bushes, and currant bushes, now stripped of their fruit, but showing that they had evidently borne a goodly crop, were the main contents. 'We've got American blackberries over here by themselves, but they do need a lot of watching, or they'd do for everything else. I never knew such things! If you leave them alone for just a week, you find an absolute *hedge* of brambles when you go back. But we've all saved a little sugar all through the year for jam, and Matey says when we gather the fruit she'll make blackberry jelly of some of it.'

'Do you think you two will be in our form when you come?' asked Nancy.

The twins shook their heads. They had no idea.

'Well, what sums are you doing?' asked Vanna practically. 'That tells a bit as a rule. We were doing adding tons and pounds; and miles and yards —not all mixed up like that, of course,' she added hastily as Fiona turned an amazed glance on her, 'but sep'rately, you know. Can you?'

Flora shook her head. 'We were doing adding money—and taking away,' she said. 'But we were efer so far on in the "Ora Maritima,"' she added hopefully. 'And Shiena—that iss our sister—taught us the Stuart kings in history before we hat to leaf Erisay. We had got to James the Fifth.'

The other four gaped at her. 'James the *Fifth*? But I thought there were only *two* of them!' cried Vanna amazedly.

'Oh, no—sefen altogether,' replied Flora decidedly.

'Eight, if you count James Edward that wass called the Old Pretender,' put in Fiona helpfully.

'And you *must* know about James the Fifth. He wass the father of Mary Queen of Scots that——'

'I know—that that old cat Elizabeth *murdered*,' Nancy finished off for her. 'But I see now what you mean. Of course, you 've been doing *Scotch* history, and they *did* have a lot of Jameses. Don't you remember, you three? Miss Burnett told us that our James the First was called James the Sixth in Scotland. Isn't that it, you two?'

'But of course we did Scottish history. What else woult we do?' demanded Fiona. 'Hafn't you read *Tales of a Grandfather* by Sir Walter Scott? That tells all apout our kings.'

'It's in the lib'ry, I think,' said Julie. 'But here, of course, we do English hist'ry. We were just going to begin William-an'-Mary when the term ended, so I s'pose we'll go on. But we only got back yesterday, and we shan't begin lessons till Monday. The day-girls came this morning to unpack their books and get everything ready for then; but that 's all we ever do till the first Monday. Then we start fair with lessons.'

'When do you think you'll come?' asked Vanna. 'Do hurry up and begin. Won't your people let you start on Monday with the rest of us? If you don't, you'll be ever so far behind us, and they might even put you into the Lower Second. If you worked hard at 'rithmetic, and your writing and spelling and reading's not too bad, they may give you a trial with us, and that would be jolly nice. You don't want to be with a lot of babies like Sybil Russell and Jackie Bettany, do you?'

Emphatically, the twins did not. They liked what

they had seen of these four, and they already knew Bride Bettany, Lady Russell's second niece, who was also in the Upper Second, which Vanna modestly claimed as being 'Not half a bad form—one of the nicest, *I* think.' Their upbringing had made them curiously childish in many ways; and they were small and slight for their age, while Julie Lucy, who 'took after' her big father, was taller than they, and Nancy and the Ozanne twins were quite as tall. To go to school and be in a 'form' with five people they already knew seemed to them to be better than to go later and have to be with people like Sybil Russell and her friends. Miss Sybil was quite alive to her importance as the elder daughter of the family, and a beauty at that, and she had rather turned up her small nose at these girls with their queer speech and shy ways when Jo had taken them to the Round House, the Russells' beautiful home, to have tea with Lady Russell's small fry. Jo herself had noticed this, and commented on it to her sister.

'Sybil's giving herself awful airs, my dear. She's getting thoroughly spoilt. It isn't even as if she were the only girl. There's Josette coming along. I think it's time some one took Sybil down a peg or two.'

'It's not my fault,' returned Madge Russell. 'Don't blame me, my dear. It's all the silly idiots of young doctors and visitors who rave about her beauty. And you must admit, Jo, that she *is* pretty.'

'Oh, she's the pick of the whole bunch—my own three not excepted—so far as looks go,' admitted Jo. 'What a pity it is people don't see what harm they do to children when they start making a fuss of them because they're attractive and taking and so on!

Sybil is a raving beauty already, I quite agree. And it's the type that'll last. She isn't just all colouring, as so many pretty children are. She has perfect features as well, and she's so dainty and graceful with it. But, for the good of her soul, I think it's time someone gave her a good squashing or two, or she'll grow into a most unbearable girl.'

'David does his best,' laughed Lady Russell. 'He really is a most disapproving brother. And I administer an occasional squashing myself when I see it's needed. She certainly isn't too polite to Flora and Fiona. I must speak very seriously to her when she goes to bed. But I think part of it comes from having so many much older cousins than herself in the house. Sybil knows she's a daughter of the house, and Peg and Rix and Bride are cousins, and she's trying to keep her end up with them all.'

'Well, I shan't bring my Highlanders here again until Sybs has learnt to be less condescending to them,' declared Jo crossly.

This being the state of affairs, the twins felt that life at school—which they knew must come sooner or later—would be much better if they were with these four and Bride, who was a sunshiny little person, very sweet-tempered, and with a small opinion of herself. And so Joey and Shiena got a shock when, on arriving home at Plas Gwyn, and after the three babies had been put to bed at their usual early hour, Flora and Fiona shyly begged to be allowed to start school on the coming Monday instead of waiting, as had been first arranged, until the half-term.

CHAPTER VI

THE TWINS GO TO SCHOOL

'GO to school on Monday?' gasped Jo, as the twins put their modest request to her and Shiena. 'But why this sudden change of tune?'

'It iss because we might be with Julie and the others, and it woult be so much nicer ass we know them a little,' explained Flora.

'I agree there. But you can go on meeting them, even if you don't go to school at once. We'd thought you'd better stay here and get accustomed to us first, you know, and not go till half-term. But if you really feel you'd like to start at once, I don't see why you shouldn't—do you, Shiena?'

'It woult be fery nice to know they are happy there pefore I must go away,' agreed Shiena. 'Yet I can see one hardt thing, and that iss how apout the uniform? We haf ordered it, but the laty said that it might be some weeks pefore it came, and what woult you do till then?'

The twins' faces fell. They hadn't thought of this. Neither had Jo, but she turned her mind on it at once, and considered possibilities.

'I think we could manage, Shiena. They'll want cotton frocks as long as this hot weather lasts. I've still got three of mine that I had my last year in school. They are almost new, because I'd had to get them as I grew so much between sixteen and seventeen. I didn't wear them out just in case they should come in useful for someone of our crowd later on, and I'd heaps of other frocks as well. They have very wide, flared skirts, and I believe if we took them to pieces and used the material carefully we could get four frocks Flora's and Fauna's size out of them. Then Daisy and Rob both have tunics they've outgrown—though Rob doesn't do *much* in the growing line, I must admit. Still, I think we could alter those. And you've both got white blouses, so there'd be no difficulty there. Yes; I think we needn't worry about the uniform question. But are you both quite sure that you want to begin at once? If you do, you'll have to stick to it, you know. No chopping and changing. We can't have that. Once you begin, you'll have to carry it through. So if, on second thoughts, you feel you'd really rather wait a few weeks, say so. It's up to you.'

But the twins were quite sure they would rather not wait, so Jo got up from her chair—they were all sitting on the lawn at the time—and went into the house and upstairs to the attic, where she routed out a trunk she had never opened since it came from Tyrol, and began to rummage in it. It proved a somewhat lengthy business, for all sorts of treasures turned up, many of which she had forgotten; and as the entire family had come with her, it took some time to go through them. Daisy—still with a badly-swollen cheek, but free from toothache for the moment—and Robin uttered wild shrieks of joy when a bundle of snapshots tumbled out, recalling for them and Jo many a wild prank, all of which had to be retailed to the Scottish girls, or else dismissed for the moment with a hasty, 'It's rather a long story. I'll tell you later.' Then a circlet of cardboard, rather badly cut about on the inside, and with remnants of silver paint still clinging to it, appeared, and Jo and Robin were at once doubled up in fits of laughter.

'Your halo, Rob! When we had that sheets and pillow-cases party the term I went back to school to teach because Peggy and Rix had measles and Madge wouldn't let me go back to the Sonnalpe for fear I caught it. Do you remember? I silvered it with a quick-drying enamel, but it didn't dry quickly enough, and what with the heat and one thing and another, it stuck and we couldn't get it off.' *

Robin chuckled. 'I should think I do! I began to think you'd have to scalp me; and your face, Joey, was a real treat. I've never seen you look so terrified—not even when we had to run before the Gestapo and were so nearly caught just before we got into Switzerland.'

'I was scared all right,' said Jo. 'I simply didn't see how we were going to get it off. Matron—that was Matron at St Agnes; we had three Matrons in those days, for we had three houses to the School—had to come to the rescue with her scissors in the end. See here—here's the ends of your curls yet, Rob.' And she pointed to two or three ends of curling black hair which still stuck to the painted cardboard.

It was eight o'clock before the trunk was emptied, and the dresses were found under everything else. Jo tossed them over a big box, and then began to

* See *Jo Returns to the Chalet School.*

bundle the other things back again. But she was stopped by the delighted twins. 'Oh, Mrs Maynard, do leaf them out, and then we can ask you apout them tomorrow,' begged Fiona. 'You do seem to haf had such funny adventures! *Pleass* leaf them out!'

Jo laughed and shrugged her shoulders. 'I can't leave a mess like this, though I'm glad to have been through that trunk. I knew I should do it, but at first I couldn't—it brought back too many memories. And then I got married, and had to settle down to housekeeping. Then the babies arrived, and we had to leave Guernsey when they were only a few months old—and a nice adventure *that* was!—and after we settled down here I've never seemed to have time for it, what with one thing and another.—Yes, Rufus, my precious? What is it? Supper-time, you think?' And she threw her arm round the neck of the beautiful St Bernard who had just padded gravely into the attic, and was gently nosing the emptied trunk with an air of deep interest, and rubbed her face in his ruff.

'Rufus knows the smell of Tyrol!' cried Daisy. 'He comes from Tiern See, you know. Just look at him!' For Rufus had sat back on his haunches, and was wagging a flail-like tail with delight.

'Yes, poor fellow!' said his mistress with a final hug. 'He had as many and as awful adventures as we in getting safe here. He's growing old now—ten years come October—but he's in wonderful condition, and we take great care of him. What a joy it was when he came back that first term * in

* See *The Chalet School in Exile.*

Guernsey! I'd had to leave him behind when we fled, and it was impossible for Madge to bring him with her. She had her hands full with all the small fry. I'd never seen him, and I didn't know what had become of him. Jockel who works at the Round House had rescued him, and, so far as I was able to gather, the pair of them wandered through Europe till Mr Flower, the father of one of our girls, found the pair of them in Bordeaux. He recognised them, and managed to send them to England, where Rufus had to spend six months in quarantine. No one told me anything about it—I gathered that Rufus was in such shape they weren't sure if it wouldn't be kinder to have him put to sleep. However, he always was a fine specimen, and he soon began to pull round, so Jack—my husband—thought it would make a nice surprise for me to have him back looking more or less like his old self. When he leapt on me in the hall at Sarres I howled like a baby, I was so thrilled to see him again. I hope he has forgotten all that awful time —eh, Rufus, old boy?'

'He never lets you go far out of his sight, even now,' remarked Daisy with a friendly thump on one big flank. 'And when you're out of the house he's always restless. Haven't you noticed it, Robin?'

Robin nodded. 'Yes; often. I don't know how much Rufus remembers of all he had to endure while he and Jockel were wandering, but I'm sure he remembers the horrors of being parted from you all those months, Joey.'

Then Joey gathered up the frocks, and they left

the attic where the light was already failing, and went downstairs. The twins and Daisy had supper with the rest, and were then packed off to bed, while their elders turned to unpicking Jo's three frocks in readiness for work on the morrow, and Rufus, his meal ended, came in and dropped at his mistress's feet with a contented 'flump!'

Thanks to hard work on the part of the two grown-ups and Robin, aided by Jo's invaluable Anna, who was another refugee from Tyrol, the two frocks were ready by Monday, and Jo announced that there would be enough material to make two more if they were careful with their cutting. The twins were small, and she had been very tall even at seventeen, and the skirts were very wide, so if they wasted nothing, there would be 'one on and one in the wash,' to quote herself, for each of the pair.

'And that's all you'll need for the present,' she told them. 'When October comes, it's to be hoped your tunics will have arrived, for you may find these cotton things a trifle chilly then. What a good thing Rob had her old blazer, and we could cut mine down for Fiona! Don't forget to ask for the hat-badges, Daisy, and we'll get these sewn on to-night.'

'It iss so kint of you, Mrs Maynard,' said Flora, looking down with delight at her brown-and-white checked skirts, and smoothing her flame-coloured tie. 'I do think they are pretty frocks.'

'They look quite well,' agreed Jo. 'But it's a mercy the sleeves are short, or we shouldn't have had enough material, I'm afraid.'

'Are you two ready?' demanded Robin, suddenly appearing at the french window. 'I've got the car outside, and unless you hurry, you're going to be late, which will *not* be a good beginning.'

Daisy, Primula, and the twins all fled to get their hats at this. Daisy would cycle as she generally did so long as the weather held; but Robin was to run the other three up in Jo's little car. Primula would stay at school, for she was a weekly boarder, the powers that be thinking her not strong enough for the daily journey; but it had been decided that as long as Shiena stayed at Plas Gwyn her small sisters were to come home each afternoon with Daisy. She would probably have joined her unit by half-term, and then they and Daisy would stay at school during the school week, only coming home for the week-ends.

Robin was an excellent driver, and she had them up at Plas Howell in good time for Prayers, which came at nine o'clock. Julie and her cousins were on the look-out for them, a 'phone message on Sunday having duly told them that the twins would be at school on the Monday, and Robin handed over her charges and then departed, since she was not at school on Mondays. Primula was in the Upper Second, too, for brains were not her strong point, though Daisy was a clever girl, and had already made up her mind to become a doctor. So the seven of them went to the Junior cloakroom, where pegs had been already assigned to the newcomers, and when they had hung up their hats and changed their shoes, they were taken to the form-room they had inspected on the Friday, and Julie introduced them to the assembled form with a simple, 'I say! These are Flora and Fiona McDonald, who've come from the Hebrides. I think they're to be here with us.'

They found themselves in a little crowd of some twenty or more small girls, among them Bride Bettany, who welcomed them with a beaming smile. They had just time to notice that Julie Lucy was the tallest of their new companions, and Primula one of the smallest, and that everyone was dressed like themselves, and then the door opened, and a short, stocky young lady with a pleasant, good-humoured face came in, and the form, standing suddenly to attention, chanted, 'Good morning, Miss Burnett,' in response to her smiling greeting. Then Julie led them up to her and explained who they were.

Miss Burnett smiled again as she welcomed them. 'I've heard about you from Mrs Maynard, and I hope you'll be very happy here among us, and that we can keep you in this form. I think there are seats over by that window for you—you'd like to sit together at first, I expect. Show them, Julie, and sit down, all of you, for roll-call. Quickly, now!'

Julie led them to the double desk, where they sat down, and then went to her own, and Miss Burnett called over the list quickly, and made the discovery that Nesta Tudor was absent, whereupon she sent Bride Bettany to find out the reason from Nesta's elder sister Myfanwy, who was a member of the Sixth. Bride returned with the news that Nesta had a cold, so Miss Burnett wrote her name on a slip of paper which she gave to Julie, and then a bell rang, and they all formed into single file at the door, and were presently marched out, and along a wide corridor to what Fiona later described to her sister as 'a simply 'normous room.' Here they passed behind a row in which the twins saw Sybil Russell standing with another small girl whose comically plain little face made a great foil to her friend's undoubted beauty. Nudging Fiona, Julie indicated this little person, hissing, 'My kid sister!' and was most properly called to order for talking by one of the big girls who stood at one side of the dais at the head of the room. Julie subsided for the moment; but, later, she explained that this was Nicole de Saumarez, a Guernsey girl, and the second prefect. Also that the prefects helped to keep order and 'all that sort of thing,' which vague statement left her new friends wondering what she could mean.

They knew, for Joey had told them, that there were nearly a hundred and fifty girls in the School, and it seemed to them as if there must be at least that number present in the room. But, to their amazement, when Prayers were ended, the door opened and a smaller party marched in, the members of which quietly took their places alongside their respective forms, while two or three mistresses, headed by one with curly white hair framing a clever face, took up positions with the rest of the Staff on the daïs. Later, they found that these were the Catholic members of the School, who had their own Prayers in another room, but joined the rest for school notices and so on. The leading mistress they came to know as Miss Wilson, otherwise 'Bill,' second mistress in the School, who taught science and geography and was a terror to evil-doers. The Head, they knew, was Miss Annersley.

Miss Annersley did not keep them long. She had already welcomed them back to school, and read out the lists of successful exam people. All she had to say now was that the village was out of bounds for the present, owing to an outbreak of measles. The only people who came from it were the daughters of the vicar, Barbara and Ursula Wallace, and Terry Prosser, the doctor's daughter. The rest of the day-girls came from round about, but these three were the only ones who lived in Howells village itself, and Barbara and Terry were Fifth Formers, and Ursula in Upper Fourth, so they might be expected to be sensible about keeping away from village children.

Then a mistress left the ranks, went to the piano and struck up a march, and, beginning with the very tiny folk from the Kindergarten, they marched out and went back to their form-rooms, where Flora and Fiona were promptly seized on by a pretty young mistress whom the rest addressed as 'Miss Linton,' and sent to a small room where they had to tackle question papers for the first time in their lives.

It is to be feared that neither of the twins did very brilliantly in those questions. They were too shy and too frightened by the strange ordeal to grasp much of what was wanted from them. As a result, they were relegated to the Upper Second instead of to the Lower Third where, by age, they really belonged; and Julie and her particular set grinned delightedly at them when Miss Linton brought them in, telling Miss Burnett that they would belong to her for the future. They were sent to their first seats, told to go to the stationery cupboard with Julie at the end of the morning to get their stationery —what, they wondered, could this mean?—and then bidden to sit still and listen to the lesson which Miss Burnett was giving on life as lived in the times of the later Stewarts.

It was all quite unlike anything they had ever called 'lessons' before, but they found it far more interesting than Shiena's painstaking little lectures on the kings of Scotland. And the French lesson that followed with jolly little Mademoiselle Lachenais was just as nice. They were thrilled with *La Vie de Madame Lapine* which would be their French book this term, and thought that school really was a most delightful place. Then came dinner, and after dinner, half an hour's rest in deck-chairs, when they were expected to read and keep silence. They were provided with story-books from the Junior Library, and Fiona revelled in *The Secret Garden*, which Julie had advised, while Flora was lost in *Five Children and It*. Indeed, they were quite upset when a bell pealed, bringing everyone out of her chair in a hurry. Books were closed and put on a shelf dedicated to their use; chairs were folded up and stacked away by two big girls who had appeared on the scene for the purpose, and they were marshalled out to the garden where their form was to have drill.

Before this happened, however, the first unpleasant happening of the day came to Fiona. Always inclined to be dreamy, she was slower than the rest in folding up her chair, and so behind the rest, keeping the remaining Senior, a slight, dark girl, with a mass of thick wavy hair and a dark, gipsy-like face, waiting. The other, whom Julie had addressed as 'Mary,' had finished her pile and vanished when Fiona carried her chair across to the waiting Senior. Unaccustomed to deal with deck-chairs, the child contrived to trap the elder girl's fingers in the bars, and received a scowl and a sharp, 'Look out, you little dreaming idiot! Can't you think what you are doing? You kids want a couple of nurse-maids with you, it strikes me. Give me that thing properly, and be more careful another time!' She snatched the chair from Fiona, paying no heed to the small girl's stammered apologies, stacked it up against the others, and then swung out of the room, still frowning, while Fiona, nearly in tears, looked at Julie dumbly.

'It's that *pig*, Betty Wynne-Davies!' said Julie, risking all sorts of penalties if she had been overheard by anyone in authority, since to call anyone a pig was strictly forbidden. 'Don't mind her, Fiona.'

'It wass an accident!' gasped Fiona, tears in her eyes. 'Inteet, Julie, I nefer meant to hurt her! It wass a true accident!'

'Of course!' Julie tucked her arm into Fiona's. 'Don't you worry, Fiona. Mary Shaw wouldn't have said anything about it—or nothing much, anyhow; but Betty's always like that. We all hate her.'

That was the only thing that marred the first day, and Fiona easily allowed herself to be comforted. The whole form united in abusing Betty heartily, and it was soon clear that all of them had suffered from her temper at one time or another. They went out to drill, and long before it was over Fiona had almost forgotten the unpleasant little encounter.

Not so Flora, however. The twins were devoted to one another, and had always stood up fiercely for each other. Moreover, Flora had always shown a most unpraiseworthy tenacity for holding a grudge. She decided in her own small mind that this horrid girl must be made to smart for being so unkind to Fiona. Just how to manage that, she could not quite see as yet, but she soon would, and then let Betty Wynne-Davies beware! McDonalds had fought to the death in feuds before this, and Flora was all a McDonald. Betty Wynne-Davies, exploding over her stinging finger to her own coterie, had no idea that her outburst of temper with a shy new girl had made her a bitter enemy of another, and that, before the term was out, she was to suffer for her thoughtlessly unkind speech.

CHAPTER VII

OLD FRIENDS REAPPEAR

'FLORA and Fauna! You *are* late!' This was Robin's greeting to the pair when they returned home from school on the Thursday evening about three weeks later. Jo's name for the twins had gone the rounds as everyone had told her it would. Daisy was an indiscreet young person, and little Primula had taken it up quite innocently. Fiona had been cross at first over the mutilation of her pretty name. Then she gave it up—after all, Daisy was known as 'Long-shanks'—and became resigned to it. Very few people ever gave her her proper name nowadays. Staff did, of course; Lady Russell always did. But to the rest, she was 'Fauna.' Small Sybil had taken it up; but Fiona retaliated with 'Red-head,' so Sybil had been rather more meek of late. She resented her chestnut locks, the more so because her brother and sister were both dark-haired, and she did not want attention drawn to them any more than she could help. So Fiona had scored there.

Now she looked up—not so very far—into Robin's face and asked, 'What hass happened? Oh, iss there a letter from Shiena?' For Shiena had departed to join the W.R.N.S. the day before. A wire received late in the evening had told them that she had reached her destination safely, and now the twins were awaiting a letter and all her news.

Robin shook her head. 'There hasn't been time yet. It takes a day and a half for letters to come, and it was nearly nine when she got there, so the last clearance of letters would be gone. We shan't hear from her till tomorrow at soonest. But there *is* some news—and quite exciting news for us. Jo wanted me to tell you as soon as you came in. I hope you'll be as pleased as we are about it.'

'What iss it, pleass?' asked Flora as she wriggled out of her gas-mask case after putting her books on the big Welsh coffer that stood in the hall. 'Iss it why you did not come to school today?'

Robin nodded. 'I had to stay to look after things here because Jo had to take the car into Armiford, and we'd no idea what time they would arrive. You've heard us talk of Jo's chum, Simone Lecoutier?'

Fiona nodded. 'She made one of their four when they were all at school. Mrs von Ahlen wass one, and the Baroness von Wertheim wass the other. Oh, iss it her who iss coming? Put I thought she lived in the north of England?'

'So she did; but André—her husband—has been moved, and to a defence area, where Simone and little Thérèse can't go. So they're coming back here and Jo is giving them the rooms Frieda and Bruno had before Frieda got Cartref in the village. It will be fun to see Simone again! And Baby Thérèse must have grown enormously. I know how our three grew at that age! They've been gone four months, and Thérèse was only three months old then. She'll be nearly twice as large now, and beginning teeth and all sorts of exciting things. Jo left word that you two were to change into fresh frocks, and be sure to wear your blazers, as it gets chilly towards evening now. She said you must get your prep done as far as possible, because she knows that when there's a baby to play with, Fauna, at any rate, won't worry too much about lessons.' She finished with a teasing glance at Fiona, who reddened and laughed.

'I know I wass bad that day; put wee Toni iss such a pet. And you were nearly ass bad ass me, Robin. You had to learn your Shakespeare all the way to school in the car next day.'

Robin chuckled. 'Well, it was the first time I'd seen him, and Gisela was so proud of having a son at last after those four little girls—Natalie, Gisel, Gretchen, and Jacquetta! And as they live at the other side of the mountains we don't get many chances of seeing them.'

'Issn't it a big family!' remarked Flora. 'Five of them! Nancy Chester hass so many brothers and sisters; but I thought people didn't nowadays.'

'They don't,' agreed Robin. She paused, and glanced at the children. Then she made up her mind. Now that Gottfried and Gisela Mensch, so long connected with the School and the Sanatorium —why, Gisela had been the first Head Girl of the Chalet School,* and Gottfried had been one of the young doctors at the Sonnalpe!—had come to Wales to join the Sanatorium which had been re-established, this time high on the Welsh mountains, it was more than likely that the families at Howells village would be seeing a good deal of them, and Gisela must not be hurt. What was more important even, Gisela's sister Maria, who was only a year or two older than the Robin's self, would be coming with them, and Maria had suffered terribly since Hitler had marched into Austria. So she added gently, 'Toni is *not* Gisela's *first* son. When she first came to England, she had a little boy, called Florian after her father. But he was a delicate baby, and he only lived three weeks. Gisela never talks of him, but I know it was a big grief to her when he died. He was named after her father, who died in a concentration camp. We were all so glad when little

* See *The School at the Chalet* and *Jo of the Chalet School*.

Gretchen came the next year, because she helped to make up a little for Baby Florian's loss. And now there is Toni, so Gisela has a son again. But don't say anything to her or Maria about it, will you, you two?'

The twins promised to be careful, and then Robin let them go, and they raced upstairs to change from school uniform into pretty woollen frocks before they came down for tea which was awaiting them. Daisy was there, too, and little Primula, and after tea they all four settled down to lessons at the dining-table, and worked steadily until the sound of the car in the drive outside brought the Venables to their feet, to tear from the room with a hasty 'Come on, you two, and help welcome Simone and the infant!' flung at them by Daisy as she raced through the door.

Shyly they followed, and were in time to see the long-legged schoolgirl fling herself on a small dark woman who looked incredibly neat and dainty, while Primula had run to the side of Jo who had just left the car, and was carrying a beshawled bundle very carefully.

'Simone!' cried Daisy after a hug, 'how lovely to see you again! And where is your daughter? These are Flora and Fauna McDonald, and we're dying to show them Thérèse.'

Simone—now Mme de Bersac—laughed as she put the big girl from her and looked up into the fresh face with warm affection. 'Daisy, you have grown again, *ma petite*. When do you mean to stop? I never thought you would ever become such a giantess. Joey has Thérèse, and she is asleep, so do not wake her up, for it is not yet time for her feed. And these are the twins from the Highlands? I am so glad to see you. But *what* did Daisy call you? Surely I made a mistake in the second name?'

'It iss mad, but Mistress Maynard will always call me "Fauna,"' said Fiona shyly. 'It iss because my name iss Fiona and my sister iss Flora.'

Simone chuckled and Jo went darkly red as she carefully handed over her burden to Daisy. 'It was tempting, you must admit, Simone. But I never meant it to go beyond the family. But it's too late now. Daisy babbled—as usual!—and I'm afraid it's going to be "Fauna" to the end of the chapter—the Chalet School chapter, anyhow.'

'"*Daisy* babbled!" Well, I like that!' cried that injured damsel. 'You gave it away yourself, Auntie Jo, when we first took them to school! You know you did! I didn't babble any more than you did!'

Simone de Bersac laughed softly. 'No need to tell me that, *chérie*. I know Joey of old. But I shall say "Fiona," for it is a pretty name, and I like it. Come and look at my baby, you two, and tell me what you think of her. Give her to me, Daisy. There! Is she not *un bijou—le petit chou*?'

The twins pressed forward eagerly to inspect the baby, who was so unlike any they had seen before, with her tiny black head, and the long black lashes making fans on her round, olive-tinted cheeks as she slept. They agreed that she was a picture, and were thrilled to be allowed to hold her while her mother greeted Primula, and tossed off hat and coat with a sigh of relief. 'Oh, how glad I am to be safely here! Thérèse was an angel on the journey, but it is so long, and so tiresome until one reaches Manchester. It is easy enough after that. And where are *your* babies, Jo? In bed? I must see them when we go upstairs—which must be almost at once. Thérèse will be rousing then, and I must put her to bed as soon as possible.'

'Let me do the putting to bed,' coaxed Jo. 'It's ages since I put anything so tiny to bed, for Frieda's small man is eighteen months old now, and my own girlies are quite grown-up persons—three next month. And Madge's Josette is past four. So I get *no* practice with a really tiny babe, and it's just as well not to forget these things.'

Simone glanced at her, but said nothing, and Jo, taking the still sleeping baby from Daisy, shooed the schoolgirls back to the dining-room to finish their homework, and then led the way upstairs to the pretty bedroom where a cot stood beside the bed, and a small, bright fire burned briskly in the grate, with a bath and towels and all sorts of baby needings before it. Simone looked at it with a sigh of content, and sat down.

'I am so thankful to be here! The journey was so long, I thought I never should arrive,' she said in the French which was her native tongue.

'Poor Simone! Never mind; you're safely at home now. Take off your things while I undress Thérèse and bath her, and she'll be ready when you are,' said Jo, sitting down in the low chair beside the bath, and beginning to undress the baby with an easy deftness that told of much practice.

Meanwhile, Daisy herded the other three back to the dining-room with a stern, 'Come on, you three!

Prep! We may as well get it over, for when Simone and Auntie Jo come down, you'll want to talk—and it's only an hour to your bedtime anyhow, Prim. Besides, it'll be as well to finish up tonight, for you never know what may happen tomorrow.' Wherein she spoke more truly than she knew, for an unexpected surprise was already on its way to them, very weary, very sad, and yet full of hope. But that was to come later. At present, the four sat down again, and while Daisy wrestled with a passage of Caesar in which she vowed there were no predicates to be found, and Primula struggled with dictation words, the twins sat with their heads together over a history book, and tried to get a few facts about Queen Anne's reign into their brains.

It was bedtime for Primula when the two old friends came downstairs later with the news that Baby Thérèse was fast asleep again, and people must be quiet when they went upstairs. Robin also joined them, for she had been tidying up the nursery for Jo, and so they were all together when the telephone bell rang, drawing an impatient 'Who on earth can it be *now*?' from Jo as she got up to answer it.

They heard her exclaiming outside in the hall, and presently she returned to the dining-room with a startled look on her face.

'Jo! Who was it? What has happened?' demanded Robin, who was sitting beside Simone, knitting at a scarf with rapid fingers.

'I wish I knew,' said Jo cryptically.

'What on earth are you talking about? You wish you knew? What *do* you mean? Who was it 'phoning, anyhow?'

'Hil—I mean Miss Annersley,' said Jo, correcting herself with some confusion. The Head of the School was a personal friend, but she was careful as a rule not to call her by her Christian name before the younger ones. So she hurried on, 'She was most queer—said she'd had a wire from London, and she couldn't make head or tail of it. She wants us to go up tomorrow, Simone. It mentioned our Peace League. At least it was signed, "Two of the Peace League," and said they were coming tomorrow afternoon, they hoped. What do you think it means?'

'Can some of our girls have escaped from the enemy? I wonder who?'

The three elder folk began to make guesses as to who it might be who was coming on the morrow, but were brought up all standing by Fiona's eager question, 'Pleass, what iss the Peace League?'

'Jiminy cricket!' cried Jo, who was famed for the variety of her exclamations. 'Do you two mean that you've been at school for three solid weeks and no one has told you about the Peace League yet?'

Flora wrinkled up her brow. 'I think I did hear someone say something apout it yesterday,' she said slowly, 'but I wass busy, and I took no notice. Iss it something to do with the School?'

For reply, Jo swung round on Daisy and Robin. 'What have you two been about not to tell them?' she demanded awfully. 'Two new girls who have been under this roof three weeks and—and four days, and they have to ask, "What is the Peace League?" and all either of them knows about it is that she's heard someone *mention* it! I'm ashamed of the pair of you!'

'Don't sound so fierce, Jo,' said Robin soothingly. 'After all, a good deal has been happening in those same three weeks and four days, and we can't tell everything in one wild burst as you always do.'

'But the Peace League!' Jo paused as if robbed of breath.

Simone began to laugh. 'Robin is quite right, *chérie*. No need to be so awful over it. As for the Peace League, you two, it is a League that was made by all the girls of the Chalet School—past, as well as present—and is a League to see that after the war we all do our best to promote peace in the world. We promise to help any member of the League, and to remember that what ever our nationality may be, we are all Chalet School girls. Joey wrote out a prayer for us, and we say it each day. You two must have copies of it so that you can learn it.'

'And,' chimed in Daisy, 'if it hadn't been for the League, we might never have got back Bruno von Ahlen and Friedel von Helfen. No one had had any idea where Friedel was since Hitler marched into Austria. Wanda and the babies were with Marie and Eugen von Wertheim in America, visiting his American relations; but Friedel just vanished from sight, and nothing was known of him for months and months. We all thought he was dead, though Wanda never gave up hope. And Bruno was sent to a concentration camp three months after our crowd had got back to England because he wouldn't do what the Gestapo wanted. Then they escaped, thanks to the brother of two of our old girls who had been made to leave the School by Hitler because they were Germans, but who stuck to our ideas for all that.'

Daisy paused for lack of breath, and Robin took up the story. 'His two cousins helped, also, for the parents of these girls were dead, and they were living with their uncle and aunt. Later on, Karl Linders, who had been forced into the Luftwaffe, crashed in the sea, and was taken prisoner. He is now on parole, for he hates the Nazis and all they stand for. Emmie and Joanna are still in Germany, of course—Emmie must be about my age, and Joanna will be fifteen, I suppose. Karl told us when Jem was allowed to visit him that their uncle and aunt were kind to them, but they were not happy. We have all so prayed that they might escape and get to England or somewhere where they will be free to live up to our ideals. We all feel we owe them so much. But they haven't managed it so far. Wanda's little Emmie who was born in the next October is Emmie Joanna after them both, because she said she felt she must do something to show how she felt about what they had done, and she could only pray for them and do that.'

Jo, who had given a sudden start during Robin's speech, now turned a beaming face on them. 'Rob—Simone—everyone! Suppose it's Emmie and Joanna got away at last!' she cried. 'Wouldn't that be marvellous?'

'It would; but would they come straight to the School?' asked Simone.

'Where else would they go? They have no relations in England that I know of—barring Karl—and *he* couldn't do much for them. I should say the School is the one place they *would* make for. How thrilling if it is!'

'Don't build on it,' Simone warned her, 'for if it is not, you may be unable to hide your disappointment, and so hurt two other girls.'

'It might quite well be some of our French or Italian people,' added Robin. 'There are a good many of them, too, you know. We can only wait and see till tomorrow.'

'And waiting is the one thing I don't want to do,' mourned Jo. 'Oh, well, I suppose it's really only a question of a few hours. And talking of that, Primula, Flora, and Fauna, what about a spot of bed? It's more than past your time. Just look at that clock! Say good-night, you three, and trot off to Anna. She has your supper waiting in the morning-room.'

As it was now nearly nine, and the three were supposed to be in bed by eight, they could say no more, so they got up, put their books away, and went off to the little morning-room where Anna had their supper of cocoa, bread-and-butter, and honey waiting for them, and then went off to bed, only just remembering in time that there was a baby in the house who was not accustomed to their chatter, and who would probably wake up if they did not moderate their voices a little. The triplets had been brought up on it, and slept through most things now.

Next morning, Simone had not come down when the schoolgirls set off through the unpleasantness of a mountain mist. Jo explained that she was tired with her long journey, and had agreed to stay in bed for breakfast.

'But we'll be up at school in time for elevenses,' she added consolingly, 'so you'll see her and Thérèse then. Now off with you, or you will all be outrageously late. Today is Friday, anyhow, so you'll have the week-end here.'

'Yess; but then we are to be weekly boarders like Primula,' said Flora regretfully.

'I know. But you couldn't go every day through weather like this; and once it's begun it may keep on. Cheer up, Flora! Half-term will be coming soon, and after that, it'll be no time before it's Christmas. Shiena may get a few days' leave then, and I'm planning all sorts of fun for it.' Jo bent down and kissed the child again as she spoke, and so they departed.

They found the School in a very ferment of excitement over the arrival of the unknown members of the League, and many and wild were the guesses as to who they could be. Only Betty Wynne-Davies and her coterie held aloof from the general expectations, and of them, as Elizabeth Arnett scornfully remarked, nothing else was to be expected.

Once upon a time, Elizabeth and Betty had been bosom friends, and partners in crime. Many had been their sins, and evil had been their career. At fifteen, however, Elizabeth had come under the influence of Miss Linton, once the Head Girl of the School in the former's wicked Middle School days, and Gillian Linton's outlook on life had made a great difference to the girl of whom it had been said with truth, 'Elizabeth *thinks* of awful things to do, and Betty *does* them—with frills on.' As a result, at seventeen Elizabeth had developed into a most helpful and responsible member of the School, and was even spoken of as being likely to be the next Head Girl unless she left with the present one.

Betty, on the other hand, was less easily influenced. She had bitterly resented the change in her friend, and instead of trying to walk with her had held herself far from any such thing; quarrelled fiercely with her; and, to all intents and purposes, set herself more stubbornly 'agin the government' than ever before. As a result, though well over seventeen, she was in no position of trust, nor was it likely that she ever would be. A good many people had wondered how it was that she had escaped expulsion so long, for some of her exploits had been outrageous. But the authorities at the Chalet School were long-suffering, and felt that if they could do anything for the embittered girl, they must, so long as the rest of the School did not suffer. Betty had a strong character, and she had her own following though it was not a large one. Still, there were one or two somewhat empty-headed people in the Fifth and Sixth who were ready to follow her lead, as well as a few in the two Fourths who admired her gipsyish prettiness, or were overawed by her sharp tongue. Of late, Miss Annersley had been seriously considering whether or no she should request Betty's guardian to remove her at the end of term, for this party did not make for any good in the School, and her patience was nearly exhausted. But the fact that this must be the girl's last year, as well as her lack of parents, had so far deterred her. Still, as Elizabeth, Mary Shand, Nicole de Saumarez, and Biddy O'Hara, the leading members of the

Sixth, shrewdly surmised, it behoved Betty to take care what she did.

'It would be nice to see Emmie and Joanna again,' observed the last-mentioned of the School's grandees. ''Tis real good friends Emmie and meself were in Tyrol, and I'd like fine to see her again.' Biddy spoke with a fascinating touch of creamiest Irish brogue. Once her English had been thick with it, but nowadays, unless she purposely put it on, there was just a hint to remind anyone that she had been a waif, adopted by the Middles of her day* seven years before. It had at first been decided to train her as a lady's-maid; but Biddy was clever, and soon showed that she would repay any pains spent on her education. So she had stayed at the School, where she had done brilliantly, and the Russells had been responsible for her. She was to sit for a scholarship to Oxford this year, and looked forward eagerly to a university training, for Lady Russell had told her that even if she did not win the scholarship, she should have her three years at Oxford. Biddy was straining every nerve to prove herself deserving of such treatment, and the whole School expected her to add to its laurels.

When Daisy, Robin, the twins, and Primula appeared, she called Robin to join their group with an eager, 'Robin! Come here, will you? Does Joey know who these Peace Leaguers are?'

The two big girls—Daisy had followed Robin, although she was a member of the Fifth only—shook their heads. Then Bride Bettany and Nancy Chester appeared, and the twins and Primula heard

* See *The Chalet School and Jo.*

no more. They ran off to join their own clan, and shortly afterwards the bell rang, and once Prayers were over, there was no more gossip for anyone. The School insisted on lessons being periods of hard work, just as out-of-lesson time was made to be play-time. Many of the girls were the children of one or both delicate parents, for many of them had joined the School because father, mother, or some other relation was at the great Sanatorium over the mountains; so work and play were carefully regulated, and the health of the girls was closely watched.

Eleven o'clock brought Joey and Simone, but the babies had been left at home as the heavy fog continued. They were welcomed with shouts, and led away to the Prefects' room, where both were closely questioned as to who the sender of the mysterious wire could be. They were there when a message came for the Sixth to come down to the library to welcome the members of the Peace League, and so were the first to see the rapturous greeting of Biddy when she entered the room to be confronted by a slight girl with fair hair, and startlingly blue eyes under black lashes and black brows, who ran forward crying, 'Biddee! At last—at last! We are here, and safe, *Gott sei dank*!'

'Emmie!' cried Biddy, flinging her arms round her old chum. ''Tis yourself, acushla! Oh, what a joyful day! Jo said 'twould be you!'

Then the younger girl, so very like Emmie, came forward for her turn, and after much exclaiming, kissing, and hearty rejoicings, Miss Annersley suddenly remembered that it was half-past eleven, and no bell had rung for the end of Break, and laughingly dismissed the Sixth with orders to ring it at once, for a full half-hour had been lost.

'Emmie and Joanna will remain here and rest,' she said. 'You can hear their adventures later. There will be plenty of time, for Joanna, at any rate, must return to school. Fifteen is too young to do anything else. And Emmie will stay, too, if the authorities don't interfere. So go and get on with your work, and you shall learn everything later.'

'There's just one thing I should like to say,' said Emmie, who spoke English fluently still, though she had a strong German accent. 'That is that our League has helped us both more than we can ever say. And it is thanks to the League that we have escaped at last. Our uncle and aunt are gone to Portugal, but we begged to come here. It was easier for them if we did so, so they agreed. But tomorrow evening, I am to tell you all what happened to us, and before then, I hope to hear much of *your* news. But I am grateful—and so is Joanna—that we began the Peace League, for if it had not been for our vow, I am sure we should never be here.'

CHAPTER VIII

AN ADVENTUROUS ESCAPE

SATURDAY dawned bright and fair, though there was promise of rain in the clear-cut outlines of the hills. The schoolgirls all set off, accompanied by Robin, at half-past nine, for the Guide meeting was held from ten till twelve on Saturday mornings. There were two Guide Companies, as well as a Ranger Company, and two Brownie Packs; and the previous term had seen the revival of the Cadet Company. The majority of the girls belonged to one or the other, for they were all very keen on the movement; and in Tyrol, the Chalet School Guides had done good work which they were trying to continue now they were in England. Flora and Fiona were thrilled with it all, and had instantly begged to be allowed to join, though this meant that they must leave their own clan for older girls. Nancy, Julie, the Ozanne twins, and the rest were preparing to 'fly up' at the end of the term; but Miss Wilson, Captain of the Company which would receive them, had refused to take them sooner, for she had as many as she could deal with. Several girls would be leaving Guides for Rangers in December, however, so she would have vacancies for them then. Meantime, she had agreed to accept Flora and Fiona, since Miss Linton, the other Guide Captain, had even less room then herself, and would lose only two of her Guides before Christmas. The twins had put in three attendances now, and were all ready for their Tenderfoot test, which was to take place that day, so they managed to forget the exciting newcomers for a little as they walked the three miles to school, murmuring together about knots, the Union Jack, and various other tests.

'When you've been enrolled, you must pitch in on your Second-Class,' said Daisy, overhearing them. 'Take my advice and start on Morse as soon as you can. It's awful to learn. I thought I never was going to manage it when I was working for *my* Second-Class.'

'Shiena iss beginning to learn it, too,' said Fiona thoughtfully. A short letter had arrived from Shiena that morning, with promise of a longer one later, and the twins had been very thrilled with it all.

'She'll learn semaphore as well, I expect,' said Robin. 'Nan Blakeney, Julie Lucy's adopted aunt, said something to me about it, I remember.'

'I know semaphore,' Primula informed the twins.

'And whoever is training you to get her First-Class will see you know your Morse,' added Daisy. She began to laugh. 'Robin! Do you remember the fearful row there was when some bright spirit started chatting to a distant friend in prep by Morse with a tapping pencil? Wasn't it monumental?'

'That was when Gillian was Head Girl,' said Robin thoughtfully. 'Yes; the prees did rather rub it in about the dishonesty of it. Who was it—I forget now. I wasn't down at the Tiern See at the time—cold or something.'

'Betty Wynne-Davies and Elizabeth Arnett, of course. It always *was* those two in those days. Elizabeth's altered a lot since then, hasn't she?' said thoughtless Daisy.

'People usually do when they begin to grow up,' replied Robin, with a frown at Daisy to make her hold her tongue. 'I know *I* did. And as for Corney and Evvy, they became utterly different.'

Daisy laughed again. 'Didn't they do some mad things before that, though. Do you remember the Middle House band, Rob?'*

* See *The New House at the Chalet School.*

'It wasn't in my time at the Big School. I was still up at the Annexe then. But Jo told us all about it after, and said she nearly laughed herself sick. I must say the idea of Corney with a saxophone takes some beating as a joke. I only wish I had been there to see it!'

'We've got that snap of her that Auntie Jo took when she was practising,' laughed Daisy, who, it must be confessed, frequently forgot to accord Jo the courtesy title of 'aunt' which had been hers since the day, now seven years ago, when Margot Venables, Sir James Russell's sister, had been brought to the Sonnalpe, very ill, with her two little girls.* For the sake of example to Primula, Daisy contrived to remember four times out of seven; but she very often forgot, and Jo had been saying lately that it was time it dropped, now that Daisy was so much older.

At this point they turned in at the gates of Plas Howell, the big house among the Welsh hills to which the Chalet School had evacuated from Guernsey during the first spring after the war broke out. Here they were met by Lorenz Maïco, Robin's special chum, and Daisy's own great friends, Beth Chester, sister of Nancy, and Gwensi Howell, to whose brother Plas Howell belonged. Mr Howell was now a Naval chaplain, and he had suggested, on the advice of Jo's brother-in-law, Major Maynard, an old school friend of his, that the School should be housed at Plas Howell 'for the duration,' on condition that they took charge of his little step-sister. It must be admitted that, at the time,

* See *The New House at the Chalet School*.

Gwensi had deeply resented the whole thing. But the first term had shown her her mistake, and now the Chalet School had no more enthusiastic member than Gwensi Howell. She was a small, slight girl of Daisy's age to a day, very dark, with a sensitive small face and big dark eyes. Beth, on the other hand, as the eldest of a family of seven, was a doer, not a dreamer. She was far and away prettier than either of her chums, being, in fact, as Robin once remarked, quite the prettiest girl in the School, with her violet eyes, chestnut curls, and cameo-like features. Beth meant to be a gardener, and her father had promised that if she did well at school he would do his best to give her her training at Swanley, the great horticultural college for women. Daisy, it may be remembered, was set on being a doctor; and Gwensi had long made up her mind to become a writer like her adored Mrs Maynard. She had every book Jo had ever published, and had even been privileged to read one or two in manuscript. She spent most of her spare time and pocket-money on beginnings, and Jo was convinced that some day the world, even if it were only the world of girls at school, would hear of Gwensi Howell.

The older folk departed, leaving the three little girls to make their own way up the avenue, and to their own form-room, where they were seized upon by Nancy Chester and Julie Lucy, who informed them that, after parade, inspection, and Tenderfoot tests, Emmie Linders was to tell the story of their escape to the assembled Guides, and the rest of the School were also to be present as a great favour.

'Emmie's a Guide herself,' chattered Julie. 'She was one when the School was at the Tiern See, and so was Joanna. Joanna told us last night that she had just flown up from Brownies when that horrid Hitler said she and Emmie were to leave and go to a horrid Nazi school in Germany. Wasn't it hatefully horrid of him?'

'Haven't you got any other adjective, Julie?' demanded a sarcastic voice from the doorway. 'Everything is "horrid" according to you. It gets a bit monotonous to listen to you kids. You get one word and run it to death. What's the latest for the opposite to "horrid"? Come along; let's hear it.'

Julie turned scarlet, and her dark eyes flamed. It was Betty Wynne-Davies, of course. With her was the girl who was her particular friend just now, an empty-headed, fluffy-haired girl of seventeen, whose real name of Florence Williams had been turned by her friends into 'Floppy Bill.' Left to herself, there was no harm in her. But Betty was rapidly making her into a pale shadow of herself. Now she sniggered at the Junior's obvious discomfort, and the six or seven small girls in the room all glared at the pair with hatred in their hearts.

'You shouldt not listen if you do not like our talk,' said Flora, rather more Highland than usual as a result of the fury that rose in her whenever she encountered Betty. Flora had not forgotten her vow to make this big girl suffer for the way she had treated Fiona on that first day. She had found no way of doing it as yet; but she was only waiting for her chance. She meant to take it to the full when it came.

A gasp came from the rest of the Juniors. They might hate Betty and all her works with every scrap of their small hearts, but that did not alter the fact that she was a Senior, and, as such, must be treated with respect. Flora knew nothing about such niceties of school etiquette, and would not have cared about them if she had. Now she went on, 'It iss not goot to listen to other people talking privately—it iss not honourable. My brothers wouldt say you were not a shentleman.'

'How true—seeing that I am a girl and not a boy,' drawled Betty. She sounded calm enough, but her eyes flashed and her quick temper began to rise. 'Didn't they teach you to speak the King's English at your home—wherever it is. Some shieling, I suppose—a but and a ben, perhaps? No doubt *you* are entitled to say what is and what is not honourable behaviour. I presume you learnt that when you ate your first parritch.' At which piece of wit Floppy Bill tittered again.

Fiona sprang to her twin's assistance. Less fiery than Flora, she had a temper that, once it was roused, took a long time to cool. She could also be startlingly sarcastic herself on occasion, for such a small girl, and now she used her tongue. 'Ton't mindt the poor creature, Flora,' she said quietly. 'She doesn't know any petter. Poor thing! It *iss* a pity apout her, issn't it?'

It was the turn of the Juniors now, and three or four of them spluttered, even though they were almost stricken dumb at such audacity.

As for Betty herself, she was dumb, too, for a moment. Then she boiled over. Taking a hasty step forward, she boxed Fiona's ears with a right good will. Fiona uttered a short cry, for the force of the blow startled her. A deadly silence succeeded the cry, and for a second no one spoke or moved. Then Betty, breathing quickly, and still furious, drew back. 'There, you horrid, rude little beast!' she exclaimed. 'Perhaps that will teach you to treat your elders and betters with more respect!'

But by this time the rest of the Juniors had rallied to the twins' help.

'You *pig*!' cried Julie. 'If the Head knew about this, there'd be a row.'

'And *you* can't talk about saying "horrid," either!' added Nancy with a defiant glare as she rushed up to Fiona's side. 'You used it yourself this minute! Come along, Fauna dear! Come and sit down a bit.'

Floppy Bill's titters had died away. She was rather horrified at the lengths to which Betty's temper had led her. 'I say, Bets, you'd better clear out of here!' she exclaimed. 'The kids are quite right. There'll be a row about this if any of the Staff gets wind of it.'

Betty had just enough self-control left to know that her friend was right there. She turned away, not trusting herself to speak, and the pair left the room followed by the glares of those who were not engaged in ministering to Fiona's cheek, which was beginning to swell.

'I say,' said Julie anxiously, 'we'd better try to do something about it. There'd be a fearful fuss if anyone *did* find out what Betty's done.—Nan! Uncle Peter's a doctor. You ought to know what to do.'

Thus appealed to, Nancy considered. 'Water, I think,' she said at length. 'That's what he used for Dickon when he hit his head against the swing, anyhow. Oh, and butter, too. You take Fauna to the splasheries, Julie, and I'll go and try to sneak some butter or marg from somewhere.'

'I don't know where you'll get it,' said Vanna Ozanne gloomily. 'There never *is* any butter or marg to be had nowadays. Can't you think of anything else, Nancy? What about—about——'

'Any sort of grease ought to do,' chimed in her twin Nella. 'Evan Evans has a pot of something he uses to keep the wheel-barrow wheels from skreeking. I know where it is—in the woodshed. I'll go and get it while you bathe her cheek. We can't let anyone see her looking like that. Someone would be sure to ask what she'd done to her face, and then what could you say?'

'Say that that—' Flora got so far. Then she stopped. To tell the truth, her English failed her at this point; and just as well, perhaps.

'You couldn't tell tales about her,' put in Bride Bettany in rather horrified tones. 'I know Betty jolly well deserves anything she gets, but you can't *tell* anyone. Come on, Julie. Let's get Fauna to the splashery, and dab her while Nella goes to get the grease. You be quick, Nella, or the whistle will blow, and then we *can't* do anything about it.'

'I ton't want to,' began Flora, rather more calmly; but she was cried down by the rest. 'We *must*! It would serve Betty right if it did get out; but we can't go telling tales. And Fauna can't tell lies about it. So we've just *got* to see what we can do.'

With this, they led Fiona off to the splasheries, as the cloakrooms were called, and while Nancy, as a doctor's daughter, was privileged to sponge the swollen cheek with cold water, Nella tore off to the woodshed where she unearthed the big pot of yellow cart-grease Evan Evans the head gardener kept for greasing wheels, and came back with it. The evil-smelling mixture was smeared on Fiona's face when they had dried it, and she was instructed to tell anyone who made inquiries that she had 'run into something.'

'It's true, anyhow,' said Vanna. 'You *did* run into something—Betty Wynne-Davies' hand—in a way. But p'r'aps no one *will* say anything.'

As it happened, everyone was too much excited about the advent of the Linders girls to notice Fiona's face, which was certainly not improved by the cart-grease. Betty was not a Guide, having resigned from her Company two years before when she first quarrelled with Elizabeth, so she was not sitting with the Guides, and only came in, grumbling at having to do so, when eleven o'clock struck and, after elevenses, the School assembled in the big double drawing-room which served as the Assembly Hall. Floppy Bill never had been one, being too lazy to care for the strenuous efforts demanded of Guides, and she had contrived in the interim to impress on her friend the need for silence about the whole affair if Betty did not want 'the father and mother of a row.'

'You know what the Head would say if it got to her ears,' she urged. 'For Heaven's sake, Bets, let it alone! And don't take any notice of the little horrors, whatever you do. You'll get into awful trouble if anyone ever gets to hear you smacked Fauna McDonald's face like that.'

'Do you expect me to put up with such cheek?' demanded Betty stormily.

'I certainly didn't expect you to hit the little idiot,' returned Floppy unexpectedly, so far as Betty was concerned. 'Honestly, Bets, old thing, you'd better try not to lose your temper like that. I know it was maddening, but the Head won't take that as an excuse.'

Betty had cooled down a little by this time, so she allowed herself to be persuaded. Besides, she had seen the horror in her chum's face at the time, and she did not want to lose Floppy Bill — the nearest approach to a friend she could boast of at school. So she said no more, and when the pair entered Hall—which Floppy was careful to do by the further door, so that they did not go near the recruits—she was more or less her usual self. If she seemed to avoid the rest of the Sixth, they were accustomed to that from Betty Wynne-Davies.

They had scarcely seated themselves when Miss Wilson, Miss Linton, Miss Burnett, and Miss Robinson, the Guiders, appeared, followed by Miss Phipps, who was one of the Brown Owls, and Miss Edwards, who was the other. Only Miss Robinson was a comparative newcomer to the School. The others had all been in it as either Staff or pupils when it was at the Tiern See, and they were as anxious as the rest to hear Emmie's story. She herself came in later, clad in a Guide uniform which the Guiders and Cadets had managed to scare up—I quote Biddy O'Hara—among them. Joanna followed her, and Miss Stephens, another old friend who was Tawny Owl to Miss Phipps, hurried in with the rest of the Staff, for the entire School were to be present. Even Matron and her satellite, Matron Lloyd, contrived to spare time for this great occasion, and were given seats next to the Head.

When they were all settled, Emmie got up from where she had been sitting between Robin and Lorenz Maïco, and began at once.

'I want to tell you something first,' she said in a clear voice. 'That is, that we must all unite to kill the evil thing called Nazism which has infected my country. It is of the devil—come from Hell. The world can never be right until it is gone, and the men who made it are gone also. Some of you who are here know this, for you have met it already. Others only know of it from what they have heard. But I tell you that nothing you have heard—*nothing!*—can ever really show you how terrible it is. One must live with it to learn that, as Joanna and I have lived with it.

'You want to know how we escaped. It began one day when a certain friend of my uncle whispered to him one word as they passed in the street. It was just a little word, but it showed my uncle that he was suspected of working against Hitler, and would be sent to prison—maybe a concentration camp—unless we could get away in time. He came home and told my aunt so, and she at once set to work, for there was much to be done before we could go.

'Joanna was working in a shop, and I at a factory as Hitler had ordered, and when we came home, we were told. Our uncle warned us that we must say nothing. We must not even show a different manner. But they would not leave us to face the rage of the Gestapo when their flight was found out, so we must go, too, and must prepare as fast as we could.

'Never shall I forget that evening! We feared lest any should come in and find us; and always there was the fear that the Gestapo might guess something and come on us sooner than we feared. And my uncle and aunt are elderly people. I do not know if you know that my mother and father were old when they wedded. My mother was thirty-eight when Karl was born, and Joanna is six years younger than he. When she died, my mother was fifty-six, and my father followed her the next week, and he was sixty-five. They had no love for the Nazis, and it was what they had to endure that killed them. They were of the old Germans, who loved the home, and music, and brought us up to do the same. But the Nazis leave one no home. They take the children from their parents when they are yet too young to know, and teach them their own wicked thoughts. Many of our old girls have wedded and now have children, and once every good German Mädchen hoped the day would come when she, too, would have babies. *I* hoped it might never come, for my children would be taken from me, and taught things I hate and know to be evil!' She spoke this with deep conviction, and the elder girls stirred uneasily at her tone. There was so much suppressed hatred in it.

Perhaps Emmie felt this, for she went on more

calmly. 'Now, it seemed, there was a chance that Joanna and I could escape this. I was taught to love my country; but I rejoiced when I thought I could leave it. We packed just the things we would need; and I can never tell you how terrible that packing was, listening every so often to hear if any were coming—nor daring to speak lest even the walls should hear us and tell what we said. I remember starting at every footfall in the street below lest it should mean that the Gestapo were coming to us. But at last it was done, and we were ready. We had not much. We wore our warmest clothes, and a change beneath, for we dared carry neither case nor knapsack nor even a parcel. But my aunt sewed her jewellery into her dress, and made me sew my mother's into mine, so that we might sell the jewels for food and clothes and shelter in a new country. Then she brought bottles of hair-dye, and made Joanna and me brush it into our hair. It changed us very much, for our hair is naturally so fair. And she stained our skins, also. For herself, she cut short her hair, and waved it with hot irons. And she rouged her face till she did not look respectable—my good aunt, who has always so hated make-up of any kind!' Emmie's voice broke in a half-sob, half-laugh as she said this, and the Head gave her a quick glance. But she recovered herself almost at once, and went on. 'And for my uncle, he had worn a moustache, but now he gummed on a beard, almost hair by hair, so that it looked as if it really grew. And he dyed hair and beard black, and so we were ready. We slipped out of the big apartment house by the fire-escape, and none saw or heard us. We passed through the streets as silently as we could, for it was long after midnight. But ours is a small town and not of military importance. Besides, the R.A.F. had been bombing the railway works twenty miles north of us, and all who could be spared had gone there to help put out their fires. So we got out of the town, and reached the country, and then it was easier.

'For two weeks we walked to the south, till at last we crossed the border, and by that time the dye had worn from our hair, and we saw that my uncle, who had been only grey before, was now white as snow. His own beard had grown a little, so he got rid of the false one. The wave was out of my aunt's hair, and she had long since lost her rouge. We were tattered, hungry, thirsty, and dirty, and none would have known us for the Herr Doktor Grundtbaum and Frau Grundtbaum, and their two nieces.

'We had reached France, but it was occupied France, and the Gestapo is there too, so we thought it best to part. No one would expect to see my uncle and aunt without us, for it was well known in our town how they had cared for us for our parents' sake. There is little that is *not* known by the Gestapo. Nor would anyone expect to see two girls wandering. So we said farewell, and left them. They went on to the south, to seek Portugal, and we faced west to try to reach England, and Karl, and the School.

'It was not easy travelling, for we had to go on foot—we dared not take a train lest any should see and question us. We begged food by the way, and

Joanna would have sung for sous, but I would not let her. They knew in Eisenheim that she has a good voice, and we might have been known if any heard her. I tell you, what the Gestapo does not know is not worth the knowing, as you say! So it was hard, and often we went hungry; and once Joanna fainted she was so empty. But a good woman, a Frenchwoman, helped us then. She took us to her house, and hid us in her grenier, and kept us until Joanna was able to set out again. She gave us a word for her cousin who was a fisherman near St Malo, and she said he would try to help us if he could. But we were ten days reaching St Malo, and the night we got there the R.A.F. make a raid on it, and we lay in a corner of an archway, and shuddered lest we had come all this way to be killed by the bombs of those of whom we sought shelter. But all was well, and last week we set foot on English soil, and so felt safe once more.' Emmie paused here, and then she spoke again. 'I cannot tell what you have done with our vow that we all signed in Tyrol. But I tell you this. That if it costs our lives, Joanna and I will keep it, for had it not been for the memory of it and our kind School we should never have had the courage to go on as we did, and so come to safety.'

She ceased, and there was a moment's silence as she sat down. Then the Head rose quickly.

'We all thank Emmie for her story,' she said. 'I am sure that to tell it required as much real courage as enduring the adventures of which she has told us, and those which she has not told us, must have done. So far as the pledge is concerned, only Joey

Maynard knows now where it is. But she has it safely, I know. But we keep it secret, for there are many girls who signed it and who are still in enemy country, so it must not fall into the wrong hands.'—'Shust like our Chart of Erisay that holds the secrets of Erisay, and which we keep hidden,' murmured Flora to her next-door neighbour, Nancy.—'But I can assure you, Emmie, that we never forget our vow—not one of us. And we never will. Please God, when peace shall come, we may all be united again, and then, at a great meeting we hope to hold at the Tiern See of all our girls, past and present, we shall be able to show it to you, and tell you of the adventures that befell even it. And now, the Guides have work to do, I know, and Emmie and Joanna need rest and quiet still after their adventurous journey across half Europe, so I am going to take them away and leave the Guides to go on with their work. But before we separate, I will ask you to say with me our League Prayer, remembering especially those who have not been so fortunate as we here, and who must still endure the horrors at which Emmie has hinted in the enemy and enemy-occupied countries. Let us pray.'

CHAPTER IX

THE CHART

'WHAT did you mean on Saturday by the Chart of Erisay, and what secrets does it hold, Flora?' The voice was Vanna Ozanne's, and Betty

Wynne-Davies, who had been lounging in a big chair with a book in which she was not really interested, dropped it, and listened.

'I shouldn't haf said anything,' came Flora's Highland tones. 'It iss a secret in our family, and Archie and Shiena wouldt be angry with me if they knew I had spoken of it. Pleass ton't ask me, for I mustn't talk of it. Fiona wass fery angry with me on Saturday.'

'But why? A chart's only a map—sort of j'ography stuff, isn't it?' It was Nella this time who spoke, though that was not to be wondered at. The Ozanne twins did everything together, and went everywhere together.

'This isn't.' Flora spoke shortly; but Nella and Vanna usually contrived to get what they wanted, and they had no mind to be disappointed this time. Betty, hidden by the high back and deep 'lugs' of her chair, forgot that she was doing something thoroughly dishonourable, and listened with deep interest.

'How is it different?' asked Vanna. 'Go on, Flora; you might tell us. We won't tell anyone else.'

'Yess; but you *will*! I know you will tell Nancy and Julie, and perhaps Bride and Primula, too, and Fiona says Archie and Shiena wouldt be fery angry inteet if we talked of it. It iss a family secret, and we wouldt nefer haf known of it if Archie were not away, and we had to leaf Erisay, so that Shiena couldt not leaf it there. And now she iss away, too, so she said Fiona and I must haf it and take care of it for them.'

'*You* have it? Then where is it? At Auntie Jo's?' Jo had the brevet rank of aunt to all the Lucys, the Ozannes, and the Chesters.

Apparently, Flora shook her head.

'Then where? Here at school with you and Fauna?'

'Nefer you mind. It iss safe, and *we* know where it iss.'

'I'll ask Fauna,' decided Vanna. 'She may tell me more than you do.'

'Ton't you do any such thing!' cried Flora. 'Fiona will be fery angry if she knows you haf been talking about it. And she won't tell you a thing, any more than I will!'

'Well, tell us a little, anyhow, Flora—do!' coaxed Nella. 'It sounds so mysterious. Can't you describe the island to us, at any rate? *That* wouldn't be saying anything about the Chart. And we'd love to hear what your home was like.'

Thus wheedled, Flora thought hastily. It could do no harm to tell the Ozanne twins something about Erisay. They had been very good to her and Fiona, and Flora loved her birthplace dearly, and would have liked these girls to know something of its beauties—the pale clear dawns across the gleaming seas; the great black cliffs on the outer coasts, and the long, smooth green slopes down to the landward side; the tall, old house, with its stone walls which Ian McDonald 'harled' freshly every year, so that they glistened whitely in the sunlight; the nooks and crannies where she and Fiona had played all their lives; the sweet, thymy turf where they used to lie out in the sun when their lessons were done, and talk of the great world that lay beyond the leagues of slowly-heaving sea, and wonder what it was like. Well, she knew something about that, now. It was better in many ways than they had thought; not so good in others. She let herself be persuaded, and kept the Ozannes enthralled by her vivid word-pictures, until Fiona, released at last from unpacking, came into the room to join them, when they all suddenly remembered that the rest of their clan were playing games in the gymnasium, and jumped up, and ran off to join them.

Left alone, and still unsuspected, Betty stretched and yawned. 'What a lot of fuss about nothing!' she thought disdainfully as she lounged out of the room. 'Just like those little Highland idiots! Still, it might be interesting to see this old Chart of theirs. I wonder what there is that's so secret about it? Flora said that little wretch of a Fauna would be mad if anyone ever saw it. I owe that kid one for her cheek to me. I've a good mind to try and get hold of the thing and show it round our set. That would give her something to think about.' Betty smiled disagreeably to herself, and went on to join the faithful Floppy and two or three others of the same type. Elizabeth was sitting chatting to Biddy O'Hara and Mary Shand at the other end of the room, and took no notice of her erstwhile friend. Betty had too much in her to be really satisfied with the kind of girl she cultivated nowadays, and this indifference on the part of her old chum cut deep. Not that she showed it; she was too proud for that. But she felt sore and hurt, and this was what, perhaps, made her embark on a course which, in her saner moments, she would have been the first to condemn.

Meantime, in the gymnasium, the small fry played happily. It had rained all day, beginning with gentle showers which speedily became something much worse, and now the rain came lashing down with a fury which drummed on the galvanised iron roof of the big shed which had been turned into a gymnasium. The apparatus was covered up and stowed away, and the Juniors were on their honour not to touch it unless someone grown-up and responsible were with them, so they were allowed to play with very little supervision. Occasionally Miss Linton, who was on duty with the First and Second Forms, strolled down the match-boarding way which linked up the gym with the Junior Common Room, just to see that all was well; but she would not stay, having plenty to do with the younger children, and they were left to themselves, and proud to be so trusted.

The two Second Forms together made up forty-one girls, of whom the oldest were the McDonald twins, with the Ozannes running them fairly closely. Flora and Fiona had been eleven on the first of August, and the Ozannes were eleven on the first of October. These two young people possessed great force of character, which made them leaders in their own form. They ruled with a rod of iron for the most part, though their cousin, Julie Lucy, could hold her own with them, and often did so. As the eldest of five, Julie was a good deal of an autocrat herself, and the three often clashed. Nancy Chester was a sunny little person whom everyone liked. She was by no means as pretty as her eldest sister; but then, as Jo had once pointed out, Beth Chester was 'a howling beauty.' The four cousins, with Bride Bettany who was of much the same nature as Nancy, and Primula Venables whom Bride refused loyally to leave out, led the others by the nose. The remaining twenty-four of the Upper Second were nice little folk, but most of them were lacking in originality. As for the Lower Second, apart from Blossom Willoughby and the small beauty, Sybil Russell, there was no one outstanding there. So the Ozannes had a clear field until the McDonalds came. Then they found that they could neither coax nor browbeat Fiona into doing anything she didn't choose, though Flora was more amenable. The Ozannes were apt to forget the extra months between themselves and the McDonalds, and the latter pair, not used to living with a number of girls, generally gave way to them on most points. It was, therefore, a great disappointment to the Guernsey pair that they could not always get what they wanted from their new friends.

On this occasion, having played 'Nuts and May,' 'I Wrote a Letter to My Love,' and 'Blindman's Buff' till they were tired, Flora was moved to suggest a 'pretend' game.

'What shall we pretend, then?' asked Nancy obligingly.

'Let's play at the escape of Bonny Prince Charlie and Flora McDonald. We've got Flora, anyhow, and someone can be Prince Charlie,' suggested Julie Lucy, who was a keen reader.

'Bags me Prince Charlie, then!' screamed Vanna.

'You can't—you've got long hair!' pointed out

Julie, whose own curls were cropped to the nape of her neck. 'Bags *me* it!'

'Prince Charlie wasn't dark—they called him "The Yellow-haired Laddie,"' said Nella. 'And anyway, he must have had long hair, 'cos we have a picture of him kissing Flora's hand in our room at home, and he has it tied back.'

'That was a wig, silly. They wore wigs in those days,' retorted Julie.

'A *wig*! How on earth could he wear a wig when he was being hunted all over?' demanded Vanna. 'He'd soon have lost it if he did.'

'And, anyhow, he hadn't *black* hair, and yours is as black as soot!' was the cousinly retort from Nella, who always backed her twin up. 'Van's hair is fairish, anyhow, even if it isn't yellow.'

'If you come to that, the only one of us with yellow hair is Primula,' put in Bride, whose own locks were brown, and who had lately been condemned to wearing glasses, so she knew *she* had no chance of being chosen.

'That's true, but Primula's hair is short—and straight as anything. I'm sure Prince Charlie had curls,' returned Vanna. 'Hadn't he, Flora? You must be some sort of great-great-grandchild of *the* Flora Macdonald, so you ought to know.'

'I'm not—she wass a kind of cousin, though. And I ton't know if Prince Charlie's hair was straight *or* curly. And if I've got to be her, then I think Fauna ought to be him. Besides, I'm heaps taller than Vanna or Julie, and it would be silly to have Flora efer so much taller than Prince Charlie—there's the bell! What iss that for, pleass?'

'Us to clear up. Supper's ready. Oh, bother! And we haven't done anything about it. Never mind. We can play it tomorrow if it's still raining. Come on, you girls. Help to put things straight!' And Vanna began to set the chairs back against the ribstalls which lined three sides of the room. The rest followed her example. They knew well enough that if they left the gym untidy it would mean the end of their playing there.

When it was all done, they streamed off to wash their hands, and after supper, bed was the order of the day; so Flora forgot her talk with Nella and Vanna, and Fiona never heard of it—which was a pity.

The rain continued off and on for three days. Then it cleared up, and on the Thursday, the School was bidden get into its outdoor things and prepare for a long walk to make up for the lack of walking exercise they had suffered since Sunday. Miss Phipps and Miss Linton would take the Juniors; Miss Wilson and Miss Burnett were to be responsible for the Middles; the Seniors could be trusted to go by themselves. For one thing, there were not nearly so many of them. For another, all the prefects would be with them, and could be relied on to see that no pranks were played.

Miss Phipps proposed to take the Juniors towards the village; the Middles were to go down the back drive of Plas Howell, and climb the hill; the Seniors, after some debating, decided to walk up to the Round House, where they were always welcome. It was a three and a half miles walk, but they would have set out by half-past nine, and get there in comfortable time for elevenses. Miss Annersley agreed to ring up Lady Russell and tell her to expect them. They would rest there for a while and then come back in time for dinner. The walk had the additional merit—from the point of view of the Staff—of being largely along the high-road, so that laggards could get the bus one way or the other if they were really tired—which was also the main reason for Miss Phipps having chosen the village for the destination of her party.

All this being arranged, the girls raced off to the cloakrooms, where they donned caps and coats, and sensible, stout shoes. The Middles left first, and then Miss Phipps and Miss Linton set off with their small charges down the front drive. The Seniors were held up for a minute or two by the Head, who wanted to send a note and some books to Lady Russell.

The Chalet School was the property of the latter, for she had begun it twelve years before on the shores of the beautiful Tiern See in Tyrol. She had had as partner Mlle Lepâttre, and when Madge Bettany, as she then was, became Mrs Russell, Mademoiselle had carried it on as managing Head. But a serious illness, ending in a bad operation, had finished the Frenchwoman's career, and from that time till her death, she nad been forced to lead the life of a semi-invalid. Flight before the Nazis had completed what her illness had begun, and three years before this story opens, Mlle Lepâttre had quietly slipped from this world to the next, leaving many mourners behind her. Mrs Russell had, however, still kept her interest in the School, and even now, when she was as busy as a woman could well be, with her own young family, her twin brother's eldest four, her house and the farm attached, and her position as wife of the Head of the great Sanatorium on the other side of the mountains, she still found time for it. 'Madame,' as the girls loved to call her, was a power to be reckoned with at the Chalet School.

Mary Shand, the Head Girl, received note and books, and then they set off down the drive, all laughing and chatting gaily, glad of the fresh air after the three long days in the house. Mary led the way with her own special chum, Nicole de Saumarez, a Guernsey girl. The rest followed, two and two, and, last of the procession, came Betty Wynne-Davies and Floppy Williams. Hilda Hope, the third member of their set in the Sixth, was in front of them, paired off with Myfanwy Tudor, the School's musical genius, though, as a matter of fact, Myfanwy, though very good, was no great concert performer like Margia Stevens, an old girl of the School, who was already making a name for herself as a pianist. Myfanwy meant to teach, and this would be her last year at school. Then she was to go to the Royal College of Music and work for her A.R.C.M. She was the second in a family of five, and her father, a vicar at Medbury some twenty miles from Howells village, had no private means at all. Dilys, the eldest of the family, had succeeded in gaining a scholarship to Oxford the previous year, and she was reading modern languages with a view to teaching, too. Myfanwy, a pretty, fair girl, rather shy and retiring except where her beloved music was concerned, had accepted Hilda Hope as a partner for the walk without remark, though she disliked the trio of which Hilda was one. However, once they got off the high-road, and into the meadows that flanked the first part of the avenue leading to the Round House, they might break rank, and then Hilda would join her friends, and Myfanwy would link up with another of the prefects, Monica Marilliar, who also came from Medbury, and who was the daughter of a well-known doctor. So she endured her fate without comment.

When they reached the meadowland, Hilda promptly left her partner, whom she herself called 'stuffy and slow,' and joined Betty and Floppy; and Myfanwy ran on, and tucked her hand through Monica's arm with a small sigh of relief. She never knew what to say to Hilda, who was a very superficial person, with few interests apart from Betty Wynne-Davies. As Myfanwy's views on that damsel were those held by most of the Sixth, Betty as a topic of conversation was hardly possible, so talk between them had languished, and Myfanwy had been at least as bored as her companion.

Once the three were together, they left the footpath, and sauntered slowly along in the wake of the rest, gossiping among themselves. Presently Floppy, who was no more tactful than Jo Maynard herself, happened to mention Flora and Fiona. Betty scowled at the names, and her black brows drew together into an equally black frown.

'Oh, do dry up about those wretched kids!' she snapped. 'I'm sick of the sound of their names.'

'I don't see why,' replied Floppy. 'Oh, I know Fauna pinched your fingers that first day; but after all, it was only an accident, and you boxed her ears for it, so why you should keep on like this is beyond me. Don't be so silly over them, Bets. They can't do you any harm, after all.'

'They're a pair of spoilt, cheeky, impossible brats!' retorted Betty. 'Why on earth there should be all this interest in them is more than I can say. It's high time someone took them both down a peg or two.'

'Well, don't yell like that, or everyone else will hear you. And you know as well as I do that if anyone heard you'd smacked Fiona's face you'd get into a nice fuss for bullying—you know what they are!'

'Smacked her face?' gasped Hilda. 'Good gracious, Bets, you surely didn't do that?'

'Well, I did, if you want to know,' snapped Betty. 'And not before it was deserved, either. And it *wasn't* for trapping my fingers—Floppy's got that wrong. It was for downright impudence. They're always cheeking me, and I'll teach them better manners before I'm done.' She paused, and a remembrance of the talk she had overheard at the beginning of the week came back to her. She knew better than to confess that piece of dishonourable behaviour to her friends, so she went on in a milder tone, 'In one way, I suppose they're scarcely to blame for being as they are. They seem to have lived all their lives on some weird little island in the Hebrides, and never seen anyone decent. I heard Flora describing it to those Ozanne twins the other day, and from what she said they might as well have been on a desert island with no one but savages round them. Still, it seems to have been rather a lovely place,' she added, as she remembered some of the descriptions Flora had given. 'There was good fishing, too. And listen to this—both those children have been taught to shoot. They had guns specially made for them, and they shot rabbits. I heard Flora say that Fauna is quite a good shot.'

'Kids like that learn to shoot?' cried Hilda incredulously. 'Why, my young brother who is fourteen only got his first gun last birthday! How old are they—nine or ten, isn't it? Who in their senses would teach a pair of babes like that to *shoot*?'

'Oh, I expect it's an ordinary thing in the Highlands,' said Floppy, who came from Birmingham and knew very little about country life save from the light novels that were her pet form of literature. 'Isn't it all teeming with game of one sort and another? Go on, Bets. What else did the kid tell you? It sounds rather interesting.'

Carefully refraining from explaining that 'the kid' had not even known she was present, Betty repeated as much as she could remember of Flora's eager descriptions. As she had a gift of language, she was able to give even more vivid pictures than Flora, for all her love of Erisay, could do, and by the time the three had reached the gate that divided the meadowland from the woodland which ran almost up to the Round House, she had them so enthralled that it was easy for her to slip into the tale of the

Erisay Chart without their noticing what she was doing.

'Yes; it certainly sounds a beautiful place,' she said. 'And, more than that, it's interesting. Flora said something about a chart of the island which is kept a secret—or has been till now, when they've all been cleared out by the Government. She said that Shiena had charge of it as the eldest brother, who is owner of Erisay now, I suppose, is in the Air Force, and couldn't very well have it with him. But Shiena's joined the W.R.N.S., so she gave it to Flora and Fauna to take care of. It seems to be something awfully precious to them, for those two Ozanne kids did all they knew to get Flora to show it to them, but she wouldn't—just flatly refused, and said "Archie and Shiena" would be so angry with her if they even knew she'd hinted at it; and Fauna had been mad when she knew she had done so—some time or other—I don't know when. So it's pretty plain they've all been taught to make a secret of it.'

Betty's voice was clear and ringing, and carried easily through the trees, now almost bare of their leaves, since the storm of the past three days had brought down most of what had remained. A man who was coming down the avenue from the house heard her words, and his eyes lit up with a sudden light. Could it be possible that the secret Chart of Erisay was in the care of a pair of youngsters? He had come to seek it and get it if he possibly could, for his superiors had dire need of it. They had been very sure that Archie McDonald would never keep anything so valuable to the family among his kit, though they had made sure of that already. Hugh, the second brother, was in the East with his destroyer, so they had been obliged to defer any attempt on his possessions. In any case, it was most unlikely that he had it, for he had not been home for two years, and it was almost certain that until Erisay had been evacuated of the entire clan of the McDonalds the Chart had not left the Great House. There remained Kenneth, the schoolboy, who was at Loretto. No one in their senses was likely to trust an important document to the care of a schoolboy. Remained Shiena, the eldest daughter of the house, and he had been sent to find out if she had it, and if she had, to get it. He had been deeply chagrined to learn, when he had finally traced her to Howells village, that she had already left. But there was just a chance that she might have entrusted it to Mrs Maynard with whom she and her little sisters had been living, and he had his plans all laid for scraping acquaintance with that young lady. Now, judging by what this girl said, it would not be necessary. It should be an easy matter to outwit a pair of children of nine or ten. But Betty was talking again, and he listened.

'Oh, I don't know what there can be—some secret entrance to the Great House, as they call it, I expect. It would be very handy centuries ago when they were always having clan-feuds, and killing each other, and burning each other's houses, and so on'—Betty was vague as to conditions in Scotland in the earlier centuries—'or there may be some hidden cave that was useful for smuggling. Whatever it is, I bet the Ozannes, or half a dozen like them, won't get it out of Flora and Fauna. For one thing, they won't go the right way to work to get it.'

Something in her tones made Floppy turn and look at her. '*Betty!* You mean to have a shot at getting it yourself!' she accused her.

Betty laughed. 'Of course I do. I've got as much curiosity as most folk, and Flora was so hush-hush over the thing I feel I simply *must* see it. What are you looking at me like that for, Floppy? There's nothing wrong in wanting to see an old chart like that. I shan't *hurt* the thing.'

Floppy was unable to put her exact thoughts into words, but she did her best. 'I don't suppose you'd tear it up or ink it or anything like that. But you'll use it to hurt Fauna, and I—well, I think it's a bit on the mean side to do a thing like that,' she floundered.

'Don't be so silly, Florence!' Betty used the seldom-used Christian name with a cutting tone. 'I'm going to hurt neither the Chart nor the kid. I simply want to see it to satisfy my own curiosity about it. There isn't anything wrong in that.'

'If Fauna knows you've had it, when, as you say, they seem to make such a secret business of it, it'll hurt her all right. When they won't show it even to their own chums, it isn't likely they'd want *you* to see it.'

At this point they met the stranger, and he glanced at them. He saw three biggish girls—one fair and graceful, with a kind of empty prettiness in her face; one stout and flushed, and not in the least pretty; the third, dark, vivid, and with an air which told him that this must be the leader of the trio.

She was looking at her flushed companion with a little smile of scornful amusement on her lips, but her eyes were angry.

'Not a pleasant person, Miss Betty,' thought the man as he passed them, and went on down the avenue until he was out of sight. Then, moving with cat-like silence, he doubled on his tracks, and was soon close behind them, among the trees. He wanted to learn if 'Betty' had any plans for getting hold of the Chart. It was urgent for his superiors to have it, and he had an idea that if he could make an ally of this girl, it might ease his work considerably. It was clear enough that she disliked the McDonald children whole-heartedly, especially the one they had called 'Fawna.' What a curious name for a girl! Some Highland rigmarole, he thought.

However, his labour was lost, for just as he drew level with the girls, another of the older ones he had passed before meeting them called out something, and the three began to run to join up with the rest. But he had time to notice that Betty was evidently very angry, while the stout one looked ready to cry, and the third was plainly uneasy. It was no good following them further at the moment. He had already been to the Round House to deliver the letter of introduction to the great doctor with which he had been provided, and if Lady Russell saw him return, she would wonder. Once more he retraced his steps, and presently was going along the high-road, feeling that he was a long step nearer the consummation of his task than he had been at breakfast time.

CHAPTER X

RE-ENTER—A CHUM OF JO'S

MEANWHILE, the Juniors were having their own adventures. They were sent to the main village shop to buy cocoa, matches, rice, and other sundries, for the Head believed in using the local people as much as possible, since to do so was only fair to everyone. They also had a parcel to take to Mrs Maynard from Mlle Lachenais. Next month would be the triplets' third birthday, and little Mademoiselle had been dressing three dolls for the little girls. One was already in Jo's care, and this was the second. The third would follow later. Mademoiselle was deft with her fingers, and the handsome rag lady which was shown to Lower Third and the two Second Forms drew gasps of admiration from them, for she was attired in the exact uniform of a Chalet School girl, complete with blazer, beret, and even tiny gas-mask case slung over her shoulder. The School badges had been embroidered on beret and blazer pocket as a finishing touch, and even those superior young people, Vanna and Nella, were overheard to sigh for one like her—and they had rarely played with dolls at any time in their lives, being of the tomboy kind, who prefer boys' games to girls'.

This magnificent lady was duly packed into a pretty box and entrusted to the care of Gillian Linton, and it was arranged that when they reached the village, Miss Phipps would take most of the Juniors and go on to the shop, while Miss Linton, accompanied by the McDonald twins, Primula, Julie, the two Ozannes, Nancy Chester, and Bride Bettany, should turn down the side lane leading to Plas Gwyn to hand the lady over to Jo. Miss Annersley undertook to warn that young person of the proposed body of visitors, and sent a basket with bottles of milk and biscuits so that they might have their elevenses at Plas Gwyn. No one doubted the cordiality of Jo's welcome, for she always greeted them joyously, and never a week passed that she did not turn up at the School, though last week-end she had told Primula and the twins that when the bad weather began it was unlikely she would be as regular as she had been, and they must not expect it.

So it was a real surprise to everyone concerned when, just as they reached the white gate of Plas Gwyn, Jo appeared, running down the drive, her three daughters at her heels, and her finger on her lips.

'I'm sorry,' she said breathlessly as she opened the gate, 'but I can't have you today. And be very quiet, for goodness sake, all of you!'

'But we've brought our elevenses an' everything!' gasped Mollie Carew of the Lower Third. 'Milk, an' biscuits, we've got with us.'

'Well, I'm sorry, but I can't have you. At least,' she added, relenting as she saw their disappointed faces, 'if you *do* come in, you must go straight to the kitchen and promise me to be very, very quiet.'

'But, Jo, what has happened?' interposed Miss Linton anxiously. 'Has Dr Jack come home suddenly, and is he worn out? Do be clearer!'

'I only wish it *was* him!' said Jo with great fervour and equal lack of grammar. 'Not that it isn't a big thrill as it is. But come on in, all of you—tippy-toes, please, and on the grass. If you wake my guests I'll slay the lot of you! Mollie, why am I honoured like this? The Head said nothing about *you* coming when she told me who was.'

Mollie blushed. 'It was to help carry the basket,' she said shyly. 'The milk-bottles were so heavy, and Miss Linton has the dolly— Oh, I f'got!' as her eyes fell on the triplets, who were listening hard.

'I see,' said Jo. 'Well, I'm glad to see you, anyhow. Round to the back, you people, and remember what I said about making no noise.'

They followed her round to the back of the house where the kitchen windows looked out on to an orchard of apple trees that were, as she had rapturously declared, a real poem in spring, and through a narrow, whitewashed passage, and into the sunshiny kitchen, with its primrose-yellow walls, blue-and-white checked lino, and curtains, and tablecloth, and the big kitchen range in which roared a glorious fire, for Anna was baking. She looked up with a smile on her round, good-humoured face as her mistress brought the party in, and produced chairs for Mrs Maynard and Miss Linton, and patted the big settle and some stools as an invitation to the girls. She took the basket Mollie handed to her, and vanished into the back kitchen where the cooker was, to prepare chocolate for the visitors, and they sat down, throwing off coats and caps at Jo's suggestion, and then all looked at her eagerly.

'What is it, Jo?' asked Gillian again. 'Who has come?'

For reply, Jo turned to Primula and Bride, the only two of the Juniors there who had been in Tyrol. 'Do you two remember the Crown Princess of Belsornia?' she demanded. 'She came to stay with us that last summer at the Sonnalpe, and she brought with her her future husband, the Duc di Mirolani and his sister, the Contessa di Mirolani, and their aunt, the Queen of Mirania.—It isn't so bad as it sounds,' she added. 'Raphael di Mirolani is about two years older than the Queen. We liked them all so much.'

'I remember,' said Bride. 'They were jolly nice, and they thought heaps of Elisaveta. Wasn't she some kind of relation to them, Auntie?'

'Tenth cousin twelve times removed or something like that. I never can get these weird relationships clear,' said Jo. 'Didn't you meet them, Gill? Or were you away at the time?'

'We were in England,' said Gillian. 'It was just after Mother had died, and I had to go to see to business things, and Joyce came with me.'

'Then you wouldn't see them. Well, 'Veta married Raphael all right—she was Crown Princess of Belsornia, you people, so he would only be Prince Consort when she came to the throne. He was a dear, though. I saw a lot of them all, for they stayed three weeks with us; and then, in the autumn, I went to Belsornia to be 'Veta's bridesmaid, and was there another three weeks. Well, you all know what happened the next year. Hitler marched into Austria; *we* fell foul of the Gestapo and had to run for it; I was ill after that, and then married Jack; and then we started the School over again; the children arrived; we had to leave Guernsey, and what with one thing and another—principally war, of course—I've never seen any of them since, and letters have been few—sadly few—and far between. I knew 'Veta had a little son just a year after the wedding. I gathered from her letter announcing his arrival that Belsornia went nearly mad over him, they were so delighted. Then I heard no more for ages until last year when a letter came by way of the States in which she said that she had another boy, and they were all living in fear and dread of what Hitler and Co. might do. Belsornia is rich in oil and various minerals, like Roumania, and they felt sure that if it weren't that it is ringed round with steep mountains with fearful passes, he would have tried to walk in. The only thing they felt they had to fear were paratroops, and they were all watching hard for those. Mirania was the same, for though very few minerals are worked there, it's one of the most fertile places going. Roxalanne—that's the Queen—told me you only have to sow your seed in the spring, and then wait till harvest-time, and there you are!'

'Oh, I expect you have to do a little weeding,' said Gillian, as Jo paused to take breath after her lengthy speech.

'Well, that, of course. But it really is amazingly

productive, and just what old Hitler would be safe to want, only they're hemmed in by mountains, too. And then there are all the rivers with which they could, and *would*, flood the country if an enemy tried on any dodges.'

'Well? Go on. Of course, the Princess and her babies are your guests we must be so careful not to wake. But what's the story, Jo?'

Anna came in with the chocolate at this moment, so Jo waited till they were all served. Then she settled herself comfortably, and, with a steaming cup at her elbow, and a piece of cake in her hand, began her tale with enjoyment. 'It begins at seven o'clock last night, when Mrs Hughes-the-post-office rang me up to say that a wire had come for me. She read it out, and I couldn't make head or tail of it. Here; I'll get the script of it!' And Jo jumped up, dashed out of the room, and presently returned with a slip from which she read, '"Safe here what news are none myself V." Naturally, I couldn't think what it meant. Couldn't place "V" at all, and anyhow, it wasn't good grammar. Well, my dear, at ten o'clock a call from Armiford came through for me. It was someone who didn't speak much English, and that little very badly. She spoke of "Erīness" and I wondered what lunatic was trying to pull my leg. But I did just manage to gather that I could expect—either *a* visitor or *visitors*. Which it would be, I couldn't make out. Anyhow, my caller rang off after that, and as it was a public call-box, I could do nothing about it but prepare—which I did. If only Rob had been at home, or Daisy, it wouldn't have been so bad.

But Madge sent for Rob early yesterday morning to stay with the babes while she was in Birmingham for the day. They wouldn't be back till late, so would keep Rob all night, and she would return here after school. And Daisy is there, anyhow. So there was I, with only Anna to help, and a number of visitors to prepare for. I didn't know *who* they were. I didn't know *how many* they were. I knew exactly *nothing*!'

Jo paused dramatically, and Fiona, jumping up, ran to clasp her hand. 'Oh, Mistress Maynard! It is shust ass you did with us!' she cried. 'You always are so kind!'

'Rats!' said Jo. 'Besides, I did know more or less what to look for where you three were concerned. Jean Mackenzie saw to that. But with *this* affair I was in an utter fog. I put two rooms ready, and hoped for the best. Then I rang up Frieda, and had her nearly dancing with excitement until I told her to get her own spare room ready in case I had to draft off an overflow to her. I knew Madge would be no use—too far off, and coming home late, anyhow. *That* was no good to anyone.'

'Oh, Joey, do cut the cackle and come to the 'osses!' pleaded Gillian. 'Of course, it was the Princess; we all know that. But I want to know what had happened, and you do dither so!'

Jo chuckled. 'It would serve you right if I told you no more after such rudeness. I've a very good mind not to.'

'Then I'll tell the rest myself,' said a fresh voice at the door.

The party jumped to its feet, and Jo began a

stern, ''Veta! I told you to stay in bed till you were called!'

'I know you did. But I've had a good ten hours, and I'm sick of it. I never was too fond of bed, as you know,' said the Princess plaintively. She came into the room, and looked at them all, singling out Bride and Primula at once. 'Prim hasn't changed a bit—I don't believe she's even grown since I last saw her. And I'd know Bride all right, in spite of those glasses. And those two must be the Highland twins you told me were living with you.' She pointed unashamedly at Flora and Fiona, who went crimson. 'Now, who are the rest? Oh, but this must be your Snowdrop that you told me about when you had the Fairy-tale Sale-of-Work in aid of the San.* Black hair, blue eyes, rose-petal skin. There's no mistaking *her*! You *are* Gillian Linton, aren't you?'

Gillian's cheeks rivalled the twins' as she bobbed a curtsey and stammered, 'Yes, ma'am.'

'I say, *must* you?' queried the Princess. 'Goodness knows I've had enough of it by this time! Surely, now I'm a refugee I can drop it. I've tried to keep it out of the children's way, anyhow. Look here, you people, let's forget I'm a princess for the time being, at least. No one knows I'm in England—or not as *me*. I registered as Mrs Helston, which is one of my husband's family names. I'd like to remain that until I've been able to breathe a little. Besides, the chances are I never shall be a princess again. That beast Hitler has bagged my country; I don't know where my father is—or my husband either, if you come to that. The last I heard of *him*

* See *The New House at the Chalet School.*

he was making his way to Egypt, and meant to try to raise a combined Belsornian and Miranian corps on the side of the Allies. You would hear that the Nazis occupied Mirania last April? I gather they are having a very sticky time of it. The whole country was flooded, and some bright person thought of strewing salt all over the land first. It'll be *years* before that land is fit for grain again! As for our people, they destroyed all the oil-wells, smashed up all the mine-workings, and generally made a hash of everything worth while to the Germans. What we shall all live on when the war's over and we get started again, goodness only knows! I rather think I shall take in washing—I've got my laundress badge, Joey, as you may remember.'* She grinned at Jo, and Jo grimaced back. 'You needn't make faces at me like that. I've done worse things than washing since we had to scuttle, I can tell you.'

She held out a pair of beautifully shaped hands which were rough and red as if she had used them to some purpose. The nails were broken, and there were scars on them, too; but she laughed as she held them out. 'Not much like the hands of any-one royal, are they? My poor Arletta! They were the last straw for her, I think. She's wept salt tears over them. I don't care; I'm not ashamed of them. They've worked to get food and shelter for my babies, and to keep them as clean as possible, and what better work can a woman's hands do? I'll have a cup of that chocolate, I think, unless you want the lot. Oh, *thank* you!' as three people rushed to supply her wants. She took her cup and

* See *The Chalet Girls in Camp.*

a slice of cake and glanced round. 'Could you make room for a little one on that settle, do you think? Thank you! *That's* better. Now then, what do you all want to know? Dad's in hiding somewhere. He refused to go off with me—said he wasn't going to leave his people to the mercy of the Nazis. But they made him take cover somewhere once I'd gone. I know that much. As for me, they had to get me away with my last baby who was only a fortnight old at the time. Luckily, it hasn't hurt either of us, though I was a little worried about her. We got across the border into Turkey, where they had meant to get us to Constantinople and see if a British war-ship would take us off and bring us to England—at first, anyway. But things didn't pan out like that. We got up against a village quisling, and he had seen me in Belsornia, and knew me on sight. So we had to give up our little ideas and run for it just anyhow. It wasn't quite such a desperate flight as yours, Joey, but it's lasted a good deal longer. We did manage to get across the Mediter-ranean to Tunis, and a fearful voyage it was. Not that we met much in the way of war planes or submarines. But the weather was terrible. We took days and days to go—it was a little Turkish sailing-ship, and she was the world's worst roller. I never was so sick in my life. And Arletta, who managed to stick to me through it all, was worse. The children seemed to flourish on it, and Joséphine throve as neither of the boys ever did. She's a positive giantess of a baby! She's six months old today, and she's more like ten.'

'She hass Mistress Maynard's name, then?'

asked Fiona politely. You simply couldn't be shy with this jolly girl, who seemed to have laughed her way through most of her troubles.

'Of course! Joey's my very best friend. I always said if I ever had a daughter she should be "Joséphine." Her other names are "Cecilia Margaret," after the Robin and Madame. The boys are Frédéric and Charles. Strictly among ourselves, we've called them Freddie and Carl. If I'm Mrs Helston for the rest of my life, that's what they'll be. It's spelt with a "C", not a "K," so it doesn't matter,' she added vaguely.

'What happened after you left the boat?' asked Bride eagerly.

'Oh, heaps of adventures, of course. We'd been landed at a little cove, and we had very little but what we stood up in. Arletta had to pretend she was my real mother, and we walked most of the way till we got to a tiny place in Algiers, not far from Oran. We got lifts, of course—donkey and mule-back, mostly. But once a French officer in a fine car came along, and he took us up, and we made nearly a hundred and fifty miles that day. The Vichy Government should have heard him on the subject of their doings! Once he thought we were British—I do speak English decently, thank goodness!—he let himself go. He'd have taken us further, but he thought we'd be safer if he put us down at a little fishing village where we might be able to get a boat. So we did after three weeks. They put us across to another place, in Spain this time, near Malaga. Between ourselves, I rather think they were smugglers. From there we got into Portugal, and after that, it was all right. I made friends with an English journalist, and he pulled strings and got us passports and papers generally, and so we arrived in England six weeks ago. Then we hadn't a penny of money among us, and I had to go to work. I got charring to do—that's why my hands are in such a state—in a Welsh village. As soon as we'd enough money, and I'd got clothes for us all, and so on—which I did from a second-hand shop in Cardiff—we set off for Armiford, and I sent off the wire to Joey, and then Arletta rang her up. We hired a taxi, and got here last night.'

She finished her chocolate, and then held out her cup. 'More, please; I really am famished, still. What am I going to do, Gillian? I haven't the faintest idea at the moment. Rest, and try to fatten up a little first, I think. I've got on the thin side. But after that, we'll have to see. Dr Jem—I beg his pardon—Sir James must advise me. I can't get on to Raphael at the moment; and I doubt if there's much hope of hearing from my father. I'd like to stay incog. if I could; but I'm not very sure how far that is possible. Diplomatic relations—which is too long to explain at the moment—have a horrid way of tangling things up. Listen! There's Baby! I must fly! What time have you people to be back at school?'

Gillian glanced at the clock, even as the Princess disappeared, and gave a cry of horror. 'Good heavens! We should have set off twenty minutes ago! We'll be appallingly late for dinner. Come along, you people! Hurry up!'

She hustled them into their hats and caps, and marshalled them out to the garden, Joey following. That young lady had a word to say to them. 'Listen, you people. You are to say nothing at all about the Princess being here till we give you leave. Promise, please—Guide honour.'

'Guide honour we won't tell,' they all promised. Then they set off. But as they went, more than one of them reflected on what a story she could tell!

CHAPTER XI

THE SCHOOL IS BURGLED

AS it happened, something occurred two days later which made it possible for the advent of the Princess and her babies to remain a secret for some little time. Or rather, their identity remained a secret. Naturally, everyone knew that Joey Maynard had visitors from abroad; and they were told that the lady had been at the School years before * when it was in Tyrol. But that was all for the moment. It roused no real excitement, for, as Robin said later, so many of the old Chaletians were turning up, that it was quite a commonplace event in these days.

After Gillian and her charges had left Plas Gwyn, the Princess, in spite of all her gay courage, was forced to give way to Jo, and retire to bed for a while. She frightened her friend badly by fainting just after lunch, and Jo packed her in between the

* See *The Princess of the Chalet School*.

sheets, rang up for her brother-in-law, and when he came, told him everything. Dr Jem listened gravely, examined the Princess, and then ordered off all the small fry with the exception of Baby Joséphine; bade Jo ring up the School to ask the Head to keep Robin, Daisy, and the rest there until he gave leave for them to come home; told Elisaveta that she must stay where she was for the present, and then departed, taking with him Jo's small daughters; the little boys were sent to Frieda von Ahlen, whose pretty home, Cartref, was barely ten minutes' walk away. Simone de Bersac was up at the School, Thérèse with her. On the Tuesday, a frantic 'phone message from Miss Annersley had informed them that Miss Slater, who had taken Simone's place as maths mistress, had broken her leg in a bicycle smash. It would be some weeks before she could get about again, and she would certainly be unable to teach for the rest of the term. Getting Staff was more than difficult, so the Head sent an S.O.S. to her old pupil, and Simone packed up her belongings and departed to fill the breach.

On the Friday, it rained again, and no one was able to go out—which may account for what came next. Everyone was very bored with life; and after supper, some of the old Chalet girls began to tell the rest of their adventures in Tyrol. The small ones could not remember much of their own affairs, but they knew plenty of stories, and Bride Bettany, who was staying on at school, together with her elder sister Peggy, and her cousin Sybil, since Lady Russell had her hands quite full with her own Josette and Jo's trio, was moved to relate how Biddy

O'Hara, in her unregenerate Middle days, had told stories every night to a select gathering from her own and another dormitory after 'lights out.' Biddy's exploits had ended rather sadly for her. Her tale of a banshee had upset one Alixe von Elsen to the point of making her walk in her sleep, uttering such wails and moans as any real banshee might have envied. The entire Middle House had been roused, and Jo, who at the time was Head Girl, had come out to see what was wrong, got a full view of Alixe's very creepy performance, and fainted incontinently. Inquiries made next day had brought out the truth, and Biddy had been condemned to spend a week or more sleeping with Miss Wilson—which had cured her of telling stories out of hours again.*

'Fiona can tell fery fine tales, too,' said Flora thoughtfully.

'She can!' agreed Bride, who had heard several of Fiona's stories. She cocked her small head on one side, and looked at Fiona consideringly. 'We can't exactly have stories after lights out, I know. But what about our *rushing* to bed, and Fauna telling us some then?'

'That's all very well. What about *us*?' demanded Vanna Ozanne.

'You're next door. If you like to risk being caught—but there'd be a fearful fuss if you were!—you can come in. We can try to hide you under our beds if we hear anyone coming,' said Bride kindly.

'How would it be for Fauna to take our dormies night about?' suggested Nella—even as one of Biddy's friends had suggested in the old days.

* See *The New House at the Chalet School*.

'Inteet and I won't do any such thing!' returned Fiona hotly. 'It would pe all fery well for you; but I shouldt get into bad trouble.'

'Fauna's right,' said Julie Lucy, who was one of the lucky ones to be in the same dormitory as the twins. 'Why should she have to do the entertaining *and* p'r'aps get caught, too. No fear! If the rest of you folk want to listen to her, you can jolly well run the risks yourselves. Anyhow, we'll all get it hot if anyone catches us.'

'But we'd get it hottest for being out of our dormies,' protested Blossom Willoughby, who combined an angelic little face with an imp-like disposition, and who was at school partly because when she was at home she led her small sister, Judy, into such awful scrapes that their mother vowed it was a wonder her hair wasn't white with worry. Blossom was the same age as Julie's small brother John, but she was a clever little thing, and was in the form below the Ozannes and Co.

Now, at her protest, Julie grinned at her. 'You've got to risk that if you want to hear the stories. Rows don't worry *you*, anyhow, so why are you making such a fuss? You get into at least one every day.'

'Yes; but Daddy said if I got another bad report like last term he'd take my bicycle away for a year,' protested Blossom, 'and that would be horrid. We'd see Fauna didn't get caught. Won't you, Fauna? Oh, *do*!'

But Fiona was proof against all the coaxing of Blossom and her room mates, and they had to give it up at last. If they wanted to hear the tales, they must risk being caught. 'Or I couldt tell you stories before bedtime if you like,' offered Fiona. 'But I won't leaf the dormy.'

In the end, it was decided that those who wished to listen must come to the Blue Dormitory, and the members thereof would do their best to shield anyone if they were caught.

Accordingly, Matron and her satellites were amazed at the speed with which the Juniors got through their washing that evening. Usually, they had to intervene, or someone would have been left out. On this night, everyone had finished in double-quick time, and the bathrooms were cleared before ever the Lower Third came upstairs.

'I don't believe you 've washed properly,' she said to Julie Lucy. 'You haven't had time. Here; let me look at the back of your neck and your ears!'

'I have, Matron—truly I have!' Julie was righteously indignant. But she had to stand still while 'Matey' swept up her curly mop from the back of her neck and surveyed it critically. There was no fault to find, so she was sent off to her dormitory, rage in her small heart at the indignity.

'Those imps are up to something,' said Matey to her assistant, Matron Lloyd. 'You might keep an eye on them, will you? I want to take two temps, and look at a tongue or two. Some of the Lower Second didn't make much of a supper I noticed, so there must be something wrong with them.'

Matron Lloyd promised; but as small Nesta Tudor chose the five minutes after Matey had gone off to 'San' to be sick, the wicked Juniors were able to carry out their plans, and the Blue Dormitory was crowded for a good half-hour, until the sound of a clock striking warned them that time was up, and 'lights out' would be going in a minute or two. The visitors reluctantly took their leave, and the Blue Dormitory settled down in their beds, as good as gold.

It was a fascinating affair. Fiona possessed a real gift for story-telling. Had she lived in the morning of the world, she would certainly have been an honoured member of her tribe, sitting before the fire during the long winter evenings in the caves, spinning tales and legends, while the flickering light lit up wonderful drawings scratched on stones with sharpened flints, and fell on the faces of the listeners as they sat with one ear open for the sound of any danger.

On Saturday, the rain continued with undiminished ardour, and when bedtime came, the Juniors were even more ready for the treat. The Highland twins had been brought up on all sorts of folklore, and the Juniors were thrilled with stories about the Kelpie, Seal-Women, Black Hares, which were really wizards or witches, and the doings of the fairy folk. Fiona sometimes varied her tales with accounts of old clan feuds, and the very prosaic Blue Dormitory became the home of gallant clansmen, clad in tartan, with plaids and kilts swinging, and skean-dhus sharp and ready for the foe, while the music of the pipes seemed to echo eerily, dirgily, round its walls. Sometimes she told them of her brave ancestress, Flora Macdonald, and the adventures of Prince Charlie—the Juniors, needless to state, were Jacobite to the core—and, told in the soft Highland tones that could swell with triumph, or wail with sorrow, the stories lost nothing in the telling. On one occasion, she had the whole dormitory on the verge of tears as she told of Culloden's Field, and the brave lads who fell there, fighting for the Scottish heir to the throne against the men of the Hanoverian usurper, as she called him. Only the thought of what would happen if they were overheard—and most of them had not yet mastered the trick of weeping quietly—helped Julie Lucy to say gruffly, 'Don't howl, you idiots! Matey will hear if you do!' and so save the situation.

For four nights they went on and were not caught. Matron, it is true, was beginning to be suspicious. It was so unlike the Juniors to be so good about going to bed. But a bad crop of colds in the School kept her busy for the moment. The little girls certainly seemed to be all right otherwise; so she shelved the matter for the time being.

On the Tuesday, Fiona outdid herself. She told a fearsome tale of a wee lassie being chased by the Kelpie, and did it so well, that she finally succeeded in frightening not only her hearers, but herself too. It was almost a relief when the chiming of the clock brought the séance to an end. Hurriedly the guests got to their feet, and, clinging rather closely together, crept from the room. Fiona, who had been sitting up on her pillow, made haste to get under the clothes, and the rest followed her example. Matron, coming along three minutes later, found them all well and truly in bed, and more than one of the six almost completely buried. It seemed safer, somehow, to leave not even a hair uncovered!

With an exclamation of horror, she turned back

the bed-clothes with a firm hand, and tucked them in properly, scolding them for being so silly. 'I know it's cold,' she concluded, 'but it's not so cold as all that. Now lie still and go to sleep, and you'll forget all about the frost. If it continues,' she said artfully, 'you may get some sliding tomorrow. Good night, girls. Remember the silence rule.' Then she switched off the light, and went out, closing the door behind her.

To her amazement, she found very much the same state of things in the next dormitory; and there were one or two others in each of the other three dormitories along that corridor. She wondered; but she was busy and worried, and thought no more about it. It *was* a cold night, after all. No doubt the children did feel a little chilly. She resolved to see that they all had extra blankets on the morrow.

In the dormitories, the Juniors tried to forget the story of the Kelpie, and go to sleep as they had been told. Flora was the first to drowse off in the Blue; Fiona, the last. But by ten o'clock, when the Seniors came upstairs, everyone was safely 'over,' and those superior damsels had no idea what had been going on; still less what was to come.

By twelve o'clock, even Miss Wilson, who was famed for sitting up later than most folks, was comfortably between the sheets, and sleeping the sleep of the justly weary. Overhead came the droning of watchful aeroplanes, and the rising wind moaned through the bare branches of the trees, making them creak and groan.

It was half an hour later when 'Bill,' as the School fondly called Miss Wilson—not to her face, though!—

woke up, and sat up in bed with a start. Some sixth sense warned her that all was not as it should be. She pushed the curly white hair out of her eyes, got quietly out of bed, and slipped on her white, quilted dressing-gown. Then she stole to the door and opened it softly and listened.

At about the same time, Robin Humphries and Mary Shand also woke up. Mary said later that she had been dreaming, and had cried out, thus waking herself. Robin's story was that she heard someone calling her. Like 'Bill,' they put on dressing-gowns and slippers, and left their rooms quietly.

Now, for some unknown reason, a good many people were sporting white dressing-gowns just now. Robin's was a gift from Jo. Mary had got hers because her room was orange, and, as she said, an orange dressing-gown would be too much orange altogether. 'I guess I'd end up by thinking I was a pot of marmalade,' she had said quaintly. All three slept on different corridors, and not one of the three knew that either of the others was on the war-path. At about the same time, Fiona McDonald, who had been sleeping restlessly, did something she had often done as a small child, though she had been free from it for the last two years—she walked in her sleep. And Flora, with that queer instinct which seems to belong to some twins, though sleep-walking was not one of her failings, also rose—giving Julie Lucy, who was roused by the movements, the fright of her life—and followed her. Julie uttered a half-smothered howl of fear, and burrowed under the bed-clothes to the bottom of the bed, where she lay quaking. No one else in the room was disturbed, for all were deeply asleep. Thus it happened that just as 'Bill' reached the head of the corridor, she was startled to see two slim forms gliding quietly down it. Both were clad in pyjamas, and the short curly hair straying over the shoulders of the pair, as well as their general height and the direction from which they came, told her that they were the McDonald twins. Wondering if this were just a mad prank, she moved quietly towards them. 'Bill' had had experience of sleep-walkers before—notably the said Alixe von Elsen—and she knew better than to startle the children awake. At the same time, Robin, coming down another staircase, caught an unusual sound from the school-rooms, and boldly decided to investigate. On the way she met Mary, who had also heard it. So, while 'Bill' was making the pleasing discovery that she had a pair of somnambulists to deal with—she had thought at first that it was only Fiona, and Flora was following to protect her twin—the two Seniors went down to the lower regions of the house, clutching each other's hands, and rather inclined to giggle.

They were right in thinking something was going on. Robin whispered to Mary, 'What price a midnight among the Middles—Fourth, for choice?' and Mary, nodding a head covered with almost silvery fair hair, whispered back, 'I reckon you've got it. *Won't* we walk into them if it is!'

At this point the two had reached the door leading into the form-room of the Upper Second. It stood slightly ajar, and there was no mistaking it. The sounds came from there. Moving noiselessly, the two girls separated, Robin making for the Upper

Third which had a second door leading into the Lower Second, and Mary remaining where she was. Robin's idea was to prevent any flight by the far door; and in this she proved remarkably successful. She reached it without falling over anything, for the black-out was down, and the light of a full moon was streaming in at the large window which ran almost from ceiling to floor in these rooms. Once at the inner door, she paused to listen a moment, and heard distinctly the sound of one of the lockers being opened, and then a noise as though someone was rummaging. Filled with righteous wrath, she was about to fling open the door, march in, and denounce the sinners, when from somewhere upstairs came a wail so eerie that even Mary's American common-sense forsook her for a moment, and she replied with a wild shriek to which Robin responded with one as wild. The two flung open their doors, bursting into the room with the moonlight streaming through the unshuttered windows across them, while from up-stairs came shouts, the banging of doors, and all the signs of the School being suddenly wakened.

No sinful Middles met the eyes of the two Seniors as they rushed into the room. Instead, there was a far more alarming figure—a tall thin man, black-clad, with gloves on his hands, and a half-mask covering the upper part of his face. It is only fair to say that he seemed as terrified of them as they were of him. At the sudden rush of their feet, he had sprung from his half-crouching position at the lockers to his fullest height, and he was staring through the eye-holes of his mask at Mary in a way that showed his fear. It must be admitted that she was a sufficiently ghostly figure in her white dressing-gown and slippers, with the moonshine catching her fair hair, and making it almost silver, while her white face was the finishing touch.

With a gasped oath, the man swung round to the other door, to be confronted by Robin, equally ghostly-looking, for she had fastened up her hair for the night in a net of thin silver braid—a discard of Jo's—and the moonlight caught it, and gave her black aureole of curls a horrible, radiant appearance. And all the time, those awful yells from upstairs were pouring out, and shrieks and the banging of doors added to the pandemonium.

The man cast one more look at the visions at each door, uttered a terrified exclamation, and made for the window. One of them was slightly open, and he dived through it, followed at full speed by Robin and Mary, who had grasped the fact that they were dealing with a burglar—though why he should want to burgle the Upper Second's lockers was beyond them for the moment—while upstairs Fiona, roused by the noise of doors and voices, and Flora, already awake, gave simultaneous yells and grabbed each other, sobbing in terror.

It was left to Matron and Bill to deal with the situation. Matey, looking her most matter-of-fact self, caught the two shivering, sobbing Juniors, hustled them along to San—whither Matron Lloyd had already gone to see to the invalids—and had them packed into one bed with cups of hot milk almost before they realised what had happened. As for 'Bill,' she turned round on such of the School as was within her reach, and with her most baleful glare demanded, 'Well? What is the meaning of all this? Is it *quite* necessary for all of you to get out of bed on a frosty night and come crowding into the corridors, *without putting on your dressing-gowns and bedroom slippers*, just because two children are walking in the corridor in their sleep? Go back to bed at once, every one of you, and never let me see such wholesale breaking of rules again! I'm ashamed of you!'

This method of dealing with them brought the girls to their senses very quickly. The prefects appeared on the scene, accompanied by those of the Staff who slept at Plas Howell. Simone de Bersac, hugging a very indignant baby to her, came to ask furiously if the girls couldn't think for once, and *not* wake up a baby at that hour of the night by their silly tricks. Simone was really angry, for the small Thérèse was cutting a tooth, and had dropped off to sleep just an hour before, after wailing for some time earlier. She forgot her English, and poured forth torrents of French rebukes, which further reduced the girls to normality. At last most of them were returned to bed, where they lay down, feeling rather silly about their wild terror. And then Elizabeth Arnett discovered that one bed in the Blue Dormitory had a hump under the clothes, and no other sign of an owner. She turned back the clothes with a firm hand, and found Julie Lucy sobbing in pitiful terror at the bottom. It was the work of a moment to haul the poor mite out, sit down on the bed, and cuddle her up with reassuring exclamations; and Julie, still terrified, clung to the big girl until she had sobbed herself into quietness.

She had had a bad fright, and, as she afterwards owned, had made sure that the Kelpie had suddenly turned up at the School and had come for her.

Miss Annersley, who had gone into Armiford to visit Miss Slater, and had been detained by various delays, so that she had gone to spend the night at the Lucys' house, had an entertaining time next day when she heard all the various members of the Staff had to say about the night's excitement. But the funniest story of all came from Robin and Mary.

Once they knew that they were dealing with a mere burglar, both girls lost their fear, and they pursued him hotly through the park, forgetting the lightness of their attire in their excitement. While he, having once ventured to look round and seeing the white figures closing in on him, was convinced that he was followed by beings from the next world. Too frightened to make any sound, he tore through the park, stumbling over bushes, and bumping into trees in a way that made him resolve to give up his evil ways if only he could once get away. Finally, he gave a last fleeting glance behind him, and saw the taller of the two figures almost within touching distance of him. In his terror he never looked to see what came next, and with an abject howl for mercy, he took a last wild leap forward, and landed with a terrific splash into the ornamental pool, which was such a charming nook in the rose-garden. Mary got the full benefit of the splash. Robin was further away and managed to escape. As for the burglar, he remained crouching in the pool against the base of the fountain, too much overcome to think straight.

His eyes were shut, and his voice was raised in lamentations of his past, mingled with promises of future amendment.

'Get up and come out of there at once!' commanded Mary in her best Head Girl manner. But he only remained where he was, yelling for mercy, and promising all sorts of impossible things if only 'the ghosts' would let him go. Mary turned to Robin, who had come up by this time. 'What shall we do?' she asked. 'We can't leave him here, you know. Anyway, he ought to be locked up until we can get the police.'

'Won't he come out?' asked Robin. 'It must be jolly cold, as well as wet.'

'He won't budge. I reckon, judging by what he keeps saying, he thinks he's got the Old Scratch after him,' replied Mary cheerfully. 'What can we do about it, Rob? I'm not going to wade into that pool in the middle of a frosty night for all the burglars in creation. But you're quite right to say we can't leave him here. What shall we do?'

'*I'll* show you.' Robin went a step or two to the right. The fountain in the centre of the pool had been shut off for some weeks now, and the spigot that turned it on was stiff with the frost; but Robin managed it at last, and after a moment's pause, the water rose in a silvery spray from the torch held by the kneeling figure. Up it rose, lovely and tenuous in the moonlight; anything but either to the man who still crouched beneath the base of the statue, and got the full benefit of its downward swing.

It was too much. With a last howl, he leapt to his feet, scrambled out of the pool on the further side, and tore off through the shrubbery before the two girls could interfere. By this time, Robin had begun to realise where they were, and what they were wearing. She shivered, and turned to Mary. 'We'd best get back, Mary. We can't catch him now, and anyway, someone *must* have heard all that awful row. The men will catch him—or if they don't, there are any number of soldiers about. I'm cold. Let's get back to the house before they miss us, or there *will* be a fuss.'

'*Robin!* Whatever will everyone say at you being outside at three o'clock on a near-winter morning? Come back to the house at once! Jo will eat us all without salt if ever she hears of *this* performance.'

'Jo won't—not if I can help it. And you needn't be afraid. I'm not the weakling I used to be. We'll get hot drinks; and if the water in the pipes is hot, we might have a tub each. I'll ask Matey if we may. Then we'll renew our bottles, and I'll bet you what you like neither of us is a penny the worse in the morning.' Robin suddenly stopped, and began to laugh. Mary shook her slightly as they hurried on to the house.

'Do stop, Robin! If Matey hears you, she'll think you're starting hysterics or something, and dose you with sal volatile.'

Robin pulled herself together as they went in through the still open window, and stopped to bolt it securely. 'We'd better put up the black-out in case that creature comes back after whatever it was he was looking for. Oh, Matron! It was a burglar. Mary and I chased him, and he ended up in the pool, and as he wouldn't come out, we turned the fountain on him. You *should* have seen it.' And she doubled up in fresh laughter.

Matey regarded her with an exceedingly grim eye. 'Have you been out like that, Robin?'

'Well, Matron, we hadn't time to put on anything else,' began Robin in rather injured tones.

'Quite so. Well, you can go to bathroom four. The water is very hot still. Mary, you may go to bathroom nine. Both of you are to soak for ten minutes, and then you can get into your night things and go to your rooms. We'll be ready for you.'

Before the sinister meaning in her tones, the pair wilted. They used no more arguments, but melted away, and when, twelve minutes later, Matron arrived in Mary's room, she found that young lady snugly in bed, her fresh hot-water bottle hugged to her, and her eyes already becoming opaquely sleepy. Matey administered a hot drink in grim silence. Mary stayed awake long enough to drink it. Then she collapsed on her pillow with a grimace. 'What horrid stuff! What did you put into it, Matron?'

Matron relaxed her grimness not a whit. 'I'll talk to you and Robin in the morning,' she said shortly. 'Stop talking at once, and get off to sleep. Good night!' Then she marched out of the room, switching off the light, and went to see to Robin who had been already dosed. That young lady was already sound asleep, so Matron finally retired to her own bed—the last to do so—where she passed the remainder of the night somewhat sleeplessly until six o'clock when she dropped off, and never woke till nearly ten, to find that the burglar had vanished; no one seemed to be one penny the worse for the night's alarms and excursions, and Miss Annersley had come back and was already interviewing a penitent Blue Dormitory, whose consciences had been roused by all the night's events, and who were making a very full confession of all their sins.

CHAPTER XII

ROSALIE GETS A BAD FRIGHT

'WHAT, in the name of common sense, any burglar thought he would get from Junior lockers is beyond me! He couldn't get much from the Senior ones, let alone Juniors'! The man must be either burgling for the love of it—which I call highly immoral!—or else an escaped lunatic!' Thus 'Bill' the following day, when the Staff were seated in the library with the Head, drinking their after-lunch coffee, and smoking—those of them that did smoke—their after-lunch cigarettes.

'Perhaps he didn't know they *were* Junior lockers,' suggested Miss Phipps.

'My dear May! He had only to take one look at the chaos that usually reigns in the small fry's lockers, or else open one exercise-book, and he must have known they were all mere babies!'

'That's a libel on the Juniors,' protested Gillian Linton. 'Their lockers are all spick and span—at the moment, anyhow. I held a locker raid two days ago, and there were only three that were really bad.

I called the owners and promised them all sorts of horrid things if they didn't reform, so I *know* those lockers were all models of neatness last night.'

'All right; I'll apologise, then. But still, that doesn't explain why he should go burrowing in them. Judging by what I saw when I did get downstairs, he must have known there could be nothing of value there. So what did the man want? That is what *I* should like to know, very definitely.'

'It's all very worrying,' put in Miss Annersley in her quiet voice. 'And the worst of it is that no one seems to have caught him. Colonel Black was on the 'phone to me before lunch, and he said they found plenty of traces of his flight in the grounds; but nothing more once he had gained the high-road. So that looks as if he had an accomplice who waited for him with a car. And the police seem to be quite as much at sea.'

'Oh, they'll get him some time,' said Miss Burnett, the history mistress.

'You cannot be sure of that. It is war-time now,' said Mlle Lachenais from the big pouffe where she sat curled up, one hand on Gillian's shoulder, her dark eyes on the leaping fire. 'I know that your police are very clever; but now it is easy for a man to get away and hide.'

'Perhaps it's some soldier trying to get paper and pencils to write letters home to all his friends and relations on the cheap,' suggested Miss Everett, who was a visiting mistress, coming out from Armiford each day. Gardening was her subject, and the School prided itself on the vegetables it produced, never to mention flowers. Everything in that line used by themselves was grown by themselves. Miss Everett also helped them to look after the seven Jersey cows and the flourishing poultry-yard which were School possessions. The big herd belonged to Mr Howell to whom Plas Howell belonged, and his own men cared for them; but the School had its own milk and eggs, and was very proud of that fact.

The Staff at large jeered at the latest idea. They did not think any soldier would be likely to risk prison for the sake of some paper and a few pencils—especially the chewed specimens which were all the Juniors would be likely to leave in their lockers. People with good cases brought them upstairs at night by special permission, which had first been given a year ago when cases and pencils began to vanish. The losses had been traced to a temporary maid, whose brother kept a small village shop where he had been able to dispose of her thefts very profitably. It was then that the Head had said such things might be kept in the dormitories, provided there were not too many cases of forgetfulness in lessons. It affected only the Juniors and the Middles, for the Seniors had studies with locked cupboards where they could house such things. The prefects went in pairs, and the rest of the Fifth and Sixth shared one between four; only the Head Girl and the Games Captain being honoured by separate studies.

Finally they gave it up, and as the bell rang for afternoon school, departed to their several duties. Miss Annersley turned to deal with some of the correspondence which falls so heavily to the lot of the Head of any flourishing school. Miss Phipps,

Gillian Linton, Mademoiselle, and Miss Burnett all had lessons in the Middle and Junior schools; and Miss Wilson was due in the laboratory for a biology lesson with the Lower Fifth, who were taking this subject as their science subject in School Certificate this year, greatly to her joy. The Upper Fifth had remained wedded to botany, and the Sixth preferred chemistry. 'Bill' was a keen biologist and the Lower Fifth found her a most inspiring teacher in consequence. Two or three other people had coaching periods; and Miss Everett, after a glance through the windows which showed the rain streaming down again, went off to give the Sixth a lesson on the composition of soils. Only Miss Dene, the Head's secretary, and herself one of the earliest members of the School, remained. She sat by the desk, taking shorthand notes as Miss Annersley dictated them. When all the letters were done, the Head detained her for a moment or two.

'One minute, Rosalie. I am very much puzzled by the latest event. You keep in better touch with the girls than even Mary Burnett and Gillian Linton. I fancy that, as you don't teach, they feel you are—less official, shall we say?—than even those two. Have you heard anything that would give us any help in this matter of last night's burglar?'

Rosalie shook her head. 'I've no idea at all, Miss Annersley. I'm as much puzzled as anyone. What *could* a burglar hope to find in the Junior lockers? It doesn't seem to make sense!'

'You're quite right—it doesn't. And yet it was the Junior lockers in which he was interested. He had been through five others before Robin and

Mary came on the scene, and it was Julie Lucy's he was routing out when they appeared.'

Rosalie shook her fair head again. 'It is a mystery to me. As Miss Wilson says, he had only to look at one or two books to see that the lockers belonged to small children, and he couldn't hope to find anything worth while there.' She paused. Then she asked, 'Do you know which ones he had gone through before that, Miss Annersley? It might explain a bit.'

'I have the list here. Miss Phipps gave it to me when I got back this morning.' The Head fished it out from under a pile of *Hamlets* and read it out. 'Nesta Tudor—Joy Leigh—Amy West—Nora Bird—Fiona McDonald. Is it any help to you, Rosalie? Does it throw any light at all on the subject?'

Rosalie frowned and thought hard. 'Nesta—Joy—Amy—Nora—I don't see what they could have that would be of any interest. They're all English girls who have come to us since we moved here. It isn't even as if they'd been in Tyrol and might be writing to any of the foreign girls. And Fiona seems even more unlikely. If it had been little Marie le Cadoulec, or Lonka Maïco—but even they are scarcely likely to have anything—' She paused, and looked at the Head. 'You see what I mean, Miss Annersley?'

Miss Annersley looked at her in blank amazement. 'I'm afraid I don't. How could children of nine and ten have valuables at school, even if they *are* foreigners? And the le Cadoulecs are as poor as can be, as you know. Jeanne never made any secret of it when she was here. I was glad she got a scholarship to London University. She has another year, and then—I may as well tell you, for I know you won't spread it abroad—she has the offer of a very good post under Professor Rich of Cambridge. And the Maïcos have always brought up their girls most austerely. Lorenz and Lonka have very few luxuries. So I'm afraid I don't see the point of your remarks.'

Rosalie blushed and looked ashamed of herself. 'Perhaps it is rather silly and story-bookish. I was only wondering if, perhaps, it had been thought safer to give—well—important documents to the children as being less likely to be suspected.'

Miss Annersley stared at her, and then burst into hearty laughter. 'My dear Rosalie! What have you been reading lately? That is an idea worthy of Jo at her wildest. As if anyone in their senses would entrust small children with important documents! And even if any of our parents were mad enough to do so, neither the Comte le Cadoulec nor Count Maïco would be likely to have any. You forget that the Comte left the French Government before the war; and Count Maïco is in deep disgrace for quitting his country as he did, because he refused to be mixed up with their aims and politics. No; I think we must look for some other explanation than that. But what it can be I am at a loss to know.'

'He *may* have been hunting on general principles, of course,' said Rosalie, whose cheeks were still scarlet.

'I should be disposed to think that, too, if it were not that he must have realised by the time he reached Julie that he was dealing with the belongings of small girls. So I cannot understand why he didn't give it up and try elsewhere. Two doors further along he would have come to the pantry and all the forks and spoons. They are only E.P., but even they would have been more worth his while than Nora Bird's Latin or Joy Leigh's dictation books. Well, there is one thing we must do, and that is, to see that all black-out is left up until the next morning. Those french windows are rather a temptation to people who are dishonest; and our screens would give some added protection. You might put up notices to that effect when you have finished my letters. And now, you have a good deal to do, and so have I, so I must not keep you talking any longer. Get the letters done, dear, and bring them to me when they are ready. If I am not here, just leave them on the desk, and I'll sign them when I get back. I am expecting two parties of parents for interview, so I may be in the little drawing-room when you are finished. Then if you do the notices and put them up, I think that's all I shall want from you today. Aren't you going to tea with Jo and her guest?'

Rosalie laughed. 'I am dying to know who it is. Jo was most mysterious about her visitors when she rang up this morning, and no one seems to know anything. Who is it, Miss Annersley? An old girl, I'm sure. But who?'

'Wait and see, my child. There's one thing I can tell you. You will be very properly thrilled when you do know. Now I must go. Mind you keep up a good fire in your office. It is a most unpleasant day, and a bright fire is a cheering thing when one is working at top speed.'

'Thank you, Miss Annersley. But tell me; you *do* know who it is?'

'Of course I do. But I am under bond to tell no one, so I'm afraid you must wait till you reach Plas Gwyn. Don't make yourself late for tea. The stationery order and the note to the music people can wait till later so long as the rest catch the post. Oh, by the way, how are you getting back? I don't care for your walking after black-out.'

'Jo said something about running me up in the car if she had enough petrol. Don't worry, Miss Annersley. If she hasn't, I'll get the six o'clock bus, and stop at the lodge and ask Williams to walk up as far as the house with me.'

'Well, if you will do that, I shan't worry about you. Now you must go, or we shall never get through.' The Head smiled her dismissal, and Rosalie departed to her office next door, and forgot about the latest school mystery while she typed letters and orders, and then turned to the notices. Having finished, she went back to the library, but it was empty. Judging that one party of parents for interview had arrived she laid the letters on the table, took up the stamp with the Head's signature on it, and went back to stamp the black-out notices. Then she hurried round the various rooms to pin up the notices, and at last found herself free to run up to her pretty room to change for her tea-party at Plas Gwyn.

As the Head had said, she was thrilled to see Elisaveta when she got there, and in the excitement she forgot to tell Jo anything about the School's latest thrill, or that young lady might have been able to help a little. The night before she had left, Shiena had said to her hostess, 'I wass thinking of asking you to take care of something for us, Jo, but I haf gifen it to the twins. They know what it means to us, and I think it will pe fery safe with them; and you haf so much to trouple you already. But I haf told them that if efer they are in trouple ofer it, to come and ask you what they must do, and I know you will advise them.'

'Of course I will,' Jo had said. 'But remember, Shiena, anything I can do for you I will, and it's no trouble. So if, on second thoughts, you'd rather leave whatever it is in my care, please do, and I'll look after it to the best of my ability.'

But Shiena had refused to give her hostess more worry than she already had, so no more was said about it. If Rosalie had told of the previous night's burglary, Jo would have at once guessed that the burglar was after whatever it was the McDonald twins had in keeping, and have insisted on their giving it to her. Much might have been saved in that case, and Rosalie herself would have been spared a nasty fright. As it was, when Jo saw her guest off by the bus—the petrol had not come up to her hopes, and she was unable to fulfil her promise to return her old friend to Plas Howell—she bade her good-bye quite cheerfully, and went back to her warm fireside and Elisaveta, now up, though still looking rather tired, and never gave a thought to what lay before Rosalie.

Meanwhile, Rosalie sat in the bus quite happily

for the two and a half miles of the road journey, and got off it certain that Williams-the-lodge, as the people round about described him, would see her up the dark drive to the house. So it was a nasty shock when Mrs Williams opened the door, and in answer to her query told her that her husband was down at the parish Institute, taking part in a darts match. This meant that he would not be home before ten, and she could scarcely wait till then. Neither could Mrs Williams go with her. There were three Williams little folk, and they were all in bed, for it was nearly seven o'clock, and could not be left.

'If it was only Arthur and Baby, Miss, I'd chance it and come with you,' said Mrs Williams, standing with the lodge door drawn close behind her. 'But that Teddy's a regular young limb, and I dursent leave them. And the men 'aven't been to put the 'phone right, neether, or I could ring up the 'ouse for you, and someone 'ud come to fetch you.'

'Never mind, Mrs Williams,' said Rosalie. 'After all, it isn't so very far, and I can't very well lose my way on the drive, that's one comfort. If only my torch will hold out!' She glanced down at the little pocket torch she carried with a very doubtful air.

'Well there, Miss; I can 'elp you there,' said Mrs Williams. 'Me 'usband took 'is with 'im to the Ins'tute, but 'ere's mine, and a new battery in it only on Sat'day. You're welcome to it, I'm sure.'

'Won't you need it, though?' objected Rosalie.

'Not me, Miss. I ain't goin' out no more. Evan got in the wood an' coal before 'e went off, and there ain't nothin' else I want now. You take the torch, an' Evan can fetch it back tomorrer when 'e's up at the 'ouse.'

Thus urged, Rosalie took the torch, bade a pleasant 'Good night' to the lively little Welshwoman, and set off on her half-mile tramp up the long, winding drive. As she had said, she could not lose her way very well, for it was railed off from the parkland where the cattle grazed. It was lonely enough, but she was in the School grounds, and it was very unlikely that she would meet any strangers there now.

It was very dark on the drive, for the moon was waning, and as the sky was heavily overcast, there were no stars to be seen. It was not raining, which was a blessing; but Rosalie felt fairly sure that it would begin again before long. She was glad of Mrs Williams' torch, for she had hardly gone fifty yards before her own went out. She tucked it into the pocket of her coat, and switched on the other one—or, rather, she tried to do so. Nothing happened, and though she pressed and twisted, it remained blank. Clearly, the battery was out. What Mrs Williams had not known was that Teddy Williams had found it on the dresser where his mother had left it on the previous night, and had spent all the morning while she was washing, in chasing his small brother Arthur with it through the shrubbery which reached down to the far end of the lodge garden. He had gone in to dinner at twelve, leaving it switched on on the bench by the door, and had forgotten all about it till nearly tea-time, when he had seen it still burning. Guiltily, he had turned it off, and put it back where he had found it. Mrs Williams had used it two or three times since without noticing how feeble the light had become, and she had finished it.

'What on earth shall I do?' thought Rosalie nervously. 'I can't go back—I couldn't spend the evening in the Williams' cottage. Besides, the Head would have fits if I didn't turn up till after ten. She'd think someone had tried to kidnap me. If only the men had got out to mend the telephone wire! Then I could have rung up, and they'd have sent someone to take me back. Well, I certainly can't stand here, either, so I'd better get on at once. If I walk quickly I ought to get there in fifteen minutes or so. It's a straight road—it's not as if I had to go through a wood as they do at the Round House. That *would* be rather horrid!' She set off, even as she thought it, and presently she was nearly half-way on her walk. Then she suddenly heard footsteps, not behind her—though that would have been bad enough—but in the grass on her right hand. Rosalie stifled a desire to shriek and run, and forced herself to walk steadily on. She even pursed up her lips and tried to whistle; but she couldn't quite manage that, so she gave it up. The steps only sounded occasionally, as if someone were trying to keep level with her without her knowing it, but was occasionally betrayed by a dry twig under foot, or a tussock of grass.

Going steadily, Rosalie thought hard. The railings came to an end about a couple of hundred yards in front of the house—or rather, they turned, to rail off the parkland from the lawn. If whoever it was who was following her got over the railings and rushed at her, she would be too far from the house for anyone to hear her call out. Anything might happen to her out there in the dark, and no one be any the wiser.

Poor Rosalie once more repressed a wish to scream, and drove herself on. She thought that if she hesitated, or tried to turn back, this person might vault over the railings and seize her then and there. It would be bad enough at the lawn; but here, half-way between the house and the lodge, it would be far worse. So far as she could see, there was only one thing she could do, and that was to be ready as soon as the end of the railings was reached to make a wild dive up the last of the drive, and hope to be near enough to the big door before anyone could come up with her to make herself heard in one wild yell. Hastily she calculated how much further she had to go. She reckoned that she must be rather more than half-way now. She must not leave the sprint till too late, or whoever it was could leap the railings and grab her before she could get going. On the other hand, if she started too soon, it would give her idea away, and then he—she was sure it was 'he'—would simply tear forward and cut her off. So she must be very careful indeed.

As well as she could, she judged her distance, for it was far too dark to see anything. Even the house was not distinguishable save as a dark bulk faintly looming up before her. The railings were not visible. She glanced from side to side, straining her eyes to make them out, but in vain. She must trust to luck and her sense of distance.

At last—and oh! what a long time it seemed to

her!—she judged that she was about at the beginning of the lawn. She paused a moment, drew a long breath, and then set off with all her might, running as she had never run before. In her ears was the thud-thud of heavy footsteps, and she could feel a hand outstretched to grab her shoulder. She missed her way in the dark, and suddenly found that she had left the gravel and was running over turf. Then, indeed, she gave herself up for lost, for how could she ever hope to find a door now? All she could do was to run, and already her legs were tiring, and a cruel stitch was catching at her side.

An exclamation in a foreign tongue seemed the end to her. She gasped out a shrill cry, and fell fainting at the feet of the person who had spoken. And he stooped down, flashing a tiny torch in her unconscious face, and uttered a guttural word of surprise. Then he swung her up in strong arms, and carried her quickly round the house. But Rosalie knew nothing of this. She lay limp, unresisting, to all appearance dead, against his shoulder, and it was some time before she came back to life again.

CHAPTER XIII

'IT'S THE ERISAY CHART THEY WANT!'

'FIONA, dear, will you run along to the Staff-room and say that if Miss Dene has come in I should like to see her here at once.'

Fiona McDonald, who had been going along to wash her hands free of ink before the gong sounded for supper, went off obediently to the rosy room which had once been a small drawing-room, but which was now a very cosy Staff-room. It was rather an ordeal for her to enter and repeat the Head's request, for both Fiona and Flora were still painfully shy; but they were beginning to grow out of it a little, and very few of the busy people in the Staff-room who looked up at her tap on the door, guessed what she was feeling as she entered and gave the Head's message in her soft Highland voice.

Miss Wilson, who happened to be there for once, looked round the room. 'Miss Dene! Isn't she here, anyone? Do you know where she is at all?'

'She was going to Jo Maynard's to tea,' said Miss Phipps, laying down the raffia mat with which she had been struggling. 'She may not have come in yet. Shall I run up to her room and see, Miss Wilson?'

'Please do.—Fiona, run along and tell the Head that Miss Dene isn't here, but we are looking for her, and will send her along as soon as she comes. And here! Take these botany books to your form-room, will you? Where are you going, by the way?'

'To wash my hands.' Fiona spread out her hands, and the science mistress lifted her black brows at the sight of them. 'They need it, I must say! Have you been *bathing* in the ink? I hope you haven't got any on your frock. Come here and let me see.' And 'Bill' turned the small girl round to the light and scanned the brown velvet frock carefully. 'Not a spot! Well, that's a good thing. All right. Run along now. We'll see to Miss Dene.'

Thus adjured, Fiona went back to the library, where she gave 'Bill's' message to the Head, keeping her hands carefully behind her back—she had put the books down outside on purpose—and was dismissed with a kindly, 'Thank you, dear. That is all, then. You can run along now.'

Fiona left the room, picked up the books, and went her way to the splasheries, leaving them in the Upper Second en route. In the splasheries she found her twin, intent on the same errand as herself. For the first time since the previous night, they were alone, and Flora had something to say to her sister.

'Where have you been, Fiona? I have wanted to talk to you all day.' She spoke in their native Gaelic, and Fiona replied in the same tongue. 'The Head sent me for Miss Dene, but she was not in the Staff-room. What is it, Flora? Have you had a letter from Shiena?'

'No; I'd have told you about that at once. It is the burglary last night,' said Flora, soaping her hands with great vigour. 'Why do you think that man was hunting in *our* lockers?'

'He had not got to yours. It was Julie Lucy's he had reached,' said Fiona carefully. 'But I see what you mean, Flora.' For her twin had made a scornful noise. 'You think he wanted the Chart, do you not? But he might search the lockers till Doomsday, and he would not find it there.'

Flora chuckled. 'No, he would not. That was a clever idea of yours, Fiona. But I wonder how they could guess that one of us might have it.'

'I know nothing about that. At least I have said nothing to anyone—not even to Mistress Maynard—

and Shiena said we were to tell her if we were in any trouble over it. Have you, Flora—besides what you said that Saturday, I mean?'

'No; I have not said a word,' replied Flora—truly, as she thought. She had no idea that she had given their secret away to the one girl who was their enemy, and that through no fault of their own.

'Then I cannot understand it. Should we speak to Mistress Maynard?'

Flora thought of this as she rinsed her hands. 'No; I think not,' she said slowly. 'I should like us to keep it a secret to the family if we could. It *is* a family secret, Fiona, and Mistress Maynard is not a McDonald, though she has been so good and kind to us.'

'But if there is any bad trouble we *must* tell her,' insisted Fiona, who was the more law-abiding of the twins. 'Shiena told us so.'

'Yes; but there is no trouble yet—at least only that man, and he did nothing after all. So I think we will say nothing yet. And don't you do it without letting me know first, Fiona. Give me your word, please.'

'I never do!' cried Fiona indignantly. 'We're twins! We do everything together, and always have done. I would not dream of it!'

'Then that's a promise, mind. Now we'd better get back to the Common Room, or someone will be asking for us. Come along.'

'I haven't dried my hands properly,' objected Fiona as she grabbed the towel. 'Wait a minute till I do, or they will be so sore.'

'Oh, use your handkerchief. Here's mine, too.

Now come along.' And Flora led the way back to the Junior Common Room, where their clan were amusing themselves in their own ways until the gong sounded for supper. However, they had an adventure before they got there. Just as they reached the main hall, which they had to cross to reach their destination, there was a little stir beyond the green baize door that shut off the kitchen regions from the rest of the house, and then it opened, and Evan Evans, the head gardener at Plas Howell, appeared, carrying in his arms a limp body. Hastily the twins drew back into their own passage while he bore his burden to the foot of the great staircase where Matron had suddenly appeared, followed by Miss Everett and Miss Wilson with one of the Guide stretchers, on which the sturdy Welshman carefully laid his load, and then it was borne off upstairs; and Evan Evans, Megan, who was housekeeper, and the three or four maids who had come with them went back to their own quarters, leaving, unknown to them, two small girls agog with excitement as to what all this was about. They had recognised Miss Dene's fair hair and big blue coat with its collar and cuffs of fox fur. Fiona had just come back from taking her a message to the Staff-room where she had not been after all. Now, she had turned up like this, to all appearance dead. What could it all mean? Was the burglar at the bottom of it?

'That wass Miss Dene!' Flora informed her twin when Matron, 'Bill,' 'Evvy' and the stretcher had disappeared down the long gallery leading to the rooms used for 'San.' 'What *can* haf happened to her?'

'Do you think it iss that man?' asked Fiona, her eyes wide at the idea.

'But why shouldt he go for her? She hass nothing to do with it.'

'I know. But he might have been lurking about' —the tone in which Fiona made this statement was enough to send cold shudders down anyone's spine! —'and haf hit her. Do you think she iss dead, Flora? She wass so fery white and still. I did not like it at all. Oh, do you think she iss?'

Flora shook her head. 'Inteet, and I ton't know. Oh, Fiona! What shall we do apout it? It iss our fault, for it iss our Chart they are after.'

But a little common sense was returning to Fiona. 'We ton't know that it iss the Chart. And she may have fallen and hit herself, and Evan Evans found her and carried her in. It iss quite likely, you know.'

'It iss likely,' began Flora; but just then Miss Linton appeared at the other side of the hall; she stared at seeing two Upper Seconds there where they had no right to be, and gave them short shrift.

'What are you two doing out of your Common Room? Go back at once, and don't leave it till you hear the supper gong sound. Run along quickly, now.'

'Miss Linton!' Fiona had bounded across the hall, and was grasping her arm and looking up into Gillian Linton's fair face with eyes that were so wide with horror, no one could ignore them.

Gillian put an arm round the child, and felt her shaking. 'Why, Fiona? What is wrong, child?

Has someone been frightening you? Here; come with me!' She opened the door of Rosalie's little office near which they were standing, and drew the child in, Flora following. She switched on the light, and sat down, her arm still round Fiona, while Flora came and stood close at her twin's other side. 'What is wrong?' repeated the young mistress.

'Miss Dene,' faltered Fiona. 'Oh, *iss* she dead, Miss Linton? *Iss* she?'

'Dead—Miss Dene? What are you talking about, Fiona?' Gillian, of course, knew nothing about the little procession which had just taken place and she had not been in the Staff-room when Fiona had come in with her message, so she could make neither head nor tail of all this.

'They haf chust carried her upstairs on a stretcher —Evan Evans carried her in from the kitchens,' said Flora, coming to her twin's rescue. The fine black brows over the pansy-blue eyes were drawn in a rapid frown at this information. 'What do you mean, children? Has there been an accident?'

'We ton't know. But she looked dead. Matey came—and Bill and Evvy with a stretcher.' In her agitation Fiona forgot formalities, and Gillian was so startled by what they were saying that she paid no heed either. 'Her head fell—just like a dead lamb's. Oh, hass she been killed?'

But by this time the young mistress had made up her mind. Whatever had happened, her first job was to soothe these frightened children, and she set about it with a will. 'You silly children! Miss Dene has been down to Plas Gwyn to have tea with Mrs Maynard. I expect she slipped and fell and hit her head as she came back up the drive, and Evan Evans found her and carried her in. Now don't be so scared, and don't begin to cry, either of you. Stay here, and I'll go and ask, and come back and tell you. But I'm sure you're making a mountain out of a molehill'—which was Greek to her listeners, who did not know the old proverb. But her voice was reassuring and so were her eyes. The twins began to recover from their fright, and she got up and left them and went off to the Staff-room to ask what had happened. She found everyone as ignorant as herself. Miss Wilson had left the room to go to seek Megan in the kitchen department to ask her about something, and that was the last anyone had seen of *her*. No one had known that Miss Everett was still in the School. She was a visiting mistress, who made her home with the Lucys in Armiford, travelling backwards and forwards. As for Miss Dene, Miss Phipps was still hunting for her. Gillian got no news from her compeers. She left them as much agog with excitement as the twins had been, and went to seek Matron.

That lady was duly found in San, looking very worried. In response to Gillian's queries, she told her that Miss Dene had had a fall and fainted, and had not come round yet. 'And *don't* worry me with any more questions; and don't broadcast it through the School either,' she snapped at the mistress whom she had first known as a schoolgirl. 'You go and look after those children and see that they get off to bed in proper time and go quietly, and leave me to see to Rosalie. I don't like this unconsciousness. I don't believe it's concussion. There's no sign of a blow. I'm sending for the doctor, and I can't say anything more till he's been. Now, out of my way, and go and see to the Juniors!'

Gillian knew Matey. She fled before the storm, went along to Rosalie's office where she told the twins that Miss Dene had had a fall as she came home, but would be all right soon, and dismissed them thankfully as the supper gong sounded through the house. Mademoiselle, Miss Phipps, and the physical training mistress, Miss Burn, another Old Girl of the School, were on duty. So Gillian saw the Juniors into the dining-room, and then retired to the Staff-room, where she was assailed on all sides by questions. She was unable to give them much satisfaction, and no one was much wiser when the gong rang for Staff dinner.

Gillian had warned the twins to say nothing of what they had seen, so the School at large heard nothing about it till next morning, when they were told that Miss Dene was not very well, so would stay in bed for a day or two. Meantime, those of the Cadets and Rangers who were taking Clerk's Badge would have practice in the work, for they were to share it out among themselves, which gave them entire satisfaction. Betty, on hearing the news, sneered a little, it is true, but they were used to her, and no one minded what she said. Daisy even was moved to wish aloud that her seventeenth birthday was over, for then she would be a Ranger, and could have taken her share of the work. She was very fond of Rosalie, whom she had known for a good many years, and very sorry to hear of her illness.

'And when are we to go home?' she lamented

aloud. 'Who on earth can Jo be having to stay that she can't have *us* as well? I do think it's the limit—don't you, Rob? It's all very well not to want the children; but after all, you and I are old enough not to make nuisances of ourselves.'

Robin looked perplexed. 'I can't imagine who it can be. It isn't like Jo, is it? And do you know, Daisy, I've just had a note from the Round House, and the triplets are there. Jo's cleared the entire house, it seems.'

'My goodness! D'you really mean that, Rob? What else did Auntie Madge say? Does she give any hint of who Jo's guest is, for instance?'

'Not exactly. She says—here; I'll read you the bit about that.' And Robin produced the letter from her blazer pocket, and read aloud, '"I don't know if you know that I have the triplets here. With Josette to help, they keep us lively, I can tell you. Jo's visitor is beginning to pull up, she tells me, so I expect you and Daisy, at any rate, will be allowed to go home for next week-end. I don't suppose Primula and the twins will be too welcome for a week or two, though. You will be excited when you know who it is. Prepare to welcome a *very* old friend—older even than Emmie and Joanna. By the way, give those two my love, and say I want them on Sunday." That's all about that,' concluded Robin, folding up the letter and putting it back into her pocket. 'What do you make of it, Daisy?'

'It's an absolute mystery to me. I'm getting sick of mysteries!' said Daisy petulantly. 'There's the burglar one, and now this. And, talking of mysteries, have you noticed Floppy and Betty? That friendship seems to be cooling off more than a little. What is the cause of that?'

'Goodness knows! Betty does seem to quarrel with people. I've never fathomed what lay at the bottom of her row with Elizabeth Arnett, though I've often wondered. Do you know, Daisy, I'm beginning to be very sorry for Betty. She never seems to keep her friends for very long. Floppy has lasted for a year, and now, as you say, they seem to be cooling off. It must be rather horrid never to have friends you can rely on,' said Robin thoughtfully. 'I should hate it if Lorenz, and Amy, and Enid and I were like that. We've been chums for years, and I hope we always will be.'

But Daisy was younger, and by no means so thoughtful as Robin. The elder girl's speech puzzled her. 'Isn't it Betty's own fault? If she were decent, her friends would stay put. Look at Beth and Gwensi and me! We've been pals from the word "Go!" Oh, I don't say we don't have spats now and then. We've all got tempers. But it never amounts to anything much.'

'Oh, I know. But, as I said, I'm sorry for Betty. I think if she could she'd be friends with Elizabeth again; but she'll have to go a long way before she reaches her nowadays, and I don't know if she would do it.'

Then the bell rang, and they parted, Robin to go to history, and Daisy to gallop off to the cloakroom to change into plimsolls for gym. But, unknown to either, they had been overheard. Standing in the half-open door of the Upper Fifth, Betty Wynne-Davies had caught her own name, and had unashamedly eavesdropped. Daisy's frank comments made her rage; but what hurt most was Robin's clear insight. Betty's vivid, gipsy face was very black as she left the room for the history class.

It was not much good she got from it, either. All the time Miss Burnett was holding forth on the Reform Bill, Betty Wynne-Davies was thinking hard, trying to see what she could do to pay back the two girls who had discussed her so freely. She could find nothing at the moment; but a little later in the day, she chanced to overhear a new speech of Robin's which gave her an idea. This time, that young lady was with her own friends, Lorenz Maïco, Amy Stevens, who had returned to school after an absence of some weeks owing to cold, and Enid Sothern. They were a most united quartette, and Amy had to hear all the news. Seated in the Senior Common Room on one of the wide window-seats, they all talked hard, while Betty, sprawled on a near-by settee, pretended to be deep in *Prester John*.

Presently, she heard Amy ask if Fiona and Flora had settled down by this time, and how they got on at school. 'I think it must be dreadful to have lived as they did, and then have to face *masses* of girls!' finished Amy.

'They've settled down all right,' said Robin. 'It's a good thing, for really, what with one thing and another, we've all got so much on our hands that if they hadn't, I don't know how on earth we should have managed.'

'What sort of things?' demanded Amy.

'Well, Jo's always up to the eyes in work, as you

know. When it isn't her babies, it's her books, or the house. And then there are the letters to Jack. And she's never let the School go. And Daisy is working like a nigger. She's made up her mind to get a schol. if she can. Of course, there's plenty of time yet; but Jo says the competition is fearful nowadays, so she's digging in as hard as she can. And I've got all sorts of oddments of my own—school duties, as well as form work. If I had to do too much sheep-dog, I should go off my head, I think. Luckily, they've chummed up with the Ozannes, and Julie Lucy, and Nancy Chester—a nice crowd, if a bit wild on occasion. And Primula and Bride belong, too. I don't do any worrying about them now, thank Heaven! I did at first.'

'Don't tempt Providence like that, Rob,' said Enid lazily. 'If you talk like that, those blessed twins will get up to something unholy, and you'll find you have to do quite a lot of worrying about them. Touch wood, my child, touch wood! You've simply *asked* for trouble now!'

Robin laughed. 'Superstitious idiot!' she said affectionately. 'As I don't believe in rot of that kind, I'll leave you to touch the wood. But all the same, I do hope those twins will keep out of trouble, for I'm going to have a shot at Jo's essay prize—she asked me the last time I saw her. I haven't a chance, of course. Elizabeth is the most likely to get it. She really *can* write essays. I'm all right if it's a case of fairy stories, but the sort of thing they want for the Josephine Bettany is rather beyond me. But Jo asked me to try, so I will; and I don't want any extra worry to put me off my stride. It'll take me all my time to turn out something I *can* send in as it is.'

The chatter passed to something else after that, and presently the four left the room, and Betty was left alone. Her face was very evil as she lay there, thinking over what had been said. So if anything upset the McDonald twins it would put Robin Humphries off her stride for the essay prize, would it? Well, that was something to know. And if Robin were upset Daisy would certainly take it to heart. Neither of the pair was given to making a parade of their love for each other, but Betty was quite keen enough to see it was there. *And* if the twins were upset, then she would be getting back at *them*. It seemed a good plan all round. The point was, what could she do to upset them? It must be subtle, for the Staff were very much on the alert these days. Also, it must be something that could not be traced back to her. Betty had been very seriously warned the last time she had had a 'Head's row,' and she had no mind to be expelled. Her guardian, a business man with little time or sympathy for her, would certainly take a very unpleasant view of any such happening. Betty rolled round, and gave her mind up to the affair with a vim worthy of a better cause. The upshot of her thinking struck her as quite clever. The details needed to be worked out, but she felt she could give up a few days to that. And then, look out, Robin, Daisy, Flora, and Fauna! Betty would pay off all scores, and then, perhaps, people would leave her alone.

She got off her settee, and went to seek her writing-case. Sitting down at a table, she set to work to write a long letter to a friend of her dead mother's. Mrs Graves would be able to help her, Betty felt sure, and she was in the habit of writing two or three times a term to the lady who, for her mother's sake, showed a certain interest in her. The letter was duly posted with the rest, and three days later, the reply came. Betty, knowing the hand-writing on the address, almost snatched it up from the letter-table when she saw it, and lost no time in seeking a secluded spot in which to devour its contents.

'MY DEAR BETTY,—I was very pleased to get your long letter, and to learn that you have decided to try for the Josephine Bettany Essay prize. I do hope you get it. I think you should stand a fair chance, for you can write a very good letter; and your mother used to head all the essay lists when we were at school. Go in and win! And best of luck to you!

'Now about your request. I am printing the words for which you ask. Gaelic is not too easy a language to follow. I don't quite see where your joke comes in; but I suppose I shall hear all about it later. Send me whatever it is you want posted, and I will post it for you; though I must say it strikes me as rather pointless. Still, I dare say a lot of the things *we* thought jokes when we were at school would have seemed equally pointless to *our* elders.

'I have no time for more at present, as I am very busy with the canteen, and also my fire-watching. I enclose P.O. for a pound, as I expect a little extra pocket-money won't come amiss at this season in the term.—Your loving AUNTIE PHYLL.

'*P.S.*—Uncle Harry also sends you a pound, and you are to spend Christmas with us as usual, dear. He also wishes you luck with the essay.'

Betty carefully slipped the postal orders into the breast-pocket of her blazer, noted the printed enclosure, and danced a little jig of joy to herself. Then, as the first bell rang, she went to find her hymn-book, and looked so super-angelic during Prayers, that Miss Annersley, catching sight of her, confided later on to Miss Wilson that Betty Wynne-Davies was up to something fishy, and they had better all keep an eye on her.

Nothing happened for the next few days; but on the Monday, when the twins had finished welcoming Robin and Daisy back from Plas Gwyn, whither they had been bidden for the week-end, and had finished plying the elder girls with questions about Mrs Maynard's guests, Robin handed them a letter she had picked up from the letter-table as she passed through the hall, and then took Daisy off to Senior Common Room, leaving the pair to stare at the unknown hand-writing on the envelope.

'It issn't Shiena or any of the boys,' said Flora. 'And it issn't Tibby McDonald, or Mrs. Mackenzie. Who can it pe from?'

'Open it and see,' advised Nancy Chester who was with them.

'What's the postmark?' added Julie Lucy. The Band, as Robin called them, were together as usual. 'That might show you something.'

However, the postmark was so indistinct that no one could make anything of it, so they followed

Nancy's advice, and opened it. A piece of bright blue paper, neatly folded, was inside. Flora opened it out, and Fiona hung eagerly over her sister's shoulder to read the few words written in an angular hand. To the horror of the rest of the Band, the twins went white as they read.

'I hope it isn't bad news,' said Nancy anxiously.

'What's up?' demanded Vanna Ozanne simply.

The twins stood staring from the letter to each other in a stricken way. They paid no heed to their chums, who were beginning to feel frightened. Then Fiona, with a big effort, recovered herself a little. 'It—it's shust something we didn't expect,' she said flatly. 'Come along, Flora; I want you.'

They made off, leaving their compeers to gaze after them in wonder. Nancy Chester was the first to speak. 'Well—it's no business of ours. But I wonder what has happened. They looked as if—as if——'

'As if they'd heard every friend or relation they had in the world had died,' Vanna helped her out. 'They've got one brother in the Navy, and another in the Air Force. Do you think anything's happened to any of them?'

'No. It wasn't in English, whatever it was. I believe,' said Julie with a wag of her black curled head, 'that it's something to do with their old home—what's-its-name—Erisay.'

And no one could offer a better suggestion.

Meantime, in a bathroom where they had bolted themselves in in complete defiance of rules, the twins were facing each other with frightened eyes and quivering lips, in silence at first. Then Fiona again broke it.

'Flora—oh, Flora! It's the Erisay Chart they want!'

CHAPTER XIV

THE TWINS IN A DILEMMA

THE bell rang for Prayers, and the School filed into its two separate rooms—Catholics had their Prayers in one with a Catholic mistress to take them; and the Protestants, who were in the majority, of course, had theirs in Hall with the Head—and, for a wonder, only their own form knew that Flora and Fiona were missing. Prayers ended, and the girls streamed out to the form-rooms, and still no Highland twins turned up, hot and apologetic. The first lesson began—arithmetic, in the case of the Upper Second—and Miss Edwards, who was Junior maths mistress, was so busy explaining the mysteries of reduction to her pupils that she never missed them until she finally turned from the board to bid them open their text-books and work the first three sums for themselves.

'Where are Flora and Fiona?' she demanded as she suddenly realised that she was two short of the usual number. 'Are they ill?'

'Please, Miss Edwards, we don't know,' said Vanna, who was form prefect. 'They were all right at breakfast, and after it, too. Then they got a letter, and they both went white, and they ran away, and we've never seen them since. We wondered if it was bad news about their brothers.'

'I see.' Miss Edwards left the question for the moment, and told the girls what she wanted them to do. She could not leave them till the end of the lesson, but she decided to send someone for Matron and see if the twins had gone to her. So when they were all at work, she called out Nancy Chester, gave her a note, and sent her off with it. Nancy trotted off to the back stairs which was what the lowlier members of the School used, and was just beginning to mount them when the twins themselves appeared, very tousled about the head, but still, there. She gave a little yelp as she saw them, and raced up to them.

'Where *have* you been?' she asked in a shrill whisper. 'Teddy missed you, and I've got a note here for Matey—I know it's about you. Where *ever* have you been? You'll get into a fearful row, you know.'

'Nefer you mind!' said Flora curtly. 'Are you going to take that note to Matey now you've foundt uss?'

'I'll have to. It was sent to her. I can't just sit on it, can I?' asked Nancy reasonably. 'I say! What will you two do? Come with me?'

The twins looked at each other. 'It mightn't pe apout us at all,' said Fiona slowly. 'It *might* pe something else Teddy wants to know.'

'It *might* be; but it's not very likely,' returned Nancy sceptically.

'We'd better shust go down to the form-room,' decided Flora. 'Ass Fiona says, we ton't know it's apout us. If it issn't, Matey will ask why we haf come, and we couldn't say why, couldt we?'

Nancy agreed with this. 'You'd better go to the form-room,' she said. 'But what you'll say to Teddy I don't know. I should think she'll be rather mad with you.' Then, curiosity overcoming her caution, she added, 'What *did* you go off like that for? And where have you been?'

But the twins refused to say. 'It iss a secret, and we can't tell efen you, Nancy,' said Fiona. 'It iss a family thing, you see.'

'Oh, right you are! I don't want to pry into your secrets!' Nancy sounded huffy. After all, when you have been worrying about the unexplained absence of two friends, and they turn up safe and sound and refuse to tell you why they had gone, you have a right to feel hurt. She turned away and went on up the stairs, her small back very straight, and her sunny brown head very erect. The twins looked after her miserably.

'I wish Shiena had nefer gifen it to us,' said Fiona at last.

'Put she did, and we must keep it a secret,' replied Flora. 'Come on! Teddy will be madder the later we are. What can we say to her?'

'Nothing—shust nothing at all,' said Fiona emphatically.

They went slowly down the stairs, and along the corridor, and into the form-room, where Miss Edwards greeted them with a chilly, 'Well? Where have you two been? Do you know that half the lesson is over? What have you got to say for yourselves? Do you know that I have had to send a message to Matron, as Vanna told me you had been all right at breakfast and just before Prayers, but no one had seen you since? And why, may I ask, have you come to lessons that untidy sight? Go to the splasheries and make yourselves fit to be seen at once; and then come back here and tell me what you have been doing. Go at once, I say.'

The twins turned and fled. In the splasheries, they hastily made themselves tidy, and then once more faced the angry mistress. Matron was there, too, having come down in reply to Miss Edwards' note. Nancy, in her seat, was working at reduction as if her very life depended on it—so was the rest of the form, for that matter. 'Teddy' in a temper was not to be trifled with!—and no one so much as looked at them as they sidled into the room, wondering what in the world they could say. The one thing they were sure of was that they must not mention the Erisay Chart. Beyond that they could not go at present.

Miss Edwards was now at her desk, looking very stern, and Matron was standing beside her, also looking annoyed. She had been in the middle of sorting out the laundry, and she hated being interrupted in an important job of that kind. Altogether, it was a very unpleasant position for the two, and more than ever did they wish that Shiena had not handed the precious Chart to them. There was nothing for it but to go up to the desk and do the best they could, so they *crawled* up to it, and lifted wide eyes to the angry mistress's face.

'Well? What have you to say for yourselves?' she demanded impatiently.

'It—it wass—private things,' said Flora after a pause when you could have heard a pin drop. 'Truly, Miss Edwards, we *had* to go.'

Miss Edwards could scarcely believe her ears. It sounded to her as if Flora were trying to be rude, and, for once, 'Teddy's' sense of humour was in abeyance, and she was really angry. 'What do you mean? How dare you answer me like that?' she snapped. 'What was this "private" business of yours? Your business was to be in to Prayers and then come to lessons with the rest of the form. How dare you go off like that?'

Neither of the twins had anything more to say. So they stood there, still gazing up at her, without speaking a word. Matron looked at them, and then decided to take a hand. She was not quite so angry as Miss Edwards, and she was a good twenty years and more older than the young mistress, and had had a long experience of girls which had taught her something. She turned to her confrère.

'I think, Miss Edwards, I had better take these two up to my room and see if I can get any sense out of them,' she said. 'If you don't mind, I will take them at once. They are interrupting the lesson, and wasting the time of other girls as well as their own. Will you excuse them, please?'

Something in her tone prevented Miss Edwards from snapping out the refusal which she had at first intended. 'Very well,' she said. 'Flora and Fiona, go with Matron. And when you come back, you can apologise to me for your rudeness, Flora.—*Girls!* Why are you not working? This is no affair of yours. Go on with your work at once!'

The girls, who had glanced up at Matron's words, promptly lowered their eyes to their slates, and Nancy Chester proceeded to make some startling improvements on what she had been taught, which drew down a storm on her own devoted head when Miss Edwards saw them. Matron laid a hand on a shoulder of each of the twins and marched them out, and the form was left to wonder what had been happening.

Meanwhile, the pair, with Matron between them, were being hustled upstairs to her room, where she stood them side by side, and then faced them with, 'Well, now I want to know the whole story. Hurry up and tell me, for I haven't all day to waste. You speak, Flora.'

'I can't,' said Flora simply.

It was Matron's turn to doubt her own ears. What could the child mean? She sat down in her office chair, and looked at them severely. 'I'll give you two minutes by my watch to make up your minds,' she told them severely. 'You don't stir from this room till you tell me what you have been doing; so you may make up your minds to *that*! So hurry up, and don't waste any more time, for I mean what I say.' She glanced down at her watch, and then sat waiting. But nothing came. The twins were plainly very much upset; but their lips closed firmly, and they stood silent. Matron waited till the two minutes were up. Then she returned the watch to her pocket, and swung round in her chair to her desk, and picked up her pen. 'You'll stay there till you do tell me,' she repeated. 'In the meantime, I'm a busy woman, so I'll get on with this list.'

She began to enter the number of sheets, towels, table-napkins, and so on which were to go down to the big laundry at the back of the house, and the twins eyed her back, and then turned and looked at each other. They got no comfort anywhere. They knew they must not speak of the Chart; and they also knew that Matron was a woman of her word. If she said they must stay there, stay there they must. What on earth could they do?

'Matron!' began Fiona timidly.

Matron raised her head and looked round. 'Well?' she asked.

'Please, Matron, Flora didn't mean to pe rude to you *or* Miss Edwards. It really iss that she cannot say where we haf peen. It iss private—private family pusiness, and we were told not to talk of it—*truly*!'

Matron laid down her pen. 'What private family business can you possibly have at school?' she demanded. 'And who told you not to talk of it?'

'Shiena—our pig sister.' Fiona never meant to be funny; but in her upset, she was more Highland than usual, and her 'b's' were even more of 'p's' than usual. It struck Flora very strongly, after so long in England, and she began to giggle. It was more than half nervousness, but to Matron, who was already annoyed, it looked like impertinence, and she fixed the giggler with her most awful glare.

'I must confess I can't see why you should giggle like that, Flora,' she said. 'And I'm afraid if that is all you have to say, Fiona, I have no time to listen to it. When you are ready to obey me, you can say so.'

Silence fell once more. The twins changed their standing position from one leg to another, and then the bell sounded for the end of the first lesson. Matron took no notice. She went on with her lists, and Flora and Fiona looked at each other once more. Were they *really* to stay there till they had told everything? But they couldn't! And they certainly couldn't tell anyone about the Erisay Chart. Shiena, in giving it to them, had warned them never to mention it to anyone, and they had promised her. They could not break a promise. Whatever were they to do?

Still busy, Matron suddenly spoke again. 'You may bring those two chairs from the other side of the room and sit down,' she said. 'You have stood long enough, and you don't seem ready to obey me yet.'

Meekly they brought the chairs and sat down. Then silence fell once more, only broken by the sound of Matron's pen. She finished her lists and rang the bell at the side of her desk. A young maid came in, took the lists, and went out again. The bell rang for Break and elevenses, and Matron got up and left the room, to return in a few moments with a tray containing three cups of cocoa and three half-slices of bread-and-margarine—the usual elevenses during the winter months nowadays. She gave the twins their share, sat down at her desk and ate hers, and then, when they had finished, collected the cups, put them on the tray and set it outside the room for a maid to take away. Then she went to the huge mending-basket, chose some work, and sat down in the wicker chair by the window, and fell to darning one of Enid Sothern's sheets.

The twins were very tired of her room by this time. The bell had rung for the end of Break, and the next lesson would be botany, which they both loved. Miss Wilson had promised to show the Upper Second the baby bud in its soft blankets in a chestnut leaf bud, and they would miss it. But what could they do? If only, *only* that horrid letter in Gaelic had never come! If only Shiena had kept the Chart herself—or given it to someone else. And yet, to whom could she have given it? Archie and Hugh were away, and Ken was at school. Anyway, Ken never knew where anything was. No one would ever have dared to give him anything so important to take care of. They had felt so proud when Shiena had trusted it to them, and now they were so miserable. It was a horrid—what was that word Miss Linton had used the other day? Fiona screwed up her face in an effort to remember, and Matron, looking up from her work, caught the grimace and felt crosser than ever, for, to tell the truth, she, too, was beginning to feel badly puzzled. Never before had any girl braved out a silent imprisonment in her room so long. Even Betty Wynne-Davies, on the two occasions it had been necessary to use it on her, had given in after an hour of it. But it began to look as if these children meant to hold their tongues all day, and, indeed, *for ever*!

'Fiona! Stop making faces!' she said sharply. 'That sort of thing won't help you at all. I can tell you that much. And remember; the sooner you make up your minds to obey me, the sooner you'll get back to your form. *I* don't want to have to spend my time here with two naughty children.'

Fiona straightened her face. Besides, she remembered the word now. Miss Linton had called it a 'dilemma,' and she had explained just what it meant. *This* was a dilemma all right, for what could they do? Would Matron let them wire to Shiena, perhaps, and ask leave to tell? But Shiena might not be at her billet, and might not get the wire till late that night—too late to reply. Must they spend the *night* here? How awful!

Fiona nearly gave in then. She just managed not to, and her thoughts wandered off to something else.

Meanwhile, Flora too was wondering if they would have to go to bed here. She looked round the room. There would be no room for them. It held Matron's desk and office chair, her wicker chair, the two on which they sat, and a humpty, as well as a table, the big mending-basket, shelves laden with books, and a radio set. Matron's own bed turned into a settee by day, and stood along one wall with a light over it, and there was no room for anything else. What *could* they do? And why *was* Fiona making such awful faces? It was at this point that Matron looked up, and ordered Fiona to stop it. Flora sat meekly, with her hands folded in her lap, and wished herself anywhere else but here. If only they hadn't had to leave Erisay! If only they had never come to this horrid England! But then they would never have known all the girls—and Nancy and Julie were dears—Bride and Primula, too. And Vanna and Nella weren't so bad if you stood up to them and let them see that they weren't going to boss you—from all of which it will be seen that Flora's English vocabulary had grown considerably. And there were Robin and Daisy. And, best of all, Mrs Maynard and her triplets. Mrs Maynard was such a dear— And at this juncture Flora looked up with a sudden light in her eyes. Mrs Maynard would help them! She wouldn't ask any questions—or at least none that they need mind. She had a wonderful way of understanding that there were some things you must not talk about; and others you *couldn't*. Flora spoke.

'Pleass, Matron, we can't tell you or anyone at school; but couldt we tell Mistress Maynard? She wouldt understand, and it might pe petter.'

'If you think Mrs Maynard has nothing else to do but run about after babies like you, you're making a bad mistake,' said Matron severely.

But Flora stuck to her point. 'But, Matron, if Miss Annersley wouldt let us ring her up, it wouldt not pe asking her to run here to us. And she wouldt help us—I know she wouldt. Oh, pleass do let us!'

Like the twins, Matron found herself in a dilemma. Having said they should stay in her room till they told her where they had been and what they had been doing, she couldn't very well go back on her words. At the same time, no more than they did she want them for the night there, and it began to look as if that might be the outcome of this. If Jo could help, it might be just as well to let her. The Fiona child had mentioned her big sister. Just possibly Shiena had said something to Jo about this weird 'secret' the twins were so bent on keeping. In that case she would certainly clear up matters if she could. Anyway, it could do no harm. Matron folded up her work, and got up briskly.

'I'll give Plas Gwyn a ring myself,' she said. 'Of course you can't go to the 'phone during school hours. No girl is ever allowed to do that unless the Head sends her herself. But I'll go down and see if it is free, and if it is, I'll ask Mrs Maynard if she can help us. If she says it is all right, you can apologise to Miss Edwards for being so rude and discourteous to her, and we'll let it go at that. But if not, I shall keep my word, and here you'll stay till you do as you're told.'

She left the room, and the twins were alone for a moment. Fiona sent a grin of admiration to her twin. 'It wass a grand idea,' she said softly. 'Oh, Flora, if we haf to sleep here with Matron, I shall die!'

'So shall I. Did you think of anything, Fiona?'

'Only that they might let us wire to Shiena to ask her to let us tell, and it might pe no use. If she wass away, she might not get it for efer so long, and we wouldt haf to stay here till tomorrow—for I will not say a wordt to anyone unless she or Mistress Maynard say we may.'

'Nor will I,' agreed Flora. Then they heard the sharp tap-tap of Matron's heels in the passage outside, and fell silent again.

They looked eagerly at her as she came in, but when she shook her head their faces fell. So Jo had refused to help them? But it didn't seem like her, somehow. They had been so sure she would either say something that would tell them what to do, or else come herself. They felt that they could tell *her*, and Shiena would not mind in the least. But Matron spoke.

'Mrs Maynard is out at present,' she said. 'I left a message, asking her to give me a ring as soon as she came in. And now, as you have wasted quite enough of the morning, you may as well help me a little. Flora, this sheet has to be turned sides to middle. It is already tacked in place. You sit at this end. Fiona, you take the other. Here are needles for both of you, and here is cotton. You can make use of your time by running it up. Mind you take small stitches, and keep them even.'

This was the end of all things. Not even Jo Maynard herself in her most unregenerate days had hated a needle more than did Flora and Fiona. Both were capital knitters; neither could sew 'fit to be seen,' as Miss Linton, who was responsible for the needlework in Upper Second, had once wailed. Matron nearly got her way then without having to wait for either Jo or Shiena to come to the rescue. Only the remembrance that it was a family secret, and they were sworn never to give it away, kept them from yielding when Matron put those instruments of torture into their hands.

Mercifully, it was not for long. There came the sound of swift, springy steps down the corridor. Then there came a rap at the door, and it opened and showed Jo herself, clad in her big coat and brown beret. With one accord, the twins cast aside the hated sheet, the needles, and the cotton, and hurled themselves on her.

'Mistress Maynard, oh, Mistress Maynard! We wanted you so badly!'

'Oh, Mistress Maynard! Did Shiena tell you about our secret? And *must* we tell? Matron says we've got to stay here till we do if you don't say it iss all right! Must we? Oh, pleass, Mistress Maynard!'

CHAPTER XV

THE SECOND SIGHT

JO was startled, as well she might be, at the warmth of her welcome, but she rose nobly to it. Flinging her arms round the twins, she swept them to one side, crying, 'Twins! What is wrong with you? Wait a moment, and I'll see to it.—Matey! See who's here!' And she drew back from the door to let her companion pass in. The twins looked up and saw one of the prettiest people they had ever seen, coming in, both hands held out, and a gay smile on the beautiful mouth as the Crown Princess of Belsornia flung herself on Matron with a shout of joy.

Matron stared. 'Elisaveta! What in the world are you doing here, child?'

'I've come to stay—for the duration if they'll let me. No one has found out where I am so far, but we can't hope for that to last much longer. I'm with Jo at the moment—her mysterious guest, you know. Robin and Daisy only knew this last week-end. Of course Madame and Dr Jem know. I've got my family here, too. Not Raphael, of course. He's in Egypt—I *hope*. But my two boys and small girl. At present I'm Mrs Helston, as that is my husband's family name. I hope I can keep to it for some time yet, anyhow.—Twins,' she turned to the twins, 'you've been little sports to keep my secret as you have done. But now the School may know. I've had to appeal to our legation—Dr Jem made me. However, they seem to think that I shall be all right here for a while, at any rate, so they won't disturb me yet. Jo, you take the twins somewhere while I talk to Matey. They've got something to say to you, I can see. Something important, too. Hop it, all three of you!'

Jo obeyed. Still clasping the twins, she led them from the room, and as the door closed behind them, they heard Matron say, 'I might have known it was you if I'd only given it a moment's thought. *Three* babies, now?' Then the door shut, and they heard no more, for Jo was drawing them down the corridor in search of a room where they could be private, and they had to go with her. She paused before a door, tapped at it, and then opened it, and pulled them in despite their protests.

'I know it's Miss Wilson's room,' she said calmly, 'but she's gone into Armiford for the day, and she'd be sure to say I might use it. So stop arguing, and tell me what has gone wrong with you. Why were you in Matey's room? And why did you greet me with such rapture?'

The twins looked at each other. Then Fiona began. 'We are in trouple, Mistress Maynard. It iss apout a secret Shiena gave us to take care of.'

'Oh? How is that?' asked Jo. 'How can Matey have anything to do with Shiena's secrets?'

'It iss this way.' And Fiona began to tell what had happened. Jo listened gravely. When Fiona ended with 'Pleass will you tell us what we must do?' she sat silent for a moment or two. Plainly this was the secret Shiena had thought once of confiding to *her*, and in which, she had promised, she would help the twins if any bother came of it.

'Can you tell me a little more?' she said at length. 'What is this thing that you feel so sure is what the burglar wanted? Why do you think it *is* what he wanted? He might just have been an ordinary burglar.'

'Oh, no,' said Flora, shaking her head till the fair hair flew. 'You see, we haf had a letter from him, and that iss why we are in trouple.'

'You've had a *letter* from him?' This didn't seem to make sense. None of the burglars Joey had ever heard of took the trouble to write to the people they had tried to burgle after the event. What could the child mean? But Fiona was already offering her the sheet which had upset them so much, and Jo took it. She scanned the words on it, and raised her brows. 'I'm sorry, Fiona. I suppose it's Gaelic; but it's Greek to me. You'll have to explain, my child. I know no Gaelic at all. What is it?'

'It iss, "Place the Chart of Erisay on the old horse-block, or it will pe the worse for you,"' said Flora gravely.

'The Chart of Erisay?' A light gleamed in Jo's

eyes. 'Now you must explain the whole thing, you two. What is the Chart? And where is it?'

'It iss a Chart which shows all the caves, and the houses, and the rivers, and eferything on Erisay,' said Fiona. 'But most of all it shows where are Na Clachan Dannsa, and how the place where they are leads into the Great House.'

'Where the *what* is?'

'Na Clachan Dannsa—the Dancing Stones. It iss some big, flat stones near the shore in a little loch. You press on one of them, and so they move, and there iss a doorway—and a passage. It leads right into our house—the Great House. Shiena said it wass a fery, fery big secret, and we must not let anyone know. Only they haf guessed we haf it, though I cannot think how they did; and so that man came to rob us of the Chart. Only he couldt not find it, for it wass nefer in our lockers—ass if we wouldt keep it there where anyone goes to get things!' Flora spoke with deep scorn. 'Put when we got thiss letter thiss morning, we were afraid and we made up our minds we wouldt take the Chart from where we haf it, and hide it somewhere else fery safe, for Shiena said we must guard it with our fery lifes if need pe.'

Knowing Shiena, Jo thought this very likely. At the same time, she was rather surprised that the elder girl should have entrusted so important a document to two small girls like the twins. If you came to that, why should the girls have it at all? What about Archie? Or Hugh? Or even Kenneth at school? Surely any one of them was more suitable than a girl? But she could scarcely say so to the twins, so what she did say was, 'I see. Then what have you done with it now?'

'There iss a wee attic right up at the top of the house,' said Fiona. 'In it there iss a little steel box, and we haf folded up the Chart fery wee, and put it in. We thought that then no mice couldt eat it, or efen if the house got set on fire, it wouldt be safer so.'

'That may be so, of course. I see your point. But why didn't you tell Matey or someone like that about it? The Head, for instance? She would have put it into the School safe, and it would have been all right there.'

'Put Shiena saidt we were to tell no one,' objected Flora.

'Then where do *I* come in? You've just told *me*.'

'I know. *You* are different, you see. We knew Shiena wouldt not mind *you* knowing—or not so much. *They* are Sassenachs, and strangers to us.'

Jo grinned. 'So far as I know there isn't one drop of Scottish blood in the Bettany family! So what price Sassenachs now?'

'You are different,' repeated Flora. 'We haf lived with you. Our home iss with you—you said so yourself. And we know that Shiena trusts you.'

'So she does the Head—and the School at large. She would never have let you go to it if she hadn't. You're worth more to her than even the Chart. Don't you see, twins? But,' went on Jo who had been doing some rapid thinking, 'I quite agree that it must *not* fall into stranger hands. Too much may depend on it. Tell me a little more, please. You say the—the Dancing Stones are in the loch. Do you mean they are in the water?'

Fiona nodded. 'Yess. They are a wee bit from the shore. It iss not much. Archie could wade to them at low tide. But *we* wouldt haf to swim to get to them.'

'What are they like? Can you give me any idea? I mean, would anyone who didn't know *see* that they had this hidden door you talk of?'

'Oh, no!' Flora was quite certain about this. 'They are shust a heap of stones—big, flat ones. Archie once said they were used for a sacrifice in the old days when our people were heathen. He said that their name must haf meant that the sacrifice wass made to dance—or, maybe, the priests danced there, too, before the sacrifice. You see, Mistress Maynard, when the sun rises, his first rays touch the stones, and that iss when whoefer wass to be killed wouldt be killed. It wass on Midsummer's Day.'

'I see. You mean that on Midsummer's Day, the sun's first rays touch the Stones. Any special one, by the way?'

'Oh, yess. It iss the one that hides the doorway. Archie thinks that where the Big House iss there wass a temple, for some of the stones in the cellar floors are so huge. He says that he thinks the victim wass kept there, and shown to the people. Then the priests wouldt lead him down the passage, and up through the doorway to the Stones. And then, you see, they wouldt either dance themselves or make him dance, while the people who had come down from the temple stood on the shore and watched. And then, when the sun's rays touched the stone of the doorway—which wouldt haf peen closed—he wouldt pe killed. It wass to the sun.'

'I see—sort of Baal-worship.' Jo was silent again, musing on this. 'Then, I suppose, when the people became Christian, the temple was flung down, and the Stones were left alone. Years after—probably centuries—how old is the Great House, by the way? Shiena didn't tell me.'

'Oh, it iss not so fery old—not *this* house. But there wass another pefore it, only it wass burned down when the Campbells came ofer one night when King Charles I. was king, and stole all our sheep and cattle, and carried off the women and children, and slew all the men till the streams ran red with blood,' said Fiona in a deep voice.

'But one man escaped, and he hid with his wife, and a little baby boy wass born later, and when he grew up, he summoned the McDonalds, and they swept down on Horonsay—that wass the island where the Campbells had come from—and he treated them chust as they had treated us!' put in Flora. 'And so we were refenged. For efery life the Campbells had taken the McDonalds took a life. And for efery cow, or sheep, or pony, they took two. And Culm McDonald looked to it that there wass no Campbell of them all left pefore he left Horonsay. And he brought back all those left who had peen living in slafery to the Campbells. It wass a mighty refenge he took for what the Campbells had done pefore he wass born.'

'And then,' wound up Fiona, 'he built the Great House which had peen left desolate on the place where the other had peen, and so the cellars are the same. But the rest of it is new. Archie says that Culm's father hid in the passage, for he wouldt know of it ass he wass the chief's eldest son, and that wass how he escaped when the rest were slain—all but the youngest boy, who wass only a wee bairn of six or sefen, and so wass taken to pe a slafe to the Campbells. Culm freed him twenty-fife years later when the McDonalds rafaged Horonsay. His name wass Kenneth, and we haf had a Kenneth efer since when there hass peen enough sons for it. The eldest iss Culm, of course. Archie is Culm Archibald, but Father wass Culm, so he had to pe Archie.'

Archie McDonald would have been edified to hear his young sisters as they pronounced his names with due reverence; but Jo was more shocked than edified. Flora had spoken with such gloating in her tones as she told of the terrible revenge the McDonalds had taken for their ravaged isle. Even Fiona's dark eyes had glowed at the telling. Some time, Jo made up her mind, the twins must be warned about revelling in such a matter. At present, she was very much more worried about the Chart. She knew, for Shiena had told her, that the Admiralty were using the Great House for certain Secret Service records and experiments. If there were a hidden entrance into it, then something must be done about it at once. She no longer wondered that the School had been burgled. If the Nazis knew anything about the Chart, they would strain every nerve to get hold of it. That might mean that the children were in danger. Someone must be told, though she was not very sure who. She must get hold of her brother-in-law and ask his advice.

Meanwhile, something must be done at once to put the thing in a place of real safety. And something must be done to safeguard the twins. The question was—what?

'I think,' she said slowly, 'that you must apologise to Matey and Miss Edwards for what looks to them like discourtesy. Yes; I know you didn't mean it that way. But that is what it looked like. And besides that, I want you to go and fetch this Chart and give it to me. It must be put somewhere well away from here. We don't want alarms and excursions every night. The School mightn't get off so easily another time. Run along and bring it here to me, and I'll see to that part of it. Be quick and get it.'

'But—what will Shiena say?' asked Fiona slowly. 'She gafe it to us to guard. We ton't want her to say that we haf failed in our trust.'

'Shiena won't say anything of the kind, for I shall let her know that I did it,' replied Jo. She saw the troubled look in the eyes of the twins and her arms went round them again. 'Dears, Shiena—yes, and Archie too—care far more for you than for any Chart. Suppose you were out alone in the garden? Someone might come and try to carry you off to make you tell what you had done with it. But if I have it and have put it somewhere, you know nothing, and so you will be safe. Don't you see?'

'Yes; but won't that make it unsafe for you?' asked Fiona.

'No; for I shan't keep it at Plas Gwyn. You may be very sure of that. And I have Rufus as watch-dog; besides which, if it seems best, I can ask

Colonel Black to give me a guard. The triplets are at the Round House, and there they may stay for the present. 'Veta's boys are at Cartref with Frieda, and there is only Baby Joséphine, and 'Veta—Anna and I can see she doesn't come to any harm. Plas Gwyn is only a small house compared with Plas Howell, and it will be much easier to guard it. So now go and get your Chart and give it to me, and I'll drive into Armiford with it and lodge it at the bank for the present. It should be safe enough there. Oh, one moment, twins! How do you think anyone has got to know about it? I mean, as Archie and Shiena made such a secret of it, how is it that anyone outside the family knows about it?'

But this the twins were unable to tell her. Nor was Shiena, when she was asked, able to help. It was not for some weeks that they found out that the secret of the Chart's existence had been learnt by a servant Mr McDonald had had three years before, who had come from the mainland. He had been on Erisay only six months, and then had left owing to having been caught pilfering by Shiena. But he had picked up enough to know that there was a secret way into the Great House, and had sold the information to his country's enemies almost as soon as it became known that the Admiralty had taken over the whole island for their own purposes. He owned that he had meant to use it himself as a means of getting in and out at night, and making a grand haul of all the McDonald treasures; only Shiena had found him out too soon. But he knew enough to give a good deal of trouble. Flora's unguarded remarks that Saturday morning, and Betty's feud with the twins, had helped a good deal. But before all this was known, much else had come to pass.

At the moment, the twins, frightened by Jo's words, looked at her, and then Fiona said timidly, 'Mistress Maynard, wouldt you not come with us?'

'Of course,' said Jo, jumping up at once. 'Come on, you people! The bell will ring for lunch soon, and you may as well make your peace with Matey and Teddy—I—I mean with Matron and Miss Edwards—before that. We must get the Chart first, and I'll stow it away. Then I'll come with you to apologise, and you'll find it'll be all right for you.'

They led her up the stairs to the very top of the house; and there, in a little box-room opening out of one of the attics, they brought to her the steel box in which they had stuffed their precious Chart. Jo took it out, glanced at it without unfolding it, and then stuffed it up her blouse—there was still a good deal of the schoolgirl in Jo Maynard, despite her family and all her other responsibilities—before she took them first to Matron, who was still chatting with the Princess, and then to Miss Edwards. The latter young lady was inclined to be on her dignity, and met them very coldly. But she accepted their stumbling apologies, and Jo's explanation, and forgave them. Matron merely said, 'Well, now, I hope you'll use your sense another time, and not waste so much good time, to say nothing about the time you've made *me* waste.'

'So that's that,' said Jo cheerfully. 'And now I'm off to the Head to suggest that she either gets a good watch-dog or so; or else demands a military guard for the next week or two. We don't want any more adventures, thank you. What Archie and Shiena will say about all this when they hear of it, I *don't* know. And there are Hugh and— Here, Fiona! What's wrong with you? Are you ill, child?'

Jo spoke in real alarm, and she had reason. Almost as she spoke Hugh's name Fiona suddenly turned white. Her eyes assumed the look of a sleep-walker, and her whole face seemed to change. At Jo's cry, Flora glanced at her sister, and then sprang up, horror in her eyes.

'Fiona! What do you see?' she gasped.

'Hugh—Hugh!' cried Fiona. 'Oh! He's gone—he's gone! The boat's been sunk! They've all gone—not one saved!'

She spoke in Gaelic, and for the moment Jo knew no more than that the girl was in a state of great mental agitation. By now Flora too had turned a ghastly white, and mumbled, almost mechanically, in English: 'It 's Hugh, our brother Hugh. Hiss ship is sunk, and no one iss saved.' And Flora burst into tears. Jo caught Fiona to her, and held her close. 'Fiona—Fiona! Wake up, darling! Wake up, Fiona!'

'It iss no good,' sobbed Flora, who had burst into tears. 'It iss the second sight, and she hass a vision. She cannot hear you, Mistress Maynard, and we cannot wake her! Oh, Hughie—Hughie!'

Jo shivered. She had heard of second sight often enough, but this was the first time she had ever met it, and she found it an eerie experience. Fiona looked like death; and low moans were coming from her. Flora was sobbing heavily, and kept well away from her sister. Jo had no idea what to do; but she lifted Fiona, and carried her to 'Bill's' bed—they had returned to her room after rescuing the Chart—and laid her on it. Almost at once the awful, grey tinge left Fiona's face, her eyes grew more natural, and she sat up, rocking herself as if she were in pain. Flora saw it, and rushed to her, flinging her arms round her.

'Fiona! What wass it you saw? Oh, say it wass not true!'

'It wass Hugh,' sobbed Fiona. 'He iss dead, Flora, dead! He wass in a little boat with sefen others, and a big ship came above the water and shot them with a gun that went rat-tat-tat-tat! The boat filled with water and she wass gone, too. Oh, Flora—Flora!'

Jo fetched Matron to the two poor children. She would have left them in her charge, but they clung to 'Mistress Maynard' as their one consolation in this horror and grief that had come to them. They were certain that Fiona had 'seen true,' and nothing that was said to them made any difference. Jo herself, having seen the whole affair, was sure they were right, too, though she made them promise not to write to Shiena as they wanted to do at first. She went and saw the Head, and Miss Annersley agreed finally to let them go home to Plas Gwyn for the rest of the week.

So it was that on the Saturday, when the wire came from Shiena, they were with Jo. She told them the news gently, but they had known it all along; and when Shiena heard what had happened, she nodded.

'Fiona iss the only one of us to have the second sight,' she said sorrowfully. 'We haf nefer liked it, and we haf tried to keep her from thinking of it, for Archie said it wass not right for her. But shust now and then she hass told us of something that hass happened, and she hass always been right. The message from the Admiralty told us nothing but that Hugh iss gone. But if Fiona said it happened like that, then it did.'

Jo kept the children with her for a few days longer. Then, as Shiena, who had had 'compassionate' leave, must return, she thought it wiser to send them back to school, where she hoped being with their friends would help to soften the blow for them a little.

Everyone was very good to them, even Betty being awestruck by what had happened. She said nothing to them; but she left them alone for the moment. Secretly, she regretted the impulse that had made her ask her mother's friend, a Highlander by birth, for that Gaelic which had so upset the twins, though she said nothing about it. Jo had kept the second sight end of the affair to herself, though she spoke of it later to the Russells when she went to fetch her daughters home; and Matron knew of it. But it was kept from everyone else. Miss Annersley had a good deal to worry her already, and there was no need for anyone else to know. But Jo was very good to the poor children, who clung to her, once Shiena had gone, as they might have clung to any older sister. She said very little to them; but she let them feel her sympathy, and after that they would have done anything for her.

It was a fortnight later that they heard that Hugh's destroyer had been torpedoed in mid-Pacific. Most of the crew had got off in her boats; but the U-boat that had done it came to the surface, and gunned the men in two of them. One had been Hugh McDonald's boat, and he and all with him had been killed, while the light gig, riddled with machine-gun bullets, had heeled over as she filled, and sank. Mercifully for the rest, the *Mosquito's* sister-ship had come up, and the U-boat had not waited for her, but dived at once; nor had they been able to square accounts with her. But all but those two boatloads and some four or five left in the *Mosquito* were saved. So the McDonalds had to mourn a fresh loss; and Archie McDonald, filled with the fire that had inflamed his young ancestor three centuries before, showed such reckless daring during the night raids over Germany, that he was later awarded the Distinguished Flying Cross, when all he was thinking about was revenge for the cowardly slaying of his brother.

CHAPTER XVI

SORROW COMES TO JO

'JOEY, when did you last hear from Jack?' Robin looked up from her seat on the hearth-rug as she put her question.

Jo, sitting by the table, busy with her new book, glanced down at the lovely face below her, and smiled faintly. 'Not for six weeks. But it can't be helped in war-time. The mails are bound to be slow. I expect I shall hear before long. Indeed, I am expecting it any day, now.'

Robin said no more, but went on with *Sir Roger* which she was reading as one of the books recommended by the Head for her Higher Certificate. But Daisy, who was helping the triplets to dress their dolls in a corner of the room, lifted her bright face to say, 'I do wish they'd hurry up a bit. It seems ages since Uncle Jack wrote.' She stopped to look at the three little girls who had just celebrated their third birthday, and began to laugh. 'Won't he see a difference in them when he does get back? They seem to have grown ever so much lately. They aren't babies any more now, are they, Auntie Jo? And look how dark Con's hair is getting.'

Jo cast a glance at her daughters. They were bonny, blooming little folks, but Daisy was quite right. They were losing their great likeness to each other. They still had Jo's sensitive mouth and long, black lashes; but except for that, they were changing rapidly. Margot kept her blue eyes and rosy face; but her hair was much fairer—almost golden in hue. Len, the eldest of the trio, had the red hair, but her eyes were definitely grey. Con, the middle one, was promising to be nearly as dark as her mother. Her hair was turning very dark, and, her Aunt Madge declared, would be black in the end. Her eyes had already become deep brown, and she had her mother's creamy skin. They were enchantingly pretty, all three; but except for a family likeness, they did not resemble each other now.

'Jack will be so glad to see them again, he won't

worry because we can tell t'other from which,' she said decidedly. 'In one way, it'll be rather a blessing. It used to worry some folk when they were babies. But you are right, Daisy. They are little girls, now. I've lost my babies. Before we know where we are I'll have to be thinking of sending them to school.'

'Oh, not before they're five, surely!' exclaimed Robin. 'That's two years ahead. You'll be able to keep them for another two years, Joey.'

Jo shook her head. 'You never know what may happen. The Head was talking of starting a nursery class next summer term as we have so many tinies of our own now, what with my three, and Josette Russell, and Frieda's boy, and 'Veta's two. And then Juliet is coming here to live, now that Donal has had to go abroad, and there are her boy and girl. Little Don is only four and a half now; and Meg will be three next week. She is just three weeks younger than my three. That would be nine to start off with—quite enough for a nice little class. And the summer term would be the very best for them to begin. If it really does start, I shall send Len and Con and Margot to it. I want my girls to be good mixers, and I'm so very busy, and shall be busier, what with one thing and another.'

'Mercy! What next are you going to take on?' cried Daisy.

Jo only smiled and shook her head. She felt certain that Robin understood, but Daisy was a baby in many ways, and there was plenty of time for her to know what was expected in the spring. She turned back to her typescript, and began to groan over her own careless typing. 'Why on earth I keep turning letters the wrong way round I can't think! It's awful!'

'Turning letters the wrong way round? But how can you?' demanded Daisy.

'Well, changing their places, then. I *will* put "c-a-h" when I mean "c-h-a," and it doesn't even make English!' lamented Jo, who had had a good deal of bother one way and another with this book, and now found that even when she was typing the fair copy she made endless mistakes.

'P'r'aps you never learnt to spell properly,' suggested Daisy sweetly.

'Daisy Venables!' Jo sprang to her feet in pretended anger. 'I'll scrag you for that!'

'You'll have to catch me first!' Daisy was up, too, and dancing defiantly behind a small table while Robin, with a shriek of dismay, grabbed her ink-well and pile of books, and flung herself against a chair to watch the fun. The three small girls, accustomed to this sort of thing, huddled together in a corner with delighted screams as their mother, transformed for the moment into a teasing schoolgirl again, went for Daisy, who dodged and squirmed and pranced all round the room, till she was caught and flung down in the chesterfield and tickled without pity.

'Ow! Mercy—mercy!' she gasped between her giggles. 'Jo! Stop it!'

'Apologise, then, wicked child, for casting aspersions on my spelling!' retorted Jo, sitting down on her to hold her still. 'Say you're sorry!'

'So I am! Get up—do! You're a ton weight, and I had a huge brekker. I'm sure it's good for no one's tummy to be sat on like this. I'm sorry—

I truly am! Now do get up, and let *me* get up.' Daisy finished with a wriggle that nearly upset Jo from her perch, and that young lady thought it both wiser and more dignified to get up and stroll off to her papers, saying, 'Don't you insult me like that again, or you'll get double.'

A knock at the front door broke in on them at this point, and Daisy sat up, and began to smooth her plaits which had suffered in the scrimmage. Anna went from the kitchen to answer it, and they heard her deep voice speaking to who ever was there. Then the door closed, and she came in, followed by big Rufus, who had been out on his own errands in the lane since breakfast time. He padded gravely over to his mistress, and stood beside her, wagging his tail, and looking up into her face with eyes full of adoration. But for once, Jo paid no heed to him. In Anna's hand she had seen an orange-coloured envelope, and at sight of it, a sudden feeling of sickness swept over her. Who could be sending her a wire just now?

The two schoolgirls caught the look, and jumped to their feet. Daisy tossed the end of her pigtail over her shoulder, and Robin kicked her books out of the way in her haste to reach Jo, who took the wire from Anna, still wearing that stunned look on her face. And yet, as Robin said later, it might have been anything. Shiena might have got leave; one of Jo's many friends might have wired to say she was coming for a brief visit. Even her brother-in-law at Pretty Maids, the old Maynard house in the New Forest, might have sent to announce his arrival. Jack Maynard had left him as trustee for Jo while he himself was away on his destroyer in the far East, and he might want to see her on urgent business. There was no real reason for her terror. And yet it was plain to see.

'Jo! *Liebchen!* Don't look like that!' cried Robin sharply, while Daisy came to slip an arm round her aunt and try to draw her down on to the settee. Jo put her gently aside, and took the wire. Anna, dread in her eyes, turned to the triplets, who were the only ones not affected by their mother's emotion, and held out her hands to them.

'Come then to the kitchen with thy Anna, my little birds, and see her make gingerbread men,' she coaxed them; and the three flung themselves on her with shouts of glee, for Anna did not encourage them to play in her kitchen as a rule. She took them off, shutting the door firmly behind her, with a look at her mistress which spoke of her sympathy, and Jo was left alone with Daisy and Robin who were not sure what to say.

'Sit down, Joey darling,' said Daisy, dropping the 'Aunt' in her anxiety. 'You don't look fit to stand. Look! Here's a chair for you.'

Jo sank down into the chair, and stayed there, the wire in her hand. Robin knelt down beside her. 'Let me open it for you, darling,' she said. But Jo shook her head. 'No, Rob. I must open it myself. But oh, girls, pray for me that I may have strength to meet whatever has come!' she said. Then she tore the envelope open and unfolded the fatal bit of paper. For a moment the printing jigged up and down before her eyes. Then it was steady, and she was able to read. 'The Admiralty regrets to announce . . .' She needed no more. Her hands dropped, and she sat staring ahead of her with white face and stony eyes. Terrified, Daisy and Robin dared not attempt to break her stillness for a moment. Then Robin plucked up courage and spoke, her arms still round the girl she loved best on earth. 'Joey, what is it? Can't you tell us, darling? Don't look like that!'

There was a pause. Then Jo spoke. 'It's from the Admiralty. Jack is dead—drowned.' The music had gone from her voice; her notes were as flat and toneless as her eyes were tearless. Robin hugged her tighter, the tears welling up in her own eyes, while Daisy, with a sob, cried, 'Oh, Joey—*no*! It can't be!'

For reply, Jo held out the wire. 'Read it for yourself. No, Rob; I am quite all right. Don't hold me. Let me go. I must be alone!' She freed herself gently from Robin's hold, and left the room, all the spring gone from her step, leaving the two to stare at each other.

'It isn't true—it *can't* be true!' gasped Daisy, dashing her hand across her eyes as she spoke. 'God couldn't do that to Jo who's always doing all she can for other people. It wouldn't be kind or fair, and I know whatever else He is, He's both kind *and* fair. Rob! Say something! Say you don't believe it! It *couldn't* happen—not *Jack*! It *couldn't*!'

Robin picked up the wire and smoothed it out. She read it slowly, the tears dripping down her cheeks. 'Oh, Daisy,' she sobbed. 'It's true. Look here. The Admiralty would never send this unless it were true.'

'I don't believe it!' repeated Daisy stormily. 'It's a mistake—it *must* be! The world needs Jack—look how clever he is, and all the work he's been doing! And Jo depends on him. She loves the girlies and us; but Jack comes first now, and we both know it. What would she do if it was true?'

'I don't know.' Robin sat crouching by the empty chair. Then she got up, pulled out her handkerchief, and scrubbed her eyes fiercely. 'We can't sit down and howl, Daisy. Jo will need us. Help me to think what we had best do—for we must do something. Jo mustn't be left alone. The wires are down, so we can't 'phone the Round House. And yet Madge ought to know. Could you—oh,' with a glance through the window, 'you couldn't—not through *that*.' And she pointed at the heavy mist which shut out everything like a thick white curtain. 'You'd never get there.'

But Daisy was up and on her feet. 'I can try, anyhow. It's just to get to the end of the lane, and then it's the high-road. If I keep to the verge it ought to be all right. And the path to the Round House is clear enough if I go carefully. But you're quite right, Rob. Auntie Madge ought to know as soon as possible. And what about Major Bob? Shouldn't we wire to Pretty Maids? Or should we wait and let someone else do it, d'you think?'

'Better wait. If you really think you can, you get off to the Round House and get Auntie Madge. I'll just try the 'phone again in case they've got it put right. But I'm sure they haven't.' And Robin lifted the receiver. But it was dead, as it had been all that morning, so she put it back. 'It's no use.

You'll have to go, Daisy. We don't know what to do, and we're too much kids to help Jo really. Madge will know what to do. You take Rufus, though. He'll look after you— Why, where has he gone?' as she looked round. 'He was here a minute ago, I know.'

'He followed Jo out of the room,' said Daisy with a final dig of her handkerchief into each blue eye. 'He may be able to help her, Rob. Don't call him. Besides, she might say I wasn't to go. You let me get off, and I'll go as carefully as I can. I know it won't help anyone if I get run over just now. What are you going to do about Anna and the triplets?'

'Anna knows—I'm sure of that. And I don't think the babies need be told yet. They're too tiny to understand. Jo will tell them herself later on.'

'Right you are, then.'

'Put your scarf on, and pull your beret over your hair. Tuck your plaits in. You don't want a bad cold *now*. You'd better take a stick, too. Now are you *sure* you're all right and can manage? You won't go wandering in the mist, will you? Be sure you keep to the path when you go through the meadow to the Round House. It may be better when you reach the wood, as it goes up all the way. You may get above it.'

'I'll be careful. Don't worry, Rob. I'll be back as soon as I can.'

Robin put her arms round Daisy and gave her an unwonted kiss. 'You *are* a lump of comfort, Daisy. I couldn't have managed alone, for I could never leave Joey by herself, and yet Madge *must* know!' Her lips quivered and the tears came again, but she brushed them away, and tried to smile. 'They'll bring you back in the car if they can, so you won't be gone so very long. Be as quick as you can, and do be careful.' She gave Daisy a final hug, and then let her out of the door, closing it softly behind her. Even her bitter grief would not make Jo selfish, and she would never have consented to Daisy's going out into that awful mist if she had known.

Daisy knew this, and got on to the grass as quickly as possible. She walked swiftly till she was out of earshot of the house. Then she got back to the path, and set off down it at top-speed. She opened the gate quietly, careful not to slam it to, and raced down the lane. As she reached Cartref she wished that she could have turned in and got Frieda von Ahlen or the Princess to go up to Plas Gwyn. But small Frédéric and his brother had begun measles two days ago, so that Elisaveta had had to go to them, and neither she nor Frieda could come to Plas Gwyn for fear of carrying infection to the triplets and Baby Joséphine. Daisy sighed for Robin left alone, save for Anna, and then turned off down the high-road. She ran fleetly and steadily, taking care to keep to the grassy verge, for, as she had said, an accident at this time would help no one. She had four miles to go to the Round House and Madge must be got to Jo as soon as possible. Luckily for her, a car driven by one of the W.V.S. people came along, and the driver pulled up when she saw the long-legged schoolgirl racing along and offered her a lift. Daisy scrambled in thankfully, and was at the field-gate leading to the avenue to the Round House ten minutes later. There she was put down, and after a brief word of thanks, set off, walking this time, for it would have been only too easy to miss her way through the meadow and lose time wandering round it. Once she had crossed it and reached the wood, she was fairly safe and, as Robin had guessed, the mist grew thinner, so that by the time she reached the little plateau on which the Round House itself stood, she was able to see the door from the edge of the clearing. Two minutes later, Madge Russell, sitting in the big round room which had given the house its name, was startled by the bursting in of a white-faced creature who glanced hurriedly round to make sure that they were alone, and then, flinging herself on her dearly loved aunt, gasped, 'Oh, Auntie Madge! Come at once, please! Jo's had a wire to say that Jack is drowned, and Rob and I don't know what to do!' And poor Daisy began to cry in real earnest.

Madge Russell, still as sweet-faced and fair as in earlier chronicles of the Chalet School, caught the girl to her, regardless of the fact that Daisy's raincoat was streaming with water, and her beret sopping. 'Daisy! My darling! What do you mean?' she cried.

'Jo's had a wire from the Admiralty to say that Jack's dead,' sobbed Daisy. 'I've come to fetch you. We couldn't 'phone 'cos a wire is down, and the 'phone's still dead. Do come at once, Auntie Madge. Jo looks *awful*!'

Madge rang a bell, and it was answered by Rosa, the nurse she had had ever since her only son had been a baby. 'Ask Sir James to come to me at once, please, Rosa,' she said. Then, as Rosa withdrew, she turned to poor, sobbing Daisy, and drew her to a seat. 'Sit down, Daisy girl. Take off those wet things. Uncle Jem is at home, and he'll come down with me at once. Just one thing, my pet. Who is with Jo now?'

Daisy gulped down her sobs, and replied, 'No one. She wouldn't let us go with her, and Anna took the girlies off to the kitchen. Rob said she guessed what it was. We wanted to go with Jo, but she said she must be by herself, and went up to her bedroom. Rufus did follow her, though.'

'Faithful old Rufus!' Madge's voice shook on the words. 'What made you come for me, Daisy? Was it your idea or Robin's?'

'Rob said you must be told, and we couldn't 'phone as the wires are down. Then she said I couldn't come because of the fog, but I said I'd try. Rob and I are too young to be much good, Auntie Madge, and we knew Jo oughtn't to be left alone like that. Even if she won't have you with her at first, she'll like to know you are there. I got a lift in a car, so it was quite easy, really. And I went slow over the meadow 'cos I didn't want to lose myself. Once you get up into the wood you get above the mist. But we had to do something, and there was no one else.'

'I see. Now here comes Uncle Jem, so run off to the kitchen and ask Rosa for some cocoa while I tell him. We'll be ready in a few minutes.'

'I'll go; but I don't want cocoa—I couldn't touch it just now.' And Daisy slipped off to the kitchen as the doctor came into the room by an inner door, his brows raised in a question which vanished as he saw his wife's face.

'What's wrong?' he demanded, taking her in his arms. 'Wasn't that Daisy?'

'Yes. Oh, Jem! Jo's had word that Jack has been killed—or drowned, rather. Daisy came to tell us as the wires are down near Plas Gwyn. I must go to Jo at once. You'll come with me, won't you? She may need you.'

'Jack Maynard drowned?' The doctor sat down in a chair rather heavily. He and Jack Maynard had been close friends for many years now. When young Maynard had first arrived at the Sonnalpe where the Sanatorium had been established, Jo had been a long-legged schoolgirl of nearly fourteen. In a week's time she would keep her twenty-fourth birthday. Eleven years of close intimacy had forged a very close link between the two men; and when Jack had married Joey four years before, no one had been more pleased than Jem Russell. Now he was told that his friend was drowned. It was a bad blow.

Madge knew what he was feeling, and she bent her head and kissed him. 'Jem, it's bad for us both—especially you, for you two were such chums, though Jack was so much younger. But it's worse for Jo. They never said anything much about it; but they did adore each other. She loves her babies, and they'll be a comfort to her presently; but just at present I know her whole soul is filled with Jack. She'll need us—badly, perhaps. I'll get you a drink, dear, and then if you could get the car out, we must get to her. We must take Daisy back, too. That poor babe came all the way here to fetch us because the lines are down and they couldn't 'phone. There's no one at Plas Gwyn but Robin and Anna and the children. We ought to get off at once, dear. I *must* go to Jo!' Madge's voice was still unsteady as she brought the drink for her husband and set it on the little table beside him. He looked up at her, and saw that her eyes were heavy with unshed tears, and the delicate pink in her cheeks had gone.

'Forgive me, dearest. I'm afraid I was selfishly thinking of my own loss. Thanks for the drink.' He swallowed it. 'There; that's better. Get a peg for yourself—you've had a bad shock, too. I'll get the car, and you collect Daisy, and we'll get down to Plas Gwyn at once.'

He left the room on the word, his shoulders slightly bowed, and Madge, picking up his glass, bore it away, and then got into her fur coat and close-fitting cap, and called Daisy, who came at once. Her eyes were swollen with tears, and she shook with sobs as she slipped into the car beside her aunt. Madge put an arm round her, and drew her close. She herself was struggling to keep down her sobs, and Daisy's need helped her.

No word was spoken as the doctor took the car as quickly as he could down the woodland drive. But when they reached the high-road, the mist was thicker than ever, and to Madge's mind, they seemed to crawl along. But Jem knew what he was about. He used his horn continually, and at long last they turned into the lane leading to Plas Gwyn, where he quickened a little, and at length they were standing before the door. Madge almost fell out in her eagerness to be with her dearly loved sister, and Robin, who had been waiting in the hall, had scarcely time to open the door for her. Then she was in the hall,

Jem following as soon as he had locked the car, and she was gripping the slight, dark-eyed girl with an anxious, 'Jo? Where is she, Robin? Have you seen her?'

'She's in her room. I've been up to the door, but I daren't go in. She seems quite quiet—she isn't crying at all,' choked Robin, who was hard put to it to keep calm now that help had come. 'Will you go up, Madge? And Jem, too. I think you two can do her more good than anyone else could. I'd have taken the girlies to her, but I didn't dare.'

'Quite right,' said the doctor. 'She won't be ready for them yet, and they must never know their mother repel them. You go on, Madge. I'll follow in a moment or two. Daisy, get your wet things off, and change your shoes and stockings. You don't want to add to our trouble by an attack of bronchitis, do you? Come in here, Robin, and tell me what you know.'

While he took Robin into the pleasant morning-room where they had been when the wire came, Madge went slowly up the stairs, only waiting to toss off coat and cap. When she reached Jo's door, she paused a moment with a brief, wordless prayer that she might be able to help her sister. Then she turned the handle and went in.

Jo was standing before the window, her whole slender figure tense. At the sound of the opening door she turned, and her sister was shocked to see the change in her. This tragic woman with white face and stony eyes was not the Joey she knew. She shut the door behind her, and sped across the room to fling her arms round the taut form.

'Madge!' Jo's voice was flat and lifeless, and there was no welcome in her eyes. She stood passively in her sister's clasp, and though the tears rained down Madge's cheeks, she had none to shed. She looked down into the loving face raised to hers, and a dreary little smile, more sad than any weeping, touched her lips. 'Don't cry, my dear. It's the fortune of war. Other women have to bear it, so why not I?'

'Joey—Joey!' sobbed Madge. 'Oh, my darling, don't look like that! Don't, Joey! Cry, darling, but oh, *don't* look like that!'

'Look like what? Cry, you say? How can I cry? I can cry for some things, but not for this—never for this. It's too deep. I can't talk, Madge. I can't think. I only know that our children are fatherless, and I am a widow. Doesn't it sound dreadful—so old, you know.' Jo laughed, a hard, unnatural laugh, and for a moment Madge felt terrified in case the shock had turned her brain. But the door opened, and Jem entered, to his wife's unutterable relief, and he took Jo in a firm grip, lifted her, and laid her on the bed.

'No hysteria, Jo! That won't help matters. Remember; you have other people to consider besides yourself,' he said sternly. 'You spoke of your children just now. You were right. You must think of them. Robin is bringing them to you—they have been away from you for nearly two hours now. Ah, here she is!' as the pit-pat of tiny feet was heard on the floor outside. Then Robin pushed the little girls in, and shut the door on them. They ran to the bed, climbing up on it, and scrambling to get to their mother. Jem's instinct had been sound. As she felt their arms about her and heard their voices, Jo sat up and held out her arms. 'Yes; come to me, my darlings! I am all you have now. I must be father and mother both to you now. Oh, my babies, my babies!' And with the last word, Jo dropped back on her pillows, hiding her face, and broke into a storm of tears and sobs which made Madge hurriedly take the children from the room.

Jem let Jo cry unchecked for a short while. He was thankful to see it, for he knew that if her calm had remained unbroken she must have been ill. All her life she had been nervous and highly-strung, and the awful shock of the news of her husband's death might have even affected her brain for the time being. Mercifully, they were spared that. But when the sobs grew louder, almost uncontrollable, he asserted himself. He had brought his syringe, and before half an hour was over, Jo was sound asleep, the merciful injection bringing her hours of oblivion when the strained mind and body rested and gained strength to meet her sorrow again.

CHAPTER XVII

FIONA TO THE RESCUE!

IT was some days before the School at large heard the sad news. Miss Annersley and Miss Wilson were told. They were old friends, and had watched over Jo since she was thirteen. But Jem considered that it was better no one else should be told for the present. When she came out of that deep drug-induced sleep, Jo was feverish and ill, and for the next few days Jem Russell and Gottfried Mensch, the two doctors, were very anxious about her. Then a wiry constitution and her quiet, regular life turned the scale and Jo began to recover. A week to the day when the wire had come, she was sitting up in her room, very wan and sad, but more like herself than she had been since she had read the wire. Then it was that the Head of the Chalet School, calling those of the Staff available together, told them what had happened, warning them to say nothing to the girls as yet. Robin and Daisy had been kept down at Plas Gwyn, for Daisy had caught a bad streaming cold as the result of her wetting; and as Anna had her hands full, Robin had to stay, too, to look after the triplets, who were also kept in ignorance. None of the little people knew yet. The doctor had advised against it. When the girls heard, they would be sure to do all they could to show their sympathy, and Jo was not ready for that yet. Later, it would help her; but just at present she was better kept quiet.

The Head had gone down on the second day after the news came, but she had said very little. Sitting quietly by Jo's bed, she had said, 'I want to read something to you, Joey.' And then, in her deep, beautiful voice, she had read the story of the raising of Lazarus. Jo listened without a word, and when it was ended, Miss Annersley closed her Bible, and bent over her and kissed her. 'Joey, dear, don't lose hope yet. He Who could raise His friend from the dead still performs miracles if we will only have faith.'

She had left after that; but it was after that that the doctors marked the slow improvement which went on steadily.

Gillian Linton had not been among those who had been in the library when the Head told them of Jack Maynard's death. She had been with the little ones. But when Miss Phipps, looking graver than anyone had ever seen her, came back, she left them, and fled upstairs to her own room. This should have been a free period for her, and she had some handwork to prepare for the afternoon. As she passed one of the bathrooms, she heard hurrying steps behind her, and turned round to see Simone de Bersac running to her, the tears streaming down her face. Gillian stopped short with a cry of 'Simone! What *has* gone wrong? Thérèse is all right, isn't she? No bad news of André?'

Simone shook her head. 'No, Gill. But oh, *ma chère*, such sad, sad news has come for our dear Jo! Come to my room and let me tell you.'

Gillian slipped an arm through hers. 'It isn't—Simone! It isn't—Jack, is it?' Then, as Simone nodded. 'Oh, what will Jo do? Jack is the world and all to her. Even the triplets have to come second-best to him.'

'Come to my room,' said Simone, controlling her voice with an effort. 'The Head has just told us, but they knew last week. Jo has been ill with the shock, and no wonder. That is why we weren't to be told before. And the girls are not to know, even yet.' She drew Gillian into her room, and closed the door behind them. But in the bathroom, a small girl who had been ordered upstairs to see what a loofah would do to her inky hands, had heard everything, and put two and two together and made a four of them. She flung the loofah down, wiped her half-washed fingers on her towel—incidentally inking it very completely—and bolted from the room. Straight to the stairs she went, and up them to that tiny attic where she and Flora had hidden the Chart of Erisay. There, she sat down to think things out and decide what she could do to help. Luckily for her it was Break, so no one missed her but her sister.

Flora, looking for Fiona to ask what she had done with their copy of *Pro Patria*, soon found that she was nowhere downstairs, guessed what had become of her, and slipped off in direct defiance of rules. Sure enough, when she reached the attic, there was her twin sitting on an old tea-chest looking the picture of woe. Flora marched up to her and sat down beside her. Fiona moved along, but said nothing. She was thinking too hard.

'What is it, Fiona, dear heart?' she asked in Gaelic.

'It is Mistress Maynard. She has had news that her husband is dead,' replied Fiona in the same tongue.

'Fiona! Who told you?'

'No one did. I was in the bathroom washing the ink off my hands, and I heard Madame de Bersac say it to Miss Linton.'

Flora looked at her twin. 'Fiona,' she said in lowered tones, 'could you—could you not—*look*?'

Now, in their fear that other people might try to use Fiona's queer gift, the elder McDonalds had impressed it on her that she was not to do so if she could help it. All the same, it had visited her at intervals all her life. When she shut her eyes and concentrated on anything, she could 'see' it, as she said. Once when Shiena had lost a valuable brooch left to her by her godmother, Fiona had shut her eyes. 'It is lying in a tangle of weeds with purple flowers, and there is a small bird looking at it. It sparkles in the sunshine,' she had said. There was only one such patch near the Great House, and it grew beside a plank bridge over a little stream that ran through the policies. Half hopeful, half incredulous, Shiena had gone to look, and there was the brooch, caught in a clump of willow-herb. On another occasion, it had been a spade guinea that Hugh had lost from his watch-chain. She had declared it was under the carpet in the drawing-room, and even led them to the spot, almost in the middle, where she said it was. It was impossible that the coin could have got there; but Hugh had gone down to the cellar beneath, and had found his coin among some chips of wood. He remembered that the day before he had been chopping up some logs into small sticks for a model ship he was making. It must have been lost then. It was after this that they had stopped her 'seeing.'

But her other visions came unbidden, and they could not prevent those. When Shiena had been going to see why their father had not come in to breakfast as usual, Fiona had caught her with a terrified cry. 'Shiena! don't go—oh, don't go! It is no use—it is too late now!' And she had 'seen' Hugh's end; of that there could be no doubt. But those were her own kinsmen, in whom ran the same blood. Could she 'see' a stranger? This was what she had been trying to decide.

'Try, Fiona!' urged Flora. 'Mistress Maynard has been so good to us. Oh, do try. It may not be true, and if it is not, then what comfort for her to know it! Do please try!'

'Well, I will,' agreed Fiona. She shut her eyes, and bent all her mind on Jack Maynard. But it was no good. Try as she might, she could see nothing but a blur of white mist, and hear nothing but the crooning of great, oily waves such as brought the seal on rare occasion to Erisay.

'I cannot do it,' she said at last, tears standing in her eyes with the disappointment. 'I have tried and tried, and I can only see mists and hear the sea.'

But Flora had another bright idea. 'Perhaps if you had something of his to hold it might help you. Let us go down to Plas Gwyn and ask for something. We will ask Miss Annersley for leave.'

No sooner said than done. The bell was ringing for the end of Break, but it might ring till its clapper fell out for all the twins cared. They tore downstairs at full speed, luckily for them encountering no one of importance on the way, and made for the library where Miss Annersley, sick at heart when she thought of Jo's bitter loss, was sitting signing the week's housekeeping cheques. She nearly dropped her pen when the door was burst open—the twins were above such courtesies as tapping for the moment—and two untidy-looking beings rushed in on her with demands to be taken down to Plas Gwyn or allowed to go by themselves at once.

'Go to Plas Gwyn?' she repeated. 'My dear girls, I can't let you do that. I'm afraid Mrs Maynard wants no visitors at present.'

'But Fiona will *look* for her!' cried Flora eagerly. 'She can "see," you know, Miss Annersley—she hass the second sight. Perhaps she can "see" Dr Maynard safe. Oh, let us go—do let us go! If he iss safe, think how glad *she* wouldt pe! *Pleass* let us go!'

Miss Annersley was in two minds about refusing. Like the McDonalds, she was a little afraid of Fiona's strange gift; and apart from that, she was not sure how the child might be welcomed. Jo was coming round; but she was very far from being herself. And then, if such a thing happened as that Fiona did 'see' Jack Maynard, it was only too probable that she would see him lying among seaweeds and shells, still and cold. Then she remembered her own last words to Jo, and felt ashamed of her loss of faith.

'Very well,' she said quietly. 'I will take you myself. I must finish these cheques first, as Matron is waiting to go into Armiford to pay the bills and order next week's supplies. And *you* cannot go anywhere looking like that. Go and make yourselves tidy, and then come back here. I shall be ready for you by that time.'

Flora leapt at her, followed by Fiona, and two pairs of arms were flung round the Head's neck, and two pairs of lips kissed her cheeks.

'Oh, you are goodt!' cried Flora. 'We will love you always for this!'

If she was a little startled, the Head kept this to

herself, though she had never before been treated this way by a pupil. She returned the kisses warmly, and then said with a rather shaky laugh, 'Thank you. Now go and get ready, and Fiona shall try what she can do if Mrs Maynard will let her. I shall be ready for you in ten minutes' time. Oh, one moment, please. How do you know anything about it?'

Fiona explained. 'I didn't mean to listen,' she pleaded. 'I couldt not help it, and then I guessed. I will tell no one else till you say.'

'Very well; that's a promise. Now run along and be ready for me in ten minutes' time.'

It is on record that two of the remaining cheques were so badly written that the bank returned them, requesting a more legible signature. But the Head was too excited to trouble much. She dashed off the last one, handed the bunch to Matron who had come for them, and then fled to get into hat and coat and change her shoes. When she came downstairs, she found the pair waiting for her in the hall. They had washed their hands and faces, brushed their hair, and put on their Sunday hats and coats. Miss Wilson was also there, asking where they were going, and why they were not in their form-room. Fiona said nothing, but Flora cried, 'We are going out with Miss Annersley. She said so. Here she iss!'

In a few words the Head explained, and 'Bill's' face grew disapproving. 'I don't like it, Hilda. It's meddling with powers best left alone.'

'If it were anything else, I would never agree to it,' replied the Head swiftly. 'I don't approve of it any more than you do. But that child certainly "saw," as she calls it, her brother's death. It is just possible she may be able to bring comfort to Jo. Of course, Jo herself may forbid it and then there's an end of it. But they pleaded so to go, that I feel it better to let them. I'm afraid Fiona may worry if I don't.'

'Well, on your head be it, then. But I don't agree with it at all.'

'I shall not allow it again. But I would give a good deal to bring help to Jo. You haven't seen her yet, Nell. She is like a broken thing—all the joy and life out of her. Madge says the only time she smiles is when the children are with her, and that it's almost sadder to see her then than when she is alone or with Madge and Jem. Can you picture it?—Joey, who was always bubbling over with laughter and joy!'

Nell Wilson's face underwent a change. 'No; I can *not*. If Fiona can do anything to change that, I suppose we must let her try. But you *will* forbid it for the future, won't you, Hilda? I do feel it's wrong.'

'I'll forbid it. And I shall forbid them to tell the others about it. It must be between ourselves and Jo. If she allows it, I am sure she will never speak of it to anyone unless it is to Jack himself if—*when* he comes home. Now I must go. Pray for us, my dear, that it may be all right.'

'Of course. I've got a "free" the next two periods, so I'll go to my room and say a rosary for Jo and Jack. And that's better than any amount of "seeing," even if it *is* second sight.'

Miss Wilson went off, still looking disturbed, and the Head joined the impatient twins, who had moved out of earshot to the hall door when the mistresses began to talk. There was very little petrol, so they had to walk, but it was a fine day, with plenty of pale November sunlight. It was a pleasant walk to Plas Gwyn, but none of the three saw anything of it, they were so anxious to get there. Very little was said until they turned into the lane. Then the Head stopped, and faced round on her companions. 'I don't know if Jo will permit it, Fiona. But if she does, I want you both to give me your word of honour that you will never speak of it to anyone—not even to your sister. Will you promise me that?'

'Of course,' said Flora readily. 'Besides, Shiena and Archie haf told us that we must not speak of it. They do not like it—and, inteet, I am a little afraid of it myself. It—it makes Fiona—strange to me.'

'Very well. And you, Fiona? Will you promise?'

'Oh, yess. It iss not a thing I can talk apout, and I nefer do.'

'Then we will go on. Come, children.' And she took a hand of each.

At Plas Gwyn, the triplets were playing in the garden with Robin looking after them. She stared when she saw the trio walking up the drive, but the triplets raised a shout, and came running towards them.

'Fauna, Flora!' cried Len. 'Come an' see! Len got a ball!'

'An' so has Con!' added that small person. 'Look! A wed ball!'

'Me, too; me got a lella ball.' Margot was not going to be left out.

'I'll—I'll stay and play with them,' said Flora hurriedly. As she had told the Head, she was always rather afraid of her twin at these times. There was not an atom of second sight about Flora, who was a matter-of-fact little person, which was just as well perhaps. Her common sense would always keep her twin's feet more on the earth.

Fiona took no notice of them at all. Her whole being was concentrated on what she had come to do. A queer light burned in her dark eyes, and she looked very white. The Head saw it, and felt half afraid. She wondered if she were right to allow the child to do this. Then she knew that she was. If Fiona were denied, she would almost certainly fret herself into a fever. Let her try, and it would be over, and she would return to normal. She turned to Robin.

'Where is Jo, Robin? Fiona wants to see her very urgently.'

'She's still in her room, Miss Annersley. She would love to see you, I know; but I'm not certain if——'

'Ah! It is Fiona who must see her. I don't matter this time,' said the Head quietly. 'Stay with the children, Robin. Or, if you like, you can go and ask Anna to make cocoa for us all. I missed my elevenses; and I don't suppose Flora and Fiona had theirs, either. I'll take Fiona up to Jo. Don't worry, dear. I'll bring her away at once if I see it's too much for Jo.'

There was nothing more for Robin to say. She stood back, and the Head, with a hand on Fiona's shoulder, went into the house. It felt strangely quiet once they were in the hall, with the door shutting out the triplets' merry shouts. Fiona shivered as she followed the Head up the wide, shallow stairs, so easy for baby feet, and along the corridor. They passed the room where she and Flora slept when they came 'home.' Then they were at Jo's door. The Head rapped gently, and a weary voice bade them 'Come in.' They entered, and there was Jo, lying on the sofa drawn up to one side of the fireplace. The long week had made a big change in her. She was much thinner, and she looked very white and sad. Fiona felt a feeling of awe creep over her. This pale woman with the stricken eyes was not the 'Mistress Maynard' who was always so jolly, and who had helped them so tenderly when Hughie had gone. But Jo had seen her, and was holding out a hand to her.

'Have you come to see me, Fiona? Come and kiss me, dear. The doctors are such tyrants they insist that I must lie here for a few days longer. I wish they would let me get up and do something.' And a restless look came into her face as she spoke.

But Fiona had got over her awe. She ran forward, and dropping on her knees by Jo's side, gave the asked-for kiss eagerly. 'Mistress Maynard, I haf come to ask you something—to do something for me. Will you?'

'Can't say till I know what it is.' A little interest had come into Jo's face, and her voice had lost its dreary ring. 'I'm buying no pigs in pokes, Fiona. Tell me what you want, dear.'

'Shust something that Dr Maynard hass worn—something he hass worn often. I can "see," you know, Mistress Maynard. You were with us when I "saw" Hughie. I shust *know* Dr Maynard issn't dead. It iss a mistake. Let me "see" him for you. I haf tried and tried alreaty, but I cannot. He iss not a McDonald, you see. But if I had something of his, then I think maybe I couldt. Do let me try for you—oh, do let me try!'

Jo lay back against her pillows, frowning. She could see that this was no silly joke, or even that the child was half pretending. Fiona quite plainly believed what she said. Then another thought came. Suppose she were right! Suppose Jack were not dead! There *had* been mistakes made. And the letters she had received on Saturday had merely said that he had been swept overboard by a wave, and as it was so stormy they had been unable to send out a boat for him, though the attempt had been made more than once before it had been given up. Her eyes fell on the row of red, leather-bound Kiplings which she had collected through the years. That sort of thing had happened to the unpleasant youth in *Captains Courageous*. Of course, in these days of wireless it was less likely to happen. Still, one could never be sure; and this was war-time, anyhow. She sat up, a light in her eyes that had not been there before, and a faint pink staining her cheeks.

'Do you really mean it, Fiona? You really feel that Jack is alive?'

Fiona nodded. 'I am sure of it. I haf been sure efer since I heard it. Gif me a coat or something

Dr Maynard often wore, and let me be quiet. I will try efer so hardt to "see" him for you.'

'I can do better than that.' Jo got off her sofa, and, swaying a little as she walked, for she was still very weak, she went to a beautiful prie-dieu standing in a corner of the room, and from it took a rosary of cornelian beads, with silver links. 'Here is Jack's rosary—the one he used until he went away. I gave him a new one then, and he left this with me. He used it every day from the time he was a boy at school. Take this, Fiona.'

Fiona took it, twining the beads about her fingers. She shut her eyes and remained perfectly still. Jo got back to her couch, and sat limply down on it. The Head, with one eye on her, and the other on the child still kneeling there, her eyes shut, the crimson beads caught round her hands, her lips parted, looked round hastily for the bell in case she needed aid. Then she stopped. Fiona's eyes were open, but she quite clearly saw nothing in the sunny room. Her lips were moving, and then she began to speak in a sing-song voice. 'He iss not dead, but he iss ill. He hass been fery ill, and he iss fery weak now. But he iss alive. He iss in a wee room with wooden walls, and it iss falling and rising, oh, efer so much. There iss a big man with a plack peard peside him, and he iss watching him. He iss a foreigner, but he means well. He iss gifing him something to drink. Now he iss lifting his head. It iss bandaged, and the man iss taking the bandage off. He iss putting on a new one.' Her voice changed subtly, though she was still seeing things the others could not. 'Now it iss white and misty, and I can see no more. But he *iss* alife, and he iss getting better, though he hass peen fery, fery ill. Soon, I think he will pe with you.'

Her voice died away, her eyes closed again, and she swayed and nearly fell. But the Head had been watching, and her arms were ready to catch the child. She lifted her, and laid her on Jo's bed, drawing the eiderdown over her. 'Can you ring for Anna, Jo?' she asked quietly. 'Fiona must have a hot drink, and then she must rest for a while.'

Still rapt in a sudden dream of hope, Jo stretched out her hand, and then Anna, blessedly solid and matter-of-fact, appeared at the door and was sent to bring hot milk for Fiona, and coffee and cake for Miss Annersley. The Head kept a finger on the child's pulse; but it grew steadier as Fiona lay still, and by the time her milk had come she was, though still very white, more like herself. As for Jo, she had lain down among her pillows and was sobbing happily into them. Hope had revived. Something in Fiona's performance had made the young wife sure that her husband was safe, even if she had no means as yet of knowing where he was. Lying there, Jo cried away all the bitter grieving, and when the Head decided that Fiona would be able to get home if they could catch the half-past one bus, she was herself again, and the smile on the lips she offered for their kisses was a real smile.

Meanwhile, Robin had seen that Flora had elevenses, and then had played with her and the triplets, though she was frantic with curiosity to know what all this was about. Daisy was still in her own room, as she was still infectious, so knew nothing of it all. In answer to Robin's queries, Flora merely said, 'Miss Annersley made us promise not to tell,' and after that, there could be no further questioning for Robin.

When the Head came down the path with a still white Fiona clinging to her arm, she nodded cheerily at the elder girl. 'All is well, Robin. Leave Jo alone for an hour, and then you can go to her. Anna has taken her some soup, so she will be all right till then. Take the triplets in and give them their dinner. By that time Jo will be ready for you.' Then she had summoned Flora, and the three went off, just in time to catch the bus.

Fiona was sent straight to bed when she got in. Miss Annersley decided that as Matron had seen what had happened when Hugh McDonald was killed, she might safely be confided in. So she was told, and Miss Wilson heard, and the three rejoiced that some measure of hope had come to Jo, though 'Bill' still disapproved strongly of the method, and did not spare to say so. Matron frankly doubted how much Fiona could know. She said nothing to the child. But she hustled her off to San, and kept her there for the rest of that day and all the next. When Wednesday came, however, Fiona rebelled. She wanted to get back into school. The parts for the usual Nativity Play had been given out, and though she was only a shepherd with about two lines to speak, she had no notion of being out of it. Flora, who was to be an angel, quite agreed. She missed her twin badly, and Matron had not allowed her to go to Fiona except in the morning and evening.

So Fiona returned to school, and in answer to her own class's curious questioning as to why she had been in San, she merely said that she had not been well. With that, they had to be satisfied. Not that anyone paid much heed to it. It was the third week in November. They broke up on December 18th, and the play would be given on the previous Saturday. That meant hard work, and rehearsals every other day, as well as odd bits at any time. Jo had written this one, and everyone had determined to do their best to make it a huge success. Madge Russell had written all they had done before this. But now she was so busy that she had cried off, and begged her sister to do her best with it. Jo had evolved a charming play, and quite original, too. The village hall had been taken, and if it were a success, they would try to get the theatre at Armiford for the next Sunday afternoon. Indeed, the Head had already been in treaty with the manager, though very few people knew of this, and it was more than likely that the play would have its two performances—the one at Howells village in aid of the great Sanatorium over the mountains, and the other in Armiford in aid of the local hospitals. It was not likely that Fiona liked being out of all this fun, especially now that her mind was at rest about the Maynards. Nothing had been heard of the doctor yet; but she was certain that he was safe.

'P'r'aps he'll get home for Christmas, and wouldn't that be fun?' she said privately to Flora. 'And Shiena may haf leaf then, too. Oh, I do think that it iss going to be efer so nice!'

CHAPTER XVIII

RETRIBUTION!

'IF you please, Miss Phipps, may the girls go to Hall? Miss Annersley wants them. She has sent for the whole School, and we are all to go as quickly as we can.' Thus Joanna Linders, who had been placed in Lower Fifth and was now working steadily with a view to School Certificate as soon as she could catch up with the girls of her own age. As she was a hard worker, and had her fair share of brains, this seemed likely to be within another term or so, even though she was a good deal behind the others when she had arrived from Germany. She already looked a different being from the scared girl who had come that sunny day at the beginning of term. Regular hours, peace of mind, and happy friendships renewed, had done a great deal for her, and would do more. In her neat uniform, with her long, fair hair swinging in a great plait down her back, she looked much like the rest of them. Her English was coming back very quickly, and there was little, even in her phrasing nowadays, to remind the others that she had left the School nearly five years before.

Emmie, being older, had suffered more, for she had understood how things stood far better than her young sister, and she was slower to recover tone. But even she was making headway at last. She was to try for her Certificate in the summer, and then they hoped to get her into a nursery training-centre. She had vowed her intention of doing her best, so that when the Nursery class the Head was projecting had begun, she might come and help. The idea had been mooted abroad, and already several people in the district, who possessed tinies under five, were asking when it would start. Jo's suggested nine would be almost double that number by the summer, even if no more came; and it seemed more than likely that it would be trebled or even quadrupled.

Miss Phipps, brought up short in a geography lesson on how the people of the Steppes lived, looked up, and nodded. 'Very well, Joanna. Form, stand! Out of your desks and to the door—quickly! Leave your things where they are. You will be coming back soon. Nella, put that pencil down. You won't want that. Are you all ready? Forward—march!'

The form marched briskly out of the room, along the passage, and across the big hall into the enormous drawing-room which had been turned into Hall for the School. They filed quietly into their usual places, and stood there waiting and wondering what all this was about. Most of the Upper School were already there, and the prefects were moving about, keeping order. The Lower Second came in in a moment, and the rest of the little ones followed. The Upper Fourth were last. They had been over in the big garage which had been turned into a chemistry laboratory, and had had to get out of overalls and wash their hands before they came, as they had been busy with an experiment. Then the

Staff filed in, and took up their places on the far side of the dais. Lastly, the door at the top of the room opened to admit the Head, Colonel Black, the officer in command of the troops in the neighbourhood, the Chief Constable of Armiford, two policemen, and a tall, thin man who walked between them, and, to the intense excitement of the School, was handcuffed to one of them. A heavy scowl darkened his face, as he glanced down the noble room and saw the rows of bright young faces before him.

The Sixth, standing at the opposite side of the dais to the Staff, were as much thrilled as anyone, despite their added years and graver outlook on life. Only one girl showed any signs of anything but interest. This was Betty Wynne-Davies. She went deathly white, and gave a tiny gasp. No one noticed it, for all were too much occupied in staring at the group on the dais and wondering what on earth it all meant.

Betty made a wild clutch after her senses, and contrived to pull herself together, though she still looked ghastly. Luckily for her, she was very much shorter than most of the Sixth, and she made haste to get behind big Monica Marilliar, who stood five feet nine in her stocking-feet, and was broad to match. Then the Head gave the order to sit down, and they sat down on the plain prie-dieu chairs that filled two-thirds of Hall, and there was silence.

The Head came forward, and looked at them all with deep gravity. 'I am sorry to have to tell you,' she began, 'that there is a traitor among us. I use the word because I am afraid the girl, whoever she is, has been both treacherous and deceitful. Another girl—two or three, in fact—has forgotten that it is well not to chatter in war-time. As a result of this, a most important document might have got into enemy hands, and if it had done, it might have been a very grave thing for our country.' She paused. Then she spoke again, this time in a different key, 'Fiona and Flora McDonald!'

The twins rose, almost paralysed at being brought to public notice like this. They gripped each other's hands, and waited dumbly for what she might have to say.

'I understand that the Chart which this man,' she indicated the prisoner sitting between his two guardians with a scarcely perceptible movement of her hand, 'has been seeking, and to get which he broke into the School a week or two ago, belongs to you. Is this so?'

'Yess, Miss Annersley,' said the twins as one girl.

'Where is it now?'

'We do not know,' said Fiona quickly. She knew now that it was Flora that the Head meant when she spoke of people who talked, and she was going to give her twin no time to give anything more away. Not that she need have worried. Flora was too much overcome by what she had done to speak. Her head was sunk, and her cheeks were crimson with shame.

'You don't know?' The Head's voice was sharp, but she was very much worried by the present events. She was also fairly sure that Rosalie Dene's unpleasant experience, which had given the girl some days in bed and left her still nervous and unlike herself, had come from this.

'No, Miss Annersley.' Fiona spoke up bravely, though she felt very frightened. And if Flora got into trouble for talking, what should they do? They could scarcely go to Jo just now. Though much better, she was still far from well, and they could not bother her with their affairs. So Fiona gripped her twin's hand, and did her best for her.

'Do you mean that you have lost it?'

'No, Miss Annersley. Someone we couldt trust hass it, and hass put it somewhere safe. But we ton't know where that iss.'

The frown between the Head's brows relaxed. 'I see,' she said. 'And you are sure that it is in safe keeping now?'

'Oh, yess, Miss Annersley. It iss fery safe, I know.'

'Then you may sit down. Oh, one moment, though! Which of you spoke of it in public?'

Fiona became dumb. She was not going to give her twin away, whatever happened, and Flora was too much overcome to speak, even now. The tears were hanging on her long lashes, and her lips were trembling.

The Head repeated her question, but Fiona shook her head. Miss Annersley nodded. 'Very well. I will see you both later on in the library. You may sit down. Now, with Colonel Black's permission, I will finish this part of the business. Will those girls who have heard of the Chart of Erisay stand up.'

The Band rose lingeringly to its feet. Nancy Chester looked ready to burst into tears; the small faces of Julie, Vanna, and Primula rivalled Flora's for colour, and Bride and Nella looked scared. The Head surveyed them all judicially.

'You six? I see. And which of you has talked of it to other people?'

The Ozanne twins' hands shot up, and were followed by those of Nancy and Bride. Only Julie and Primula remained still.

'I see,' said the Head again. 'Well, when I have finished with Fiona and Flora, you four may come to the library too, and we'll have a little talk together. But just now, I want you to remember that because you gossiped as you have done, you might—you *might*, I say—have been the means of bringing about the deaths of very very many of our men—your own fathers and brothers among them. You may sit down now.'

The six sat down, and made themselves very small. They had not liked the way the rest of the School had looked at them. Nancy, whose father was now an army doctor, and Bride, who was Jo's niece, and who adored her Uncle Jack, were biting their lips and winking their eyes to keep from crying. Besides, Bride's sister Peggy, who was in the Upper Third, had turned such a look of horror on her as appalled Bride's small heart. Oh, whatever would Peg say to her later? And Auntie Madge and Auntie Jo would be so horrified too! It was almost more than Bride could bear.

But the Head had finished with them, and what she had to say next drew the School's attention away from the small sinners at once.

'That is the least of the trouble,' she was saying.

'One expects small girls to make silly mistakes sometimes. They are still too much of babies, perhaps, to understand the seriousness of what they have done. But I have something much worse to do, now. One of the elder girls has also talked; and not from carelessness, as the little girls have done; but, or so I understand, from sheer malice. This is a terrible thing, and I can only mark my feeling about it by pronouncing the heaviest punishment I can upon this girl. I am now going to ask Colonel Black and Mr Dunnett to permit their prisoner to look at you all, and point out the girl who deliberately told him of the Chart.'

The two policemen rose, their prisoner with them, and the Chief Constable and Colonel Black followed suit. The thin man stared slowly at the front row of tinies who were sitting staring solemnly at him. He shook his head, and looked at the next. Then on his gaze travelled till it reached the Upper Third. Then he turned and spoke to the Head, a certain insolence in his hard, clear voice.

'I regret that I am unable to see the bigger young ladies at the back of the room. Perhaps I might go down and look at them?'

The Head glanced at the two big men in charge, and they nodded, so she said, 'Very well. Or, better still, as it was none of the younger children, I will send them back to their work, and the older ones can march, form by form, past you. Will not that be better, Colonel?'

'A lot better,' replied the Colonel grumpily. He hated this business of letting this man stare at these bonny, decent girls in his insolent way. But it had to be done. The prisoner had declared he did not know the name of his informant, and it was necessary that it should be known, as she would have to give evidence against him, for they must have the evidence of the girl who had, by what he had told them, given away the secret of the Chart to satisfy her own private malice and ill-feeling.

Miss Wilson jumped up here, however, and interfered. 'One moment! May I make a suggestion. Perhaps if the girls were asked, the guilty one would own up and then we need not go to this extra trouble.'

The Head welcomed the suggestion with relief. She wondered she had not thought of it herself. The truth was, she had been so stunned by the news Colonel Black and Mr Dunnett had brought that she was, even now, unable to think clearly. She turned back to the girls. 'Kindergarten to the Upper Third, stand! Turn! Forward—*march*! Go straight to your form-rooms.'

The Juniors marched out, and as each form left the room, the mistress in charge of it left the ranks and tailed on. As soon as the girls reached their rooms, they were taken severely in hand. No talking was allowed. They had to settle back to work at once, and they were all kept hard at it. The Upper Second managed to cast various looks at the eight members of the Band; but Miss Phipps caught Nesta Tudor at it, and called them to order at once. 'Girls, get on with your work. You have quite enough to do with that. Nesta, don't let me see you taking your eyes off your book again. Stand up and begin to read where Nora left off, please.'

As Nesta had naturally lost her place, she was unable to obey, and got a sharp scolding which took all the starch out of her, and left the entire form only anxious to avoid Miss Phipps' tongue for the rest of the day.

Meanwhile, in Hall, the Head was appealing to the girl who had been the cause of all the trouble. 'Will the girl who has done this thing please stand?'

There was no response. Betty was usually plucky enough, but she literally dared not give herself up now. She remained cowering behind Monica's broad back, and hoping that when the prisoner reached the Sixth he would not recognise her. It had been dusk when she had encountered him in the kitchen-garden that October day, and she had worn her beret pulled well down over her head. It had been gardening day for the Sixth, and she had been sent back to collect a trowel and fork she had left out. She had seen this man coming to her, and had attacked him as a trespasser at first. But he had seen enough of her to know that she was the girl he had seen in the wood at the Round House who had spoken of the Chart and the McDonald twins with such bitterness. He had his own methods, and he had speedily placated her. Then he had questioned her very cautiously, and Betty, unguarded in the hatred she felt for the twins, had told him more than she had realised at the moment. When he began to ask her plainer questions, she had tried to draw back, but he told her brutally that she had already given away enough to be of great help to him, and if she did not tell what he wanted to know, he would find ways and means of letting her head mistress know how much she had already told. Betty was badly frightened, for she remembered all too well Miss Annersley's words at that last interview she had had with her. 'This sort of thing must end, Betty. I cannot let it go on. If I have any more complaints of you, you must go. You are having a bad influence in the School, and I cannot sacrifice the School for one girl.'

He had seen that he had made an impression, and had followed it up by reminding her of the way the twins had annoyed her. This was an excellent chance to punish them. Only let her tell him what she knew about the Chart, and he would see to the rest. It would be the finest punishment of all to them, since they clearly regarded it as something very precious. He assured her that it would do no harm to anyone if he took it. He would make no bad use of it.

Betty, badly frightened at the thought of what the Head would say if the whole story came out, and even more afraid of what her guardian would say, had yielded to his coaxing, and told him that she knew that the twins had it. She told him where the Junior lockers were, and even agreed to contrive to leave a window of the room unlatched if she could, so that he might get in quietly. It was an easy matter for her to slip in after the prefects had locked up and fasten back the latch of the french window. That was all she had done, and she had assured herself that more than likely no harm would come of it. The twins would never leave such a thing in a locker. And there, she had been right.

Now, all this had come of it. Expulsion was all she could expect if her part in the affair came out, and she simply could not face it. So she slumped down in her chair, and hoped against hope that it would be all right.

It was a vain hope. Form by form the girls were marched in front of the dais, and the prisoner's cold blue eyes wandered over their faces. He recognised none of them. Each form, as it was done with, marched straight out to its form-room, till at last only the Upper Fifth and the Sixth were left. Upper Fifth marched up, stood in a long file before the group on the dais, and the prisoner looked them over. His gaze lingered for a moment or two on Gwensi Howell's face. She was as dark as Betty, and much the same height and build. He stretched out his free hand.

'I do not know—this may be the young lady who so kindly helped me with information. She is the same size, and she is dark, too.'

'Indeed, then,' flashed out Gwensi at her very Welshiest in her anger, 'I never did such a thing! I have never seen this creature before, look you!'

His hand dropped. 'A thousand pardons, gracious lady. It is not the voice nor the accent. I have made a mistake.'

'Fifth Form—turn! Forward march to your form-room,' said Miss Annersley wearily. There was only the Sixth left, and surely, surely none of the Sixth had done this thing!

The Upper Fifth marched out, Gwensi still boiling with rage at the bare idea that *she* could be thought to have done anything so vile, and the Head turned to where the Sixth sat at the side of the dais. 'Sixth Form, stand! March!'

They filed along before her, Betty whiter than ever, and took up their places. The man stared at them. His eyes widened in recognition as they fell on Robin's lovely face, but he made no comment. He passed from her to brown-haired Lorenz, and then to Cornish Enid, whose blue eyes were bright with anger. Monica Marilliar came next, but he wasted no time on her. Monica was much bigger than the girl he had seen. Jocelyn Redford—Biddy O'Hara—Nicole de Saumarez—they were all too big, though Biddy and Nicole looked small beside Monica and red-haired Elizabeth Arnett. Floppy Williams came next, but she, too, could not be the girl. Then came Betty, and he looked at her, an unpleasant smile on his lips, and she stared back at him like a rabbit staring at a snake. He bowed to her. 'Fräulein,' he emphasised the title, 'I make you my apologies. Both of us are in hands too powerful for us. Believe me, I would not have told of you if I could have helped it.' He turned his head towards the Head. 'Gracious lady, this is the *gnädiges Fräulein* who gave me my information. I deeply regret that I must acknowledge it, but so it is.' He stepped back as he ended, with another low bow; but Betty was too far gone to see it or to heed its mockery. With a bitter little cry, she threw up her hands, and swayed forwards. The next moment Elizabeth Arnett had sprung forward and caught her. She could not support the dead weight, but she lowered the fainting girl to the floor, while the Colonel and the Chief Constable, thankful to get away, gave a signal, and the prisoner was marched out at once, leaving the horrified Sixth alone with Miss Wilson, Matron, and Miss Annersley.

The Head paused not a moment. Jumping lightly down from the dais, she stooped over Betty. 'Matron!' she said urgently.

Then 'Bill' acted. Swiftly she marshalled the Sixth out of the room and bore them off to their own form-room, while Matron and the Head ministered to Betty, and later lifted her and carried her between them to the small isolation ward in San, where she found herself when she had fully recovered consciousness.

The Head was bending over her, and Matron was near, a glass in her hand. 'Don't talk, Betty,' said the Head quickly. 'Drink this, and then go to sleep. I will see you later.'

But Betty rebelled. 'I *must* talk! Oh, Miss Annersley! What have I done? What have I done? I never meant it to come to this. Only Elizabeth——'

A third person moved forward. Wonder of wonders! Elizabeth was stooping over her, and Elizabeth was speaking gently to her. 'Don't, Betty! I know I'm to blame as much as you, if not more. I should have stuck to you. It's my fault as much as yours.'

Betty stared at her. Then, as Miss Annersley slipped an arm under her shoulders and lifted her, she suddenly burst into tears. 'Oh, Elizabeth!' she sobbed.

CHAPTER XIX

'THE MESSAGE OF CHRISTMAS'

FOR the next few days Betty stayed in isolation. There could be no question of rescinding her sentence. Elizabeth went to the Head, and begged her to do it, but Miss Annersley shook her head.

'For Betty's own sake I can't, Elizabeth. What sort of life would it be for her when the whole School knows what she has done? You need not tell me that you elder people would try to make it easy for her; I am sure you would. But even so, you could not help feeling, at times at any rate, that she was not to be trusted, and it would show. Betty is not a thick-skinned person, and she would feel it, however much you might try to hide it. And the Middles and the Juniors would scarcely even try to do it. And apart from that, I must mark my deep displeasure and grief as much as possible. Do you realise, I wonder, what might have happened if that man had got hold of the Chart? The Great House on Erisay contains secrets of national importance. The Admiralty know nothing of this hidden passage —or they *knew* nothing of it. Naturally, they have been told now—and an enemy might have stolen on them unawares and taken the secrets. He might even have destroyed the place and all in it. No; Betty must go.'

Elizabeth looked troubled. 'I didn't know it was of such tremendous importance, Miss Annersley.

Yes; I see your point. But Betty is so afraid of her guardian. It isn't as if she had a father and mother to go home to. It would be bad enough then; but she has no one. And Mr Irons is so stern.'

'Perhaps, knowing Betty's character, he feels that sternness is the best thing for her. He may feel that she needs a very firm hand over her.'

Elizabeth shook her head. 'It isn't that. He just doesn't bother with her. He isn't married, and he doesn't like girls. He sent her to school when she was only five, and she's been at school ever since. I've often heard her say that if it hadn't been for her mother's friend, she would never have known what a home *could* be like.'

The Head looked troubled in her turn. She knew Mr Irons, of course, and she had never been struck by any show of fondness he had for the girl. He had seemed to look on her as a trust, certainly, and one for whom he must do all in his power from a monetary point of view. But he had never spoken of her as if he had the slightest feeling for her other than that she was a trial to him, and a bother. She could well imagine that Betty dreaded facing such a man, and yet, for the moment, she could not see what to do. She dismissed Elizabeth, and, pushing her papers to one side, set her mind to work on this problem. Finally, she lifted the telephone receiver and dialled the Plas Gwyn number. Jo, with her wide understanding of girls, might be able to help. It would be good for her, too. They all knew that what she had just gone through had left a scar that would never fade. On that day when the wire had come, something had died in Jo that could never be brought to life again—her schoolgirl side had gone. But she was riper now, and she might be able to help.

Jo answered the telephone herself. On hearing of their problem, she promptly declared her intention of coming up to school at once. 'I've been thinking about it, and wondering what could be done, Hilda. I know you can't go back on your word. But I've *seen* Mr Irons! I should hate to be in his hands as Betty is. Brrr! He made me shiver all over. He's as hard as his name—and he looks just like a bit of iron, too,' she added. 'I'll be with you as soon as I can. I've plenty of petrol, for a wonder, so I'll get Boanerges out, and hop up ek dum.'

Jo was as good as her word, and just after she had arrived, little Mrs Lucy was announced, and her chum insisted on getting her to join the conference too. 'Janie's so human, she'll be able to give us a hand.'

So Janie Lucy came in, and after kissing Jo with unusual warmth, sat down, shelving her own business of Julie's dress for the play, and the trio set to work to see what they could do to help Betty.

'You say Elizabeth says that the only real home Betty has ever known is this Mrs Graves'?' asked Jo after the Head had told them the whole story. 'What's she like, Hilda? Any idea? She might help if she would. Has she ever been to the School? Oh, you must tell Mr Irons, I know. He *is* Betty's guardian. But if Mrs Graves could be coaxed to have her there for a little, it might tide things over. And then Betty is nearly eighteen, isn't she? That means she will be called up before long. Look here; I'll tell you what! Get Mrs Graves' address if you can, and tell me, and I'll write to her, and ask her—oh, hang! I can't have her to stay at present. We're chock-a-block with 'Veta and the babies.'

'I can, though,' said Janie eagerly. 'If you'll write to her, Jo, I can put her up for a few days. You can tell her so when you write.'

'Good for you, J.! I knew you'd turn up trumps. Yes; I know you could shove her in here, Hilda, but I think we'd better talk to her away from the School. It makes it less official. If she's really fond of Betty she ought to come to the rescue. Then Nan's got a spot of leave, hasn't she, J.? If you could take Betty, too, she might talk to her—get her to join the W.R.N.S.—if they'll have her. At any rate, it's an idea.'

'It is,' agreed Miss Annersley, her brow clearing. 'Very well; I'll ask for Mrs Graves' address, and you can write, Jo. Then if she will come, and Mrs Lucy really will put her up, we might come in and have a chat with her, and see if she will help us out. I must confess, I never exactly took to Mr Irons on the occasions on which I met him. Betty is a difficult girl. It seems to me that she has come to a crossroads in her life, and what she becomes will depend largely on the way she is handled now. But I couldn't, as you say, Jo, go back on my word.'

'Of course not,' agreed Janie. 'But if we *can* help the silly child, I'll be glad to do it.'

So it was settled. Mrs Graves was written to in Jo's most persuasive strain, and Miss Annersley had the much more unpleasant task of informing Mr Irons of his ward's latest doings. Both replied—Mr Irons in a cold business letter which chilled the Head as she read it; Mrs Graves with deep sorrow in every line. Mr Irons said that he was unable to get away from business for at least a week. If the School could keep the girl till then he would be glad, as the military had taken over his house and he himself was living in rooms where he could not have her. He must have time to make some arrangement for her. There was not one word in the letter that could bring any hope that he would try to treat the affair except as a tiresome piece of business which he detested.

Mrs Graves, on the other hand, grasped at Janie Lucy's invitation eagerly, and said that she was dropping everything at once, and would come by train on the day following the arrival of her letter at Plas Gwyn, if that would be convenient. A wire was promptly sent, welcoming her, and Betty was fetched from school the same day and installed in the little bedroom next to Nan Blakeney's, so that she might be there to greet her mother's friend. She was very quiet and subdued; even her hair seemed to have lost some of its rampant curliness, and she was thin and white. Janie was kind to her, but left her to herself. It seemed to her that it was far better for the girl to realise how far her spite and malice had carried her.

Only Elizabeth said good-bye to her. The rest refused with one accord. The Head had been quite right when she had said that if Betty were kept at school, her life would not be worth living. What hurt the girl most, perhaps, was Floppy Bill's refusal to have anything more to do with her. That young lady had had a bad shock, and she was of too shallow a nature to recover from it at once. She had no pity for the girl she had called her friend, and who had fallen so far, and when the Head sent for her and told her that she might see Betty for a few minutes, she shook her head. 'Thank you, Miss Annersley, but I'd rather not. I never want to see her again.'

'Florence,' said the Head gently, 'I know you have had a shock; but how much better are you than Betty that you should judge her so hardly?'

Floppy Bill flushed. 'I never set up to be a pattern good girl,' she said sullenly, 'but I've never done the things Betty has done, and I'd rather die than do them. After all, it was only an accident in the beginning, and Fauna—I—I mean Fiona—couldn't help it. I think it's downright mean to be so hard and unforgiving as Betty has been. And to risk all she did just to pay the kid out is beyond everything.'

'That may be. But Betty has never done *you* any harm, and you have been close friends this past eighteen months. Do you think you have any right to try to push her further down than she already is?'

But Floppy Bill stuck to her guns. 'I'd rather not, Miss Annersley.'

Miss Annersley gave it up after that. But it was with a stern face that she told Betty that her erstwhile friend would not come. Betty said nothing. Perhaps she had expected this. But her lips quivered, and the Head went away sadly. She left the School an hour later, when the Sixth were all in the Sixth form-room, and when Monica said in subdued tones, 'There goes Betty,' Floppy Bill turned her back on the window, and went on talking hockey feverishly with Hilda Hope.

Joey and Miss Annersley went to the Lucys to tea on the day after Mrs Graves had arrived, and found her a kindly, middle-aged woman, with greying hair brushed back from a pleasant, sensible face. She was very much upset by the whole thing, and blamed herself for not having seen more of Betty. She told them that Mr Irons and Mr Graves had been left as joint trustees for the girl, but as she and her husband had been in India at the time, Mr Irons had been appointed the child's guardian. Betty's parents had died within a few days of each other of influenza, and she had been barely five then. Mr Irons had sent her to a good boarding-school, where she had also spent most of her holidays. When the Graves had left India ten years later, Mrs Graves had seen what she could of the girl, and had supplemented her rather meagre pocket-money, but she owned that she had done little else.

'George Irons is an upright man,' she said. 'My husband tells me that, financially, he has cared for Betty's interests to the best of his ability. When she comes of age she will have quite a good income—seven or eight hundred a year, I believe. And there is a house which is, at present, let on a long lease to good tenants. But he was the last person to have charge of a girl. You know, Miss Annersley, I feel I've failed Jessie Wynne-Davies badly over her girl. Perhaps if I'd taken more trouble all this would never have happened. As it is, my husband and I are willing to assume complete responsibility for the child from now on. But it will lie with George Irons. My husband is writing to him about it, and will try to go and see him. But if he agrees, Betty's home will be with us for the future—until she has one of her own.'

As it turned out, Mr Irons was more than willing to resign to their hands his post as Betty's guardian. He had not even a house now to which he could take the girl. He had only accepted the task from friendship towards her long-dead father. He would continue to look after her interests, and she was to make her home with the Graves, who were childless themselves, and would be very good to her. The Head warned Mrs Graves not to pet Betty too much at first. She must realise what an awful thing she had done. But the mere fact that she would not have to go back to her former guardian to live, and her 'Auntie Phyll's' grief over her downfall and warm-hearted welcoming of her to their home, broke down Betty's defences. She cried bitterly in Mrs Graves' arms, and whispered promises of good behaviour which, if they were kept, would go far towards making up for what she had been and done in the past. She was bound to see Mr Irons, and his contempt for her conduct, and his curt, 'Well, Beatrice, I think I need not tell you what I feel about you. I am too much disgusted with you to have patience to speak to you. I only hope Mrs Graves' kindness will not be repaid by a similar outbreak later on!' cut her to the quick.

After that, she went away to try to build a new life for herself, and, in the event, she succeeded. Later, she ventured back to see Jo and Janie, and the Betty who came to them then was a very much nicer girl than the one who had left them. One thing, she said, had forced her to do her best, as well as Mrs Graves' goodness to her. At Christmas time, a letter in script had come for her, and when opened, proved to be from Fiona. That young lady had taken the lesson of Jo's Christmas play to heart, and she wrote to say that she was sorry she had ever annoyed Betty. And as for the Chart, she was not to think any more about it. Fiona's spelling was wild, and her writing none too good; but her meaning was clear enough. Betty never knew that the elder twin had done her best to get Flora to join in; but Flora refused to forgive so easily, and, indeed, called her sister 'a soft' for doing it. But then, as I have said before, Flora was all a McDonald, with all a Highlander's proneness to hold grudges till they were paid.

Meanwhile, once Betty had gone, the School at large turned to the Christmas play, and, as Daisy said, pitched in at rehearsals with all its might. When the School was in Tyrol, they had had quite a name for the beauty of the Nativity plays they had produced each Christmas term in aid of the big Sanatorium, up on the Sonnalpe, of which Sir James Russell, then plain Dr Russell, was the head. Too much had happened during their first term in Guernsey for them to do anything about it; but the next year, however, they had given one of the old ones—'The Bells of Christmas.' This year, Jo had been prevailed on to try her hand, and as it was her first play, they were all keen to do well in it. It was quite a change from those they had done previously.

As Jo said when she handed it over, 'Madge and I think along different lines sometimes.' But for all that, it was quite charming.

Lessons got rather pushed to one side in the next fortnight for rehearsals of both the play and the carols in it. Jo had written two or three original ones, and they had been set by Mr Denny, the School's somewhat eccentric singing-master, and old Herr Anserl, who had been music-master almost since they had begun. He had escaped from Austria at the time of the Anschluss, and had continued his work till the end of the last summer term. Then he had settled down to a well-earned retirement, saying he had taught for fifty-five years, and he needed a rest now. But he had been delighted to give the School his help in this, and Miss Denny and Miss Ames, who were now responsible for the piano side of the School's education, declared that they intended that any examination candidates should perform before the irascible old man before the actual exam.

'If they can pass Vater Bär,' said Miss Denny, giving him the nickname by which naughty Jo had christened him years before, 'they can pass any ordinary examiner.'

Joanna had been a great stand-by in this play. Hitherto, they had had Jo's golden voice to depend on for solos, as well as two or three other people; and even last Christmas, Jo, at the urgent request of the entire School, had taken her old part of the Spirit of the Bells. But she had flatly refused to be in it this year, and the School was rather badly off for good voices for once. Robin had a charming mezzo, but it was not strong. Daisy's sweet, high soprano was an asset; and Monica Marilliar owned what promised to become a good contralto. But otherwise they had very little, and no one with a voice like Jo Maynard's. Hers possessed something of the unearthly sweetness of a choir-boy's, and when she sang, few people could resist her. Joanna's had something of the same quality, though less marked as yet, and, with one accord, she had been chosen for chief soloist when the parts were given out.

'We are *slafes* to the play,' announced Fiona McDonald at Plas Gwyn the Saturday before it was given. 'And this week we shall do *no* lessons!'

'Bless me!' cried Jo. 'What ever sort of reports will you all get?'

'Lessons more or less ended this week,' said Daisy, who was perched on the fender-stool, knitting hard at a grey scarf. 'But we shall have *some*—most of the morning, you know. But after half-past eleven, we are to have choir-practice every day; and rehearsals every afternoon. *And* there won't be any prep. We'll have to make up for it next term, Fauna, so I don't know that we get much out of it that way.'

However, the busy days passed—all too quickly for those who were responsible for the production—and Saturday came at long last.

'What's the weather doing?' was the first question for most people when they woke up, for overnight it had threatened to snow. However, very little had fallen, and the sky was clear; so they got up, dressed, and went downstairs to breakfast in fine fettle. There would be no Guide meeting that morning, as every minute was wanted for the arrangement of the village hall and all the oddments that always crop up at the last moment. Rosalie Dene and Miss Wilson had to motor into Armiford for more crinkled paper, for one of the Juniors had contrived to spill red ink over her wings during the dress rehearsal the night before, so fresh ones had to be made. Miss Linton and Miss Stevens turned to as soon as 'Bill' and Rosalie got back, and the wings were ready in time—but only just. Every row of 'feathers' had to be stitched on, and it took some doing. Miss Phipps personally searched the village billiard-room, where the Juniors were to dress, to make sure that anything like ink was not there before she left the hall that morning.

Dinner was at half-past twelve; and half-past one saw the School marching in at the back-door of the hall. On the morrow they would all go to Armiford, for the Head had decided to risk it, and the play was to be given at the local theatre in aid of the Armiford General Hospital on the Sunday. At two o'clock the doors opened, and the door-keepers—Miss Denny, Miss Slater, back again for this, though she still had to use a stick, and Miss Everett—had a hard time of it. By a quarter to three the place was nearly packed, and still people were coming.

'We'll have to put up "House full" notices if this goes on,' said Miss Everett with a chuckle. 'Have the Round House party come yet?'

'All but Sir James. He sent word to say that he would be here by three all right, but not a moment before,' replied Rosalie Dene, who had come to bring her more change. 'The thing that's puzzling me,' she added with a frown, 'is that Jo hasn't turned up yet.'

'Perhaps she 's funking it. It must be rather awful to have to sit through your own play. I know *I* couldn't do it.'

'Jo could, though. I hope there 's nothing wrong.' And Rosalie went off to another job, still looking anxious.

It was just two minutes to three when the sound of Sir James' big car told the watchers that he had arrived, and the Head went out to meet him, reproaches on her lips, for he was to explain a little about the play before the curtain went up. But the reproaches died on her lips. For out of the car came Joey, her eyes shining, her cheeks pink; and following her, still very gaunt and white, and with his head strapped up, was—Jack Maynard!

They learned later that he had flown home from Mauritius, near which he had been picked up by a tiny fishing-boat when he had been swept away that night. He had struck his head on an iron stanchion as he went, and had been ill for weeks. But the half-caste crew who had rescued him were very good to him, and here he was again—still with many weeks of convalescence before him, but Jack himself!

There was no time then for explanations. The Head rushed the party to their seats, and Jem Russell complained later that he had barely locked the car doors before he found himself on the platform before the curtains, with Joey and Jack just squeezing into their seats below him. He cut his speech very short, merely saying that all present knew it was in aid of the Red Cross. As this was a Nativity play, there must be no applause from beginning to end. Then he vanished, and had just got to his seat when the little orchestra, made up of three violins, one viola, one 'cello, a harp—Frieda von Ahlen was an expert harpist—and the glocken-spiel, played by Herr Laubach, struck up the first carol, and voices from behind the scenes took it up with a will. It was the Welsh carol 'Seren Bethlehem,' which may be freely translated 'Silent Bethlehem.' The School sang an English version, Welsh being beyond the powers of most of them. As it finished, the curtain was raised, and there was the stage, with a tower-like building at one side. Before it stood an old man dressed in the flowing robes of the East, and round him stood three or four others, similarly attired. They all shaded their eyes with their hands, and looked anxiously across the stage. Then the curtains at the far end parted, and a younger man, also in flowing draperies, these caught up in his girdle, limped in. Clearly, he had come a long way, for he looked dis-hevelled and worn and footsore. He was followed by a stalwart young negro, and then Melchior welcomed Caspar and Balthasar to his tower, where all three had met to speak of the strange new star they had seen in the heavens and what its portent might be. They finished by singing together the old Flemish carol, 'Three Kings are here.' Then the curtain descended, and the choir at once filled the hall with the lovely music of the German 'Song of the Ship.'

As the last notes died away on the air, the curtain was raised again, this time to show the 'shepherds abiding in the field, keeping watch over their flocks by night'; and, to the great delight of all the little people in the audience, there was a mother-sheep with her two baby-lambs beside her. This was a great surprise, as lambs, even round Howells village, are not as a rule born before the end of January. But Mr Griffiths-the-Court-Farm had sent round three nights before to say that they had arrived, and if the School would like to have them, he would bring sheep and lambs down to the hall for the shepherds' scene. He himself was also on the stage, got up rather hurriedly in a loose burnous and Palestinian head-dress, lent by one of the doctors at the Sanatorium, who had been some years in Palestine. Big Rufus, with his wise face laid on his paws, was also there, watching the very new babies with deep interest. The mother-sheep seemed rather nervous, but Mr Griffiths had kept her and her babies with him ever since they had arrived, and she knew her master. Luckily, there was only a brief time, for this was a tableau, with the shepherds looking amazed at the great group of angels with soaring wings and folded hands, and eyes and faces uplifted at the far end of the stage. The curtain was raised long enough for the audience to see the beautiful picture. Then it fell, and while Mr Griffiths took off his charges to the Rectory glebe for the present, the choir burst forth into 'Out of your sleep arise and wake!'

The next scene was quite a surprise. It was a room in a factory—a full room, with girls in overalls and caps, very busy packing something into cylinders. Across the random chatter as they worked, came the sound of the old English carol, 'The First Noel,' and the girls stopped to listen. They spoke of Christmas, and one—Daisy Venables—said how little like Christmas this year's would be.

'Why, we're even going on working!' she concluded. 'Besides, men have forgotten what Christmas means nowadays. They only think of it as a time to have presents, and a good feed. That's all it means now.'

As if in reply to this, the curtains at the back of the room parted, and an angel, all in white, with thick fair hair raying out from under a silver halo, stood before them. The orchestra whispered soft notes through the air, and the angel sang.

Perhaps because she had been through so much, Joanna's voice was full of tears as she sang Jo's words.

Christmas is near. Oh, man, cease work and hear
    The song the angels sing.
Though war has hushed each bell, yet angel voices tell
    How Christ from Heav'n took wing.

Christmas is near! Good Christians, have no fear.
    Ye never may forget
The Maiden Mother fair, the stable cold and bare—
    Ye have them with you yet.

Christmas is near! To Christ all men are dear,
    To each He whispers, 'Come!
My children, come and see Me, born to set ye free,
    And bring ye to My Home.'

Joanna's voice soared up, fresh and lovely, with a soft lilt in it that suited the quaint words and air, and those who knew what she had gone through, felt tears pricking at the backs of their eyelids. Then she ended, the curtains closed before her, and once more the girls in the workshop renewed their talk. But it was different now. And when the bell rang for the end of work, they began pulling off caps and overalls and saying that they would go and seek the little Christ Who was born into the world to bring peace to men of goodwill. The curtain fell on this, and the choir sang the Flemish carol, 'Sing, good company, frank and free,' with its gay, lilting tune.

Once more, as they ended, the curtain rose, to show a modern school-room, full of children between the ages of seven and twelve. They were talking of Father Christmas, their Christmas stockings. Then Sybil Russell came forward, and with eyes full of gravity, said, 'And my mummy says we give Christmas presents because God gave the First Christmas Present to us—Jesus in the manger.'

At once, her cousin Peggy Bettany replied, 'Oh, but that's ages ago!' and again the curtains at the back were drawn to show a bevy of baby angels with the big one behind, and Joanna sang her second solo, the enchanting 'How far is it to Bethlehem . . .,' with the babies joining her. The effect was lovely, and there was a great silence as they ended and the curtains closed before them, leaving the little people in the school-room to agree that the First Christmas Present still belonged to them.

Then the curtain fell once more, and this time the choir sang another of Jo's carols to such a jolly tune that heads and feet in the audience went a-wagging, and before it ended, everyone was joining in the refrain, 'Laus Deo!' so that a great volume of music rolled out.

> The bells across the ages ring—laus Deo!
> And in the sky the angels sing—laus Deo!

For Christ is born on earth today;
He sleeps amidst the flowering hay,
Laus Deo—laus Deo—laus Deo!

* * * * * *

O, let us join in gladsome song—laus Deo!
That to this world of grief and wrong—laus Deo!
God's Son has come to set us free,
Right merry may we surely be.
Laus Deo—laus Deo—laus Deo!

There were seven verses of it, and so insistent was the happy air, that for days afterwards, boys in the streets might be heard to whistle it, and it rang out over the bare fields as the men went about their work, much to the gratification of Mr Denny who had composed it.

When the curtain went up this time, it was on a scene in the village hall in an evening. Men were there, lounging about; others in groups, talking, and others throwing darts. In various corners sat women, knitting or sewing and chatting, and all the talk was of prices of food, the need for the munitions factories working on Christmas Day, and the difficulty of getting toys for the children. Not one word was spoken about the true Message of Christmas. Then a big fellow—how Monica did revel in her soldier's uniform!—got up and said he ought to be going for his bus. Anyhow, *he* meant to have a good Christmas. He was going to stay in bed till twelve, and then would go to a dance at night.

An old gaffer in a smock-frock piped up—and no one recognised Elizabeth Arnett for some moments—'Ah, Christmas ain't wot it was in my time. Us didn't stay abed then; us got hup and went to 'ear Parson preach, and sing the Christmas 'ymns.' Whereupon the young man replied, 'Oh, we've finished with all that, grandpa. 'Itler 'as seen to that.' Once more the angel appeared for her third and last solo—the quaint Angevin, 'Voisin, d'où venait ce grand bruit?' only she sang an English version of it made by the poetess Eleanor Farjeon.

The folk in the parish-room stared, then, when she had vanished, they began to get up and go out with subdued good-nights, and the curtain fell on an empty stage.

What was to come next? The audience wondered. As for Madge Russell, she was almost stricken dumb. She had never imagined that Jo could produce anything quite like this. It was certainly very different from her own, which had always leant to the picturesque and historical. She had never dreamed of being quite so modern as this.

But when the curtain rose for the last time, she found that Jo had not departed from the old ways. This was the stable at Bethlehem. The Manger stood in the centre, with the bambino in it. Over it stooped the Madonna, Robin, looking lovelier than ever in her blue robes, with the tender look on her face. Behind was Joseph, played by Emmie Linders. The angels knelt before it, or clustered in graceful groups near by. To one side stood the shepherds, Mr Griffiths with a tiny lamb in his arms, and Fiona with her hand on Rufus' thick mane. At the other side knelt the three kings, offering their treasures. Two or three of the children knelt beside the baby angels, and groups of munition-workers and village men and women were there; and at the widely-opened door thronged the rest, making a big company. At almost the same moment, the orchestra struck up, and at once everyone got to their feet, for it was the old 'Adeste Fideles,' which the School sang with all their hearts. Joey's lovely voice rang out in the beautiful Latin words, and many others joined in, for the Rector had insisted that the choir learn it in the original Latin for this Christmas, and there were few homes which did not know at least part of the words. As the last 'Venite adoremus' rang out, the curtain fell for the last time, and the play was over.

'Why did I feel ass if I must cry?' asked Fiona of Jo that night just before she went to bed.

'I don't know,' said Jo thoughtfully. 'It always makes me feel that way, too.'

'And the message of Christmas——' began Robin.

'Is that Christ is always with us, and came to bring peace to men of goodwill,' said Jo softly.

'But there is fighting going on now,' said Flora, who was standing by Jack Maynard.

'Yes; but when the war is over, we shall try to forgive—*if* we are of goodwill,' said Jo. 'Then we shall, indeed, have peace.'

'I see. But *must* we forgive?'

'If we want peace,' Jo's voice lingered over the word, 'we *must*. If we don't, then we are of *ill*-will, and no peace can be ours. Don't you remember our Peace League and its vow?'

Flora said no more. Fiona took up the tale. 'Anyhow,' she said slowly, 'the war hass done one coot thing.'

'And what is that, pray?' demanded Jack Maynard.

'Why, if it hadt not peen for the war, we shouldt nefer haf come here and that would haf peen a pity, for now we are used to it, I like it fery much. I know you haf not had a good time, Dr Jack; and we haf lost Hughie. Erisay iss taken from us, and we cannot go there now, though we shall after the war. Put efen with all that, I am fery gladt to pe here, and I hope we may stay till we are big enough to leaf school.'

'I expect so,' said Jo. 'And now it is past your bedtime, and you have another exciting day coming tomorrow. So say good-night, and be off with you—Primula, too. Daisy and Rob will be coming in an hour's time—oh, yes, you are!' as Daisy began to protest. 'I want Jack to myself for a little.'

'We'd better go at once,' laughed Robin. 'Come on, Daisy! We'll say good-night, and get off.'

But when they had all gone, and only the two remained in the pretty drawing-room, Jo lifted her face as she stood in her husband's arms. 'Jack, I nearly had a fit when I got Jean Mackenzie's letter. But oh, I too am glad the Highland twins came to the Chalet School, for if it had not been for them—or for Fiona, anyhow—I don't think I could have lived through the awful time before I got your cable saying you were safe. So I say—Thank God they came—and once more, thank God for the Chalet School!'